PASSAGEWAYS: MYTHOS

A Writing Bloc Anthology

ALY WELCH   C. BRENNECKE   CARI DUBIEL

BLAIR COSBY   MAGGIE HOYT   GERRI MAHN

SKYLAR LENNOX   TCC EDWARDS

KAYTALIN PLATT   TAHANI NELSON

MIKE X WELCH   EVAN GRAHAM   JENN NEWMAN

PETER L. HARMON

WRITING BLOC
INDIE PUBLISHING TEAM

PASSAGEWAYS:
MYTHOS
A WRITING BLOC ANTHOLOGY

CONTENTS

❧ I ❧

JUST DESSERTS

A Retelling of Hansel & Gretel

Aly Welch

I smiled at my reflection in the bathroom mirror as I adjusted my blond ponytail. My parents could not afford a party, but Mama made me a new dress for my sixteenth birthday, baby blue cotton with straps just wide enough to conceal my bra straps and a circle skirt that stopped at my calves. I never had a dress that exposed my shoulders before. Daddy hadn't looked too happy about it, but it felt heavenly on a hot balmy day in June.

I reached for my small white purse on the counter. Daddy had given me just enough money to buy myself a burger, fries, and a milkshake at the local diner. Part of me wished the family could afford to dine out together. The other part was glad I wouldn't have to contend with my big brother Johnny. Maybe I'd stop by the library to check out a Nancy Drew mystery to read while I ate so I wouldn't feel so alone. Shame it was too hot for a picnic in the park. Sometimes I'd spend entire weekends exploring the neighborhood just to avoid my brother.

Johnny hadn't always been so bad, but ever since he started fixing cars at a nearby shop, he'd made friends with some of the tougher boys at school. The worst of them, Hank, was a two-time senior who always seemed to be in trouble with the local authorities. But as long as Johnny kept his own nose clean, our parents didn't interfere—even though I know Daddy was disappointed Johnny didn't want to become a carpenter like him.

Johnny was at work right now, which was for the best because he'd be even less approving of my new dress than Daddy was. Hank and the other boys, sometimes they'd stare on days I walked by the shop and Johnny would get so red-faced and angry. He'd yell at me like it was my fault whenever he caught me alone.

"Stop making eyes at Hank!" he'd say, as if I ever did anything but look straight ahead and pretend not to hear the lewd things Hank shouted while his friends guffawed. My inflamed cheeks always gave me away, and they'd just laugh and carry on even more.

☆ ☆ ☆

At least the diner was in the opposite direction of the shop. As I sat down on a red vinyl seat at the end of the counter, a group of giggling classmates walked into the diner. They paused by my chair. "Hi, Pearl," Maggie Watson said. She was tall, green-eyed, with luxurious brown curls that cascaded halfway down her back.

"Hi Maggie, hi Helen, hi Joan," I said to Maggie and her friends, a mousier brunette and an elegant blonde. I took another sip of my milkshake. It was chocolate with lots of whipped cream that had been stained pink from the juice of the cherry I'd already eaten.

"I wish I could get away with eating all that food, but I'm afraid my dress would positively burst at the seams." Maggie gestured at her sunny yellow sundress, cinched tightly at the waist with a green satin ribbon. I think I sighed over that very same dress in a boutique window last weekend. "Yours looks like it has a lot more give." She smirked and flounced away with her friends to sit in a booth.

I swear. Maggie could be as pretty as Jane Russell if that cruel twist of her lips didn't ruin it for the rest of her face.

Every now and then Mama took me to the matinee. Daddy and Johnny would be scandalized if they knew we saw *Gentlemen Prefer Blondes* a couple years ago. Sometimes I liked to imagine that I was on holiday, traveling to exotic locales far away from mean girls like Maggie and hulking menaces like Hank. I wasn't as beautiful as Marilyn Monroe or as sly as Jane, but none of their adventures seemed half as intimidating as navigating my own hometown. What I wouldn't give to have a fun, glamorous friend like either of them.

I finished every last bite of my food. Then I looked back at Maggie and her friends sharing a milkshake and fries. I smiled and waved and turned to go. As I walked down the street indulging a fantasy of some devastatingly handsome sailor romancing me overseas, I didn't even notice Hank and his friends heading straight for me until he grabbed me roughly by the elbow.

My eyes grew wide as I looked for my brother, but he was nowhere to be found.

"Why don't you let me buy you lunch?" Hank sneered, pulling me in close.

"No, thank you." I braced my hands against his chest, not wanting to touch him but having no other way to keep distance between us. "I just ate."

"Then you can watch us eat." Hank's friends chuckled.

I could smell the tobacco and whiskey on his breath. It was all I could do not to retch.

"What's the matter? Ain't I good enough for ya?" Hank's grip tightened on my arm.

"Maybe you should let her go, Hank."

I looked over his shoulder at the speaker. A tall but scrawny kid named Jimmy or Timmy or something. He was in the year ahead of me.

"Yeah, Johnny'll be mad if he finds out you roughed up his sister," said another.

"Well Johnny ain't here, is he?" Hank snarled.

I tried to think of what Jane or Marilyn would do in my situation, but my mind came up blank. So I did the only thing I could think to do.

I brought my knee up to hit Hank between the legs. He released my arm and doubled over, groaning in pain. I ran.

"Get her!" I heard Hank growl.

I think I was two blocks away before I realized nobody was chasing me, but I slipped into the first open door I could find just in case. As I breathed in the alluring smells of fresh baked bread, and spices like anise, ginger, nutmeg, and cinnamon, I realized I was in the kitchen of the local bakery, Darby's Delights.

Someone closed the door behind me. "Who you runnin' from, sugar?"

I turned to face the town witch.

"Crazy Mabel" the other kids called her, but she didn't look crazy to me. Instead, I saw a woman of indeterminate age with smooth brown skin and faint crow's feet surrounding her kindly brown eyes. A red gingham handkerchief secured her black hair, which had only just begun to gray at the temples, and she wore a modest dress of the same fabric under an apron. Before I could open my mouth to answer, another door opened, this one separating the kitchen from the rest of the bakery.

"What are you doing back here?"

I stared at Mr. Darby, still unable to speak. His green eyes peered into mine from under bushy eyebrows. He was a short man, stout, with an intimidating gaze and balding head, but he was not, to my knowledge, unkind. He did, after all, employ Miss Mabel. She even rented the one-room apartment above the shop. I remember the decision caused a fair amount of grumbling in the community, but the Darby family went back generations and had substantial local influence. Mr. Darby and Mrs. Darby lived across town in one of those fancy ranch homes in Druid Hills. Mr. Darby drove a brand-new Thunderbird, a white one. I knew this because Johnny'd worked on Mr. Darby's car once and couldn't stop carrying on about it.

"I think she's here about the job, Mr. Darby, sir," Mabel said, her warm husky voice drawing me out of my thoughts.

"Oh, right!" A welcoming smile replaced Mr. Darby's perplexed expression. "Why didn't you come in through the front? No matter. Say, you're the Stantons' daughter, aren't ya? Patty? Peggy?"

"Pearl," I said, grateful to find my voice but worried about this new predicament I found myself in. Job? What job? I knew my way around a kitchen well enough, but nothing Mama taught me how to bake came close to the delicious breads and sweet confections from Darby's Delights. Why, his baked goods were known all over the state of Georgia, maybe even the country.

"I knew it was something with a 'P'," Mr. Darby said to Mabel. "I knew Pearl when she was maybe this high." Mr. Darby knelt down a little to hold his hand at his knee. "She loved the gingerbread cookies most of all." Mr. Darby straightened his back with a grunt and turned to me. "We don't see your family in the shop much these days."

I looked down at my shoes. "Work's been slow for Daddy."

"I see." Mr. Darby gave a sympathetic nod, then smiled once again. "Pretty thing like you would be great for business working behind the counter. Do you know how to use a register?"

"No, sir."

"Mrs. Darby can show you. I know she'll be happy to have the help. This dang humidity, it's bothering her knee something awful. Guess I should go take the sign out of the window. Come along. I'll show you how I close up the shop."

Not knowing what else to do, I followed him back through the door. I think I heard Mabel chuckling softly as she continued working in the kitchen.

☆ ☆ ☆

Even though I arrived home before dinner, my parents watched me walk into the kitchen with their lips pursed together, Daddy sitting at the small dining table and Mama standing in front of the oven.

"Just where have you been? I need you to help me with the stew."

"I... I got a job," I said to Mama, casting a furtive glance in Daddy's direction.

"You got a what?" Daddy stood up from the table. He looked like his eyes were about to bug right out of his head. Reminded me of the excitable husband on *I Love Lucy*. It was all I could do not to laugh.

"A job," I repeated, stifling a grin. "Mr. Darby wants me to help at the bakery."

Mama's eyes widened. "Mr. Darby? Did you hear that, William?"

Daddy's look of consternation softened. "It's not that I don't enjoy your cookies, Pearl, but you're not exactly Betty Crocker. And doesn't he already have someone working in the back? What's that they call her? Crazy Nelly?"

"Mabel," I said. "Her name is Mabel."

"Crazy Mabel. That's it." Daddy narrowed his eyes, considering. "What's he want to hire *you* for?"

"Mrs. Darby's knee has been bothering her. She could use the extra help."

"I suppose a summer job isn't the worst idea," Daddy relented. "So long as it doesn't interfere with your chores at home."

My first job.

I wondered how much money I could save over the summer and whether or not it would help me leave this sweltering city and its rough city boys behind. I'd all but forgotten about what happened with Hank until Johnny walked in the door as Mama and I set the table.

"I thought I told you to stay away from Hank," Johnny snarled as he sank into a chair at the dining table.

"I never want to be anywhere near him." I glared, hands on my hips. "You need to tell him to stay away from me."

"What's this about Hank?" My father walked into the kitchen and sat down at the table.

"He and his friends tried to bother me when I was leaving the diner," I told him before Johnny could say anything different. Lord only knew what sort of story Hank had come up with. I'm surprised he said anything at all, the way I'd left him doubled over and groaning.

"That boy's trouble," Daddy told me.

"I know it," I said.

Johnny glared down at his food while he ate, all slunk down in his seat. I wondered if Hank had taken his anger out on him but decided I didn't care. Hank was Johnny's problem. I didn't want him to become mine.

☆ ☆ ☆

The next morning, I pulled my hair back into another ponytail, securing it with a pink scarf, and dressed in a cream blouse and pink circle skirt.

"Well, don't you look as sweet as candy," Mrs. Darby said as I walked in the front door of the bakery. She was as round as Mr. Darby with kind brown eyes and an easy smile. Mrs. Darby spent the morning teaching me how to use the cash register along with the ins and outs of running the bakery. After the midmorning rush, she sat down in a chair behind the counter. "Be a dear and help Mabel in the kitchen."

The smell of fresh baked cookies greeted me as I walked through the kitchen door. I watched as Mabel removed a pan of sugar cookies from the oven. It was at least double the size of our oven at home. Why, you could fit a whole person in there if you wanted. A sudden image of Hank doubled over on a pan with an apple in his mouth appeared in my mind. I slapped my hands over my mouth to stifle a giggle.

Mabel set the pan on top of the oven to cool, then turned to me with a quizzical expression. I shrugged, pressing my lips together. "You're a secretive one, aren't ya?" She gestured at a bowl of pale pink frosting on the counter. "You can frost these cookies once they're cool, if you like, Miss Pearl."

I watched as Mabel rolled more dough on the other end of the counter. After a few minutes, I checked the cookies in the oven. "I don't know how you make these without burning them," I said. "Mine always end up all brown and crispy on the ends no matter what I do. It's a wonder Santa doesn't leave coal in my stocking every year."

Mabel grinned. "I have a few secrets of my own."

I began spreading frosting on Mabel's perfectly round and soft sugar cookies. She made polite conversation as we worked, asking me about school and my family but revealing nothing about her own. Still, I enjoyed talking to her and felt sorry when Mrs. Darby summoned me back to the front of the bakery.

The rest of the week went on much the same. I'd help Mrs. Darby during the morning rush and again in the afternoon. The rest of the time was spent in the kitchen with Mabel. I'd glean bits and pieces of her life before Atlanta. She had worked in a cafeteria at the University of Georgia in Athens, where the Darbys' son—James Darby Junior the third—had gone to study law. An unusual friendship to be sure, but I didn't bother her for details.

☆ ☆ ☆

"I hope you aren't spending any time around that witch," Johnny told me one evening after dinner as we washed the dishes. For a moment I thought he meant that awful mean-spirited Maggie until I remembered what they called Mabel around town.

I rolled my eyes. "Those are stories made up by rude little children with more imagination than brains."

"Not just children," Johnny argued. "Jimmy said she put the evil eye on his dad, and that's why he had that accident at the train yard. And Hank said some of the girls around town sneak to her apartment late at night for love potions."

"Love potions?" I shook my head. "Honestly, Johnny. I think you've been inhaling too many fumes at the shop. You haven't been sippin' from Hank's flask, have you?" I leaned in close, trying to sniff his breath.

Johnny pulled away from me and dried his hands on a towel. "Don't say I didn't warn you." He gave me one last dirty look before lumbering out of the kitchen. I found myself wondering, not for the first time, what happened to the sweet little boy who used to explore the neighborhood with me and tell off any boy that so much as looked at me cross-eyed.

☆ ☆ ☆

The bakery was closed on Sundays, so I didn't see Mabel again until Monday.

"That poor thing's madder than a wet hen," Mrs. Darby said when I came in. "See if you can help Mabel in the kitchen."

I nodded, worried I was about to discover why so many people called her Crazy Mabel. Instead, I found her all nervous and distracted in the kitchen as she dropped this spoon and bumped into that counter. Distraught, to be sure, but not the wild-eyed witch the town painted her as.

I noticed an envelope poking out from a pocket in her dress. "What's that?"

Startled, Mabel nearly dropped her spoon again. She took a deep breath, placing her free hand against her chest before fixing her eyes on my face. "Child, you scared me half to death." I thought she would ignore my question, but Mabel reached for the envelope, her hand trembling. "I've been carrying this around since it arrived on Saturday, but I haven't been able to bring myself to open it. Could be nothing, could be everything."

Mabel clutched the envelope to her chest before holding it out to me. I took it. "It's from James Darby the third," I said, perplexed.

Mabel nodded. "He's been in touch with a former classmate of his, a private investigator, trying to help me find my son."

Somehow passing the letter to me helped Mabel collect herself. I slipped it into my own pocket. Then I helped Mabel bake, and listened, rapt, as she told me her story.

☆ ☆ ☆

James had a friend, Rudolph, but everyone called him Rudi. He was quite the charmer. Always flirting with this girl or that girl. But he would catch up to me as I was leaving work and tell me all about his day and the latest book he was reading or what he was studying. I'd listen and ask questions, and he'd tell me how nice it was to have someone he could talk to. One day he asked if I'd like to go on a picnic with him. I was surprised. People gave us funny looks as it was. He made it sound so nice and romantic. He'd pack a basket and bring candles and meet me in a clearing in the woods behind his dormitory. Only he never bothered with the basket.

Sometime later I realized I was with child. When I started to show, I lost my job. I ran into James as I was leaving and I was so upset, I told him everything that had happened. Well, I guess he confronted Rudi, but Rudi didn't have any interest in taking responsibility. Not until I had the baby and the baby was taken away. I only held him once.

I didn't see James again until years later. He's been trying to find my son ever since.

☆ ☆ ☆

"Open it," Mabel asked me when she finished her story.

"Are you sure?" My own hands were shaking as I broke the seal. Mabel nodded. I removed the letter and began to read. "Oh, Mabel." I looked up, blinking back tears. "Mabel, he found him. He's... he's in Canada."

Next thing I knew, Mabel and I were holding on to each other crying and laughing.

"Is everything alright in there?"

We untangled ourselves as Mrs. Darby poked her head in. "Everything's fine, Mrs. Darby," I told her. "Just fine." Satisfied, Mrs. Darby closed the door. I grinned at Mabel. She wiped the tears from her face with the back of her hand, then reached for the letter.

"My boy's starting college," she said, her eyes widening with pride and delight. "It was a closed adoption. No wonder it took Mr. Darby and his investigator friend so long to find him. I suppose it makes sense. An illegitimate child with someone like me wouldn't do for Rudi's career and reputation."

"What are you going to do now?"

I hadn't meant to wipe the smile from Mabel's face. She pursed her lips, thinking. "Toronto is such a long way away," Mabel said. "But he gave Mr. Darby his address. I'll send him a letter just as soon as I'm done working." Her smile returned.

☆ ☆ ☆

I couldn't stop grinning myself until a few unexpected customers walked in late that afternoon. Something about the way Hank and his friends were eyeing the bakery, it didn't sit right with me. But he was the very picture of southern grace—all "yes, ma'am" or "thank you, miss" to Mrs. Darby and me—so I forced myself to smile as I handed him his cookies. I didn't even flinch when his grease-stained hands brushed against mine. If he was still angry about what happened last week, he hid it well.

☆ ☆ ☆

Johnny was quieter and more subdued than usual during dinner, and that was saying something. Kept staring out the window, looking pensive. I didn't feel right sharing anything personal about Mabel so I was quiet, too.

☆ ☆ ☆

I think it was after midnight when a loud creaking noise awoke me from a deep sleep. Then I thought I heard the click of the front door, and sure enough, when I parted the curtains of my room to look outside, there was Johnny sneaking away from the house, dressed all in black. I suppose I should have gotten our parents. Instead, I tucked my nightie into the slacks I wore to help Mama with the gardening and pulled a light sweater over my head. I felt just like girl detective Nancy Drew as I slipped on my shoes.

Johnny was halfway down the road by the time I left the house. When he turned a corner, I followed the sound of his footsteps like breadcrumbs, grateful for the light of the full moon but careful to keep my distance. At first, I thought he was heading to the shop—my brother, a would-be car thief?—but then I realized his real destination was the bakery. I can't even pretend I was surprised when I saw him join a few shadowy figures outside the shop. I knew Hank was up to something earlier, I just knew it.

Someone tall and thin—Jimmy maybe?—picked up a rock and threw it through the window. Then he reached a long skinny arm inside to unlock the door. The four boys went inside the bakery as I moved closer, keeping to the shadows as much as I could. I watched from behind a tree across the street as they began to search the bakery.

A light turned on in the apartment above the bakery.

Oh no. Mabel!

I ran across the street and behind the bakery, but I was too late. Mabel was already opening the back door. Two of the boys were standing in the kitchen, arguing. "You can't leave that on!" I heard my brother saying. "It could cause an explosion!"

"That's the—" Hank started to say, but he saw Mabel standing in the doorway. He lunged past my brother and grabbed her.

"Let her go!" Johnny yelled. "This is going too far!"

"Nobody's gonna care about some crazy old woman," Hank snarled, only he called her something else. Mabel tried to claw at his face. Hank brought his arm up and backhanded her so hard, he knocked her halfway out the back door.

The next few minutes were a blur.

I'm not sure what I said or if I even said anything at all. I just remember yelling and running at Hank, and Johnny reaching for me, to help or to hurt I didn't know in the moment. There was a struggle. Then Hank lost his balance and fell back into the open oven, headfirst.

He howled in pain. I turned away, wincing at the smell of charred hair and flesh. Then I fell to my knees, reaching for Mabel's still body.

"Get outta here!" Johnny yelled.

"I'm not leaving her!"

"I'll get her. Go!"

So I stood up and I ran. I'm not proud of it, but I ran. There was an explosion behind me, but I kept on running until I ran inside the house. I saw the light turn on in my parents' room as I pulled off my sweater. I had barely slipped under the covers of my bed when they turned on the light in my room.

"Pearl, where's Johnny?"

I pretended to wipe the sleep from my eyes as I sat up. "Isn't he in his room?"

They shook their heads and told me to get dressed and left the room. I didn't know what to do or say as they ushered me outside. We joined other families heading in the direction of the bakery, some walking, others running. Firemen were working to put out the fire.

"We found two of 'em running from the scene," I heard one police officer tell another. "They think the other two were still inside."

My parents clung to each other as we watched the scene unfold. Ambulances arrived. "Johnny!" Mama ran to one of the stretchers. Johnny moaned. He was alive, but he was hurt. How hurt, I didn't know. Mama rode with him to the hospital.

The Darbys arrived as Mabel was being wheeled into the other ambulance.

Mr. Darby talked to the drivers.

Then he talked to the police officers.

Finally, he came to talk to my father.

"I don't know what part your son played in what happened tonight," Mr. Darby said, "but it looks to the authorities like he tried to help poor Mabel, and he's burned something awful, and well, I don't see any reason to add to his suffering." He shook my father's hand.

☆ ☆ ☆

Johnny had second and third-degree burns all over his back and the backs of his arms and legs. He stayed in the hospital for a long time. Even when he came home, we had to help tend to his wounds. Nobody talked about what happened and why. I think my parents agreed his injuries were punishment enough. I was just happy to have my sweet brother back.

Mabel wasn't burned anywhere near as badly as Johnny, but she had a concussion. I couldn't visit her in the hospital, but the Darbys let me know as soon as she was out. They didn't know if they were going to rebuild the bakery or start fresh, but they gave Mabel the money to see her son once she was well enough to travel.

The explosion was the talk of the town for quite some time, each story wilder and more outlandish than the next. I barely kept my fingernails to myself when Maggie suggested a ritual sacrifice, of all things, was to blame. Eventually people lost interest and turned their attention to some mayoral candidate in another town who was rumored to have an illegitimate son, one of mixed race no less.

I spent the rest of summer and the next two years working at the diner to save up enough money for my own ticket to Toronto, Canada. In her last letter, Mabel told me she was opening her own bakery with her son's help. He wanted to focus on cakes and cookies so they could call it "Just Desserts," but she worried if that wasn't a little too on the nose.

I wondered if Mabel could use another set of hands in the kitchen.

ABOUT THE AUTHOR

Aly Welch lives in Western New York with her husband, author Mike X Welch, and their twin sons. When she isn't writing, she enjoys acting, karate, and yoga. She also loves exploring the woods, and still hopes to find magic behind every tree and under every rock.

NEVE BLANC AND THE SEVEN MURDERED MEN

A Retelling of Snow White

C. Brennecke

Monday mornings always began with mirror time. As an on-air reporter, my appearance was under constant scrutiny, so it was best to have a well-practiced reporter face: serious, somber even, but friendly. Never unattractive. It's a fine line to walk, but if anyone in this town could walk it, it was me.

I allowed myself a slight smirk as I took in my reflection. I was especially striking that day, with my shining black hair, gleaming porcelain skin, and lips—such sumptuous lips—adorned with the perfect shade of rose red lipstick. If I hadn't gone into journalism, I could've had a walk-on part as a CW vampire. *What a waste*, I often thought, *to possess such an aesthetic bark yet none of its bite.*

But there was little reason to lament my lack of bite in my new position at Channel 7 News. No longer a lowly weather girl, as an investigative reporter my role was more predator than prey. I spent my days roaming the streets of Manhattan, camera at the ready, looking for the next big scoop. And when there was a story, I made sure I was the first to strike.

According to rumor (and don't think I wasn't aware of it), I had only gotten my job due to privilege. I'm the former mayor's daughter after all, and people assumed that my career was simply a perk. That's not true, of course; socialites aren't just *given* jobs. First, I had to be asked. Like so many things, it was all about consent. I had *consented* to my career because it's what I wanted. With my looks and my pedigree, I could have gone far in life without ever working a day. But what would be the sense in that? With a career of my own I could go even further, and all without ever cowering to the will of a man.

That was the dream, at least.

☆ ☆ ☆

It was a quiet morning, and hellishly hot, but I was whistling a happy tune that day. I had landed my first big investigative scoop and was celebrating with a red velvet frappuccino with extra whip. There had been a double murder at a surgeon's office the day before, and I just so happened to discover the scene before the police arrived. I slipped right into reporter mode and hit them with rapid-fire questions to catch them off guard, and it paid off. I was able to collect a few key details that were missing from their official report. Not only were the victims missing their heads (a fact that was readily apparent to anyone at the scene), but some of the surgeon's tools were missing as well.

Trying to shake the gory scene from my mind, I sucked down the last few drops of my drink and hailed a cab. I had a next-of-kin interview lined up for the morning and was hoping to do some research after that. I wiped a bead of sweat from my brow as a cab pulled up. *This guy better have his AC on*, I thought, rolling my eyes at the pair of rubber balls hanging from his rearview mirror.

Not one to waste time, I took out my notepad to jot down some questions during the ride. But every time I touched pen to paper, the cab would swerve violently or come to a sudden stop. After a few ruined attempts, I glanced at the mirror above the dangling balls and caught the cabbie smirking. I glared at him. "You're a real prick, you know that?"

His response was a stream of vulgar gestures and obscenities, followed by a coughing fit, possibly an asthma attack. The cab then came to a screeching halt and the driver told me, in no uncertain terms, to get out. We exchanged additional obscenities as I exited the cab. He then sped away—but not before I managed to snap a shot of his license plate.

☆ ☆ ☆

From that point on the day grew difficult. I was supposed to film a victim profile spot, but obtaining usable quotes proved impossible. No one had a single kind word to share about the older victim, a cosmetic surgeon with several malpractice suits filed against him. There were also rumors he'd blackmailed his more well-known clients for sexual favors. Everyone I spoke to—the nurses, his partners, and even his wife—every last one of them seemed more relieved than saddened by the news of his death. And a few were downright elated.

The other victim presented a different quandary. He was a delivery guy who seemed to be in the wrong place at the wrong time. It took extra legwork to find anyone who knew him, and the consensus seemed to be that he was well-liked and far too young to have met the end of his life. The only problem was I couldn't get a single quote that didn't reference the young man's fondness for pot. Though legal, it would still be in bad taste to include someone's recreational use in their victim profile.

After mining for fluff, I started asking each interviewee more investigative questions:

Did the victim fight with anyone recently? Do they have any enemies? Have you noticed any strange behaviors? Did you see anything out of the ordinary? What was the last conversation you had with them?

Nobody knew anything of substance as far as suspects were concerned, so I had to dig up names connected to the malpractice suits and blackmail rumors on my own. I wasn't expecting to find much though. Not that day at least. The police were holding a press conference that evening, which gave me only a couple of hours to finalize and film the victim profile spot after that. My plans to do research at the courthouse and hit up my gossip columnist friends would have to wait until the next day.

☆ ☆ ☆

A gory scene on the Upper East Side. Police are reporting a double homicide that took place inside a local doctor's office. Authorities are scratching their heads at who might have wanted both men dead. One was a plastic surgeon and the other a delivery driver. As far as anyone can tell, their only tie was the order of Thai food still warm when police arrived at the scene.

☆ ☆ ☆

After finishing the victim profile, I changed out of my overly starched business suit—the kind with a mini skirt (the station expected its on-air women to dress provocatively, of course)—and into a much more comfortable ensemble of shorts and a hoodie before heading home. I was oh-so-ready to veg out on my couch and get my mind off things, but first (I decided as I climbed the steps out of the subway station closest to my apartment), a nightcap was in order.

☆ ☆ ☆

The moment I plopped atop a stool at the neighborhood bar, a bright green concoction appeared in front of me, courtesy of a grinning bartender I had never met before. I raised an eyebrow. "What's this?"

"Apple martini." The bartender winked at me.

I rolled my eyes. The guy was cute, and judging by his cheesy smile, he seemed to know it. I definitely wasn't in the mood for something so saccharine, so I glanced around the bar until I spotted one of my favorite regulars, Walt. He was an older gentleman who was there almost every night. I knew once he was a few beers in, he'd drink pretty much anything handed to him. So I headed over with the martini.

With the sickly-sweet drink successfully offloaded, I slumped into a booth and flagged down a waitress. After ordering a lager, I asked her what was with the new guy.

"Cute, isn't he?" The waitress leaned in. "He started two nights ago and he's already slept with half the waitstaff."

"Impressive," I deadpanned.

☆ ☆ ☆

While working on my beer, I went over the events of the past 48 hours. It all seemed like a blur now. Things really started when I went to the cosmetic surgeon's office to drop off a payment for a friend. That's when I found the doctor... and the delivery guy. There are some parts in there I'd rather forget, but once I pulled my head together, I managed to alert the receptionist to call 911. A few minutes later the police arrived and started questioning me. Realizing the murder scene would be on the news, I went straight into reporter mode to get as much information from them as I could before they made me leave. I ran a few errands after that, before heading home for a shower and bed. Then came my celebration frappuccino, followed by interview after interview with not a single lead. After that, I attended the press conference and rushed through the filming of the victim profile. It was a lot for two days, and there was still so much to do: research, follow-ups, looking into other recent crimes to identify any similarities. At some point I needed to buy groceries as well. But that would all have to wait. First, I desperately needed some beauty sleep.

I threw back what was left of my lager and stuck a ten under the empty bottle. As I got up to leave, I glanced back at Walt to wave goodnight and noticed he was slumped over at the bar. I shook my head.

☆ ☆ ☆

Another day, another murder.

I was finishing my second coffee of the day when the familiar buzz of my phone sent a shiver through my spine. It was an alert from my office. They'd received a tip about another murder fitting the killer's MO. I sprinted out the door.

The new victim, a male cab driver, was also missing his head. They found him in the elevator of his apartment building. The police had taped off the entire lobby, and I had to wait outside. The cameraman assigned to cover the story with me had yet to arrive, so I sent him a quick text asking him to hurry.

Eventually, once a few reporters gathered, an investigator came outside to field questions. At first, the other reporters asked the standard ones—*What was the victim's name? What was the time of death? Are there any suspects?*—all of which the investigator promised would be answered in the press release. I then asked a question of my own. "Is this murder connected to the double homicide?"

The investigator cleared his throat. "We're looking into it." And with that, he walked away.

I have to admit I felt relieved that the victim's name wasn't released yet. There was already a lot on my plate, so I didn't mind putting off another victim profile until after the next press release. And the possibility of the murders being connected had turned this big scoop into a giant banana split-sized sundae. I had a lot to prepare for.

☆ ☆ ☆

The rest of the day was all phone calls and paperwork. I had to follow up on leads and outline several variations of my script, all dependent on which information the police did and did not release. It occurred to me it might be time to call my stepmother—a federal investigator—for an off-the-record statement, though I wasn't sure if the feds had gotten involved yet.

☆ ☆ ☆

"Hey, Neve."

My back tensed up at the sound of my boss's voice. I turned to face him. "Yes, sir?"

"These murders you're covering, is this a serial killer we've got?" He pushed my roller chair to the side and squinted at my monitor.

"It might be. The authorities haven't made that ruling yet."

He bent down to help himself to my trackpad and started scrolling through my drafts and open tabs. He shook his head and glanced at me with an expression that implied he thought I was stupid. "It's gotta be a serial killer. You ready for a story that big, toots? I can assign it to someone more seasoned if you want."

I grit my teeth. "I'm ready, sir. One hundred percent ready."

"Good." He stood up. "Run with the serial killer headline. Don't want anyone else beating us to the punch."

"Yes sir."

☆ ☆ ☆

After the press release came out, I tweaked a teaser for my upcoming feature report and filmed it—with the serial killer headline, even though it wasn't confirmed yet. After that I started on the cabbie's victim profile to get a jump on the next day's pile of work. Once my eyes became too heavy to stare at a screen any longer, I decided to go home.

But first, I made another quick stop at the neighborhood bar for a nightcap.

And then lather, rinse, repeat.

☆ ☆ ☆

I jerked awake several times in the middle of the night, thanks to a steady stream of nightmares. Flashes of blood, Thai food, coffee, rubber balls, police tape, and glowing apple martinis haunted my mind. The dreams left me feeling more exhausted upon waking up than I was when I went to sleep.

It was a real struggle to get out of bed. I didn't have the energy to get dolled up, so I took my phone off the charger and texted work to let them know I'd be working from home that morning. With a double espresso in hand, I turned my police scanner on for background noise while I worked. It wasn't long before an alert caught my ear. Another body at Columbus and 84th. That was close. Very close.

I threw on some clothes and raced out the door and down the block to my neighborhood bar. When I arrived, there was police tape blocking off the entire sidewalk surrounding the establishment. I decided to wait as close as I could to the alleyway behind the bar in hopes of catching the owner or one of the waitresses on their way in or out.

☆ ☆ ☆

I was still waiting outside two hours later when my phone rang. It had just started raining, so I was crouched under an overhang with a few other reporters. I moved out from under the overhang and headed towards a spot out of earshot. I reached into my pocket to retrieve my cell. "Hello?"

"What's all that noise? Where the hell are you?" A loud, gruff voice shouted on the other end.

"It's raining, sir. I'm outside."

"Outside where?"

"Columbus and 84th Street."

"Columbus and what? Damnit, you're not even close to work, are you?"

"No, I'm investigating the—"

"Never mind, it doesn't matter," my boss huffed. "Listen, when you get to the office, do me a favor and grab my umbrella. I left it hanging on the door of my office. I'm gonna need it tonight."

"You're not at the office, sir?"

"No, I'm in a cab heading home. You can handle that, right? Get my umbrella and deliver it to me? I don't have to worry about you getting sidetracked, do I, toots?"

"No, of course not, it's just that it's..."

"Good."

I let out a few choice words after he hung up on me. I couldn't believe he was still treating me like an intern in the middle of my first serious investigation. He clearly resented me for skipping that step and wanted to force that experience on me—probably because his higher-ups hadn't given him a say when they hired me. It was bullshit. And I was over it.

☆ ☆ ☆

That phone call was the last time I spoke to him. By the time I arrived at the office, reports of a murder in the Upper East Side were already coming in. A white man, mid-sixties, overweight, and decapitated. They found him dead just inside his doorway. They hadn't released a name, but I already knew who it was. My boss would be the headline at his own station that night.

I stood in front of his office door and shook my head. The umbrella still hung there, forever forgotten. Feeling overwhelmed, I booked it to the bathroom to splash some water on my face. I needed to focus on work. There would be an in-depth feature the next day, and I wanted to be the one to deliver it.

I looked at my dripping reflection and gave myself a pep talk, followed by an abridged version of mirror time. Once sufficiently calmed down, I grabbed a cup of coffee and got to it. Most of my coworkers had stayed late to commiserate together, so I took the opportunity to interview them for soundbites about his legacy. No one knew why somebody would murder him. Sure, he was an impossible-to-please hardass and an old-school misogynist, but despite that, he was well-loved. He was a mentor to many and always gave back to the community. Just enough sugar to make his faults palatable. To most people anyway.

☆ ☆ ☆

When I woke, I was still at work and slumped over my computer. My eyes weren't ready for daylight, so I squinted and blinked until they adjusted. I reached around to find my phone. It was 7:18 am. I wasn't sure what time I had fallen asleep, but I wagered it was the most sleep I had gotten in weeks. My coworkers would arrive soon—it sounded like a few already had—so I booked it to the bathroom to fix my hair, then ran to the break room for some much-needed coffee.

Back at my desk, I wasted no time in getting back to work. I was never one for mourning, and neither was my boss, so I figured the best thing to do was to get ahead of the story to make sure my station delivered the news first. As I logged into my email, an alert flashed across the screen. The police had officially declared the murder spree to be the work of a serial killer. This came as no surprise but meant that the case would now receive national attention, both on the criminal investigation side and on the media side. The Feds would certainly be involved, which meant a call to my stepmother was finally in order.

A vibration jolted through my bones. I looked at my phone. *Speak of the devil.*

"Hello. Neve speaking. May I ask who's calling?" I liked to pretend I didn't know my stepmother's number when she called. It seemed to irritate her.

"It's Ingrid. Listen, I need to talk to you about this serial killer case. I've just been assigned to it and I'm getting caught up on the details now. Is this right? That you were the one that discovered the first murder scene?"

Dear Step-Mommy was all business as usual. She didn't even pretend she cared about me, which was the least she could do considering how abruptly she'd inserted herself into my life. My father had a ring on her finger mere days after the first anniversary of my mother's death, and if Ingrid had gotten her way, I'm sure it would have happened even sooner.

"I'm fine, thanks for asking." I rolled my eyes. "And yes, I already gave my statement to the police." I resolved not to give her any more information than that. If she wanted details, she'd have to work for them.

"Well, that was their investigation, and this is mine. I'd like to bring you in to answer a few questions."

"I really don't have time for that right now. I've been assigned this story as well."

"It's not a story, Neve. These are very serious crimes."

"Tomato, to-mah-to."

The voice on the other line sounded unamused. "Neve, it's really in your best interest to cooperate with the investigation."

I sighed. "I really can't meet with you today. There's just way too much on my plate. The best I can do is tomorrow."

"Tomorrow morning it is. I'll send a car for you."

"Fine." I hit the red icon and ended the call.

☆ ☆ ☆

Everyone in my branch of the office was sent home early that day. The higher-ups had decided we all deserved time to mourn. That was the story at least. Everyone knew they were scrambling to figure out a temporary replacement for my boss and were holding interviews that afternoon. In any case, I decided to make the most of the break and stopped at the market on my way home to pick up groceries for a nice home-cooked meal.

"Hey! Snow White!" a gruff voice called out from the alley.

My hand tightened around the pepper spray in my pocket. *It's just a fan*, I told myself. He had called me Snow White, after all, a nickname some of the locals had coined back when I covered the blizzard beat. I glanced towards the alley, forcing a smile.

No one was there. *Strange.*

Then came a slurping sound from the shadows, followed by mumbling that ended in a single, sickening word: "Thick."

The "ick" sound rang in my head, dripping with spit. *Ick. Ick. Ick.* It was as if he only saw me as a mindless piece of meat. No brain, no soul, no will. Just a body to consume. His view of me was all wrong, and he was about to find that out.

Soon I was in the alley and out of breath, wrapping my thick thighs around the man's frail neck; one knee locked around the other and squeezing with all my might. The man struggled, of course, but his middle-aged arms were no match for the thickness of my thighs. I held the position easily; all I had to do was wait.

Fucking sicko, I muttered, reaching for his wrist to check for a pulse. Once I was sure there was none, I relaxed my grip and let out a sigh. *What the hell am I supposed to do with him here?* I gave the body a kick.

It was the first time something like this had happened out on the street. Usually I could lock a door and close the blinds while I went to work removing my victims' heads. But not this time. This time I'd have to hide the body and come back later with the doctor's tools. I'd need to bring a change of clothes and some wet wipes to clean myself up with too. *What a nuisance.*

☆ ☆ ☆

That evening, as I was serving dinner—a feast of ham and roasted apples —I glanced at my newest guest and stopped. I gave the visage a courteous smile, then repositioned my fork and knife. A thin slice of meat would not do for him, no, no. *Sicko* preferred his meat thick. The slab of ham hit Sicko's plate with a thud, splatting the fresh face with specks of clove-infused grease. I glanced around the rest of the table with a smile on my face. My found family was certainly a motley crew.

It had all started with a run-in with a Hunter, a middle-aged man who had followed me around town for months and months. I had spoken to the police about him several times—I'd even pleaded with Ingrid to put some pressure on them, yet they never took any measures to stop him. So I took matters into my own hands and began stalking him back. I followed him all the way home to his apartment one night, and after surveying his digs long enough to determine he lived alone, I gave his door a knock. After that, well, one thing led to another, and soon Hunter was laying there naked. And dead. Not one to love 'em and leave 'em, I hoisted Hunter up and into his current position at the head of the table, where he sat slouching and reeking most foul.

Along both sides of the table sat the severed heads of my other victims. There was Dick, the cosmetic surgeon who dared to tell me to get on my knees under threat of him leaking my cosmetic history to the press. Then young Pothead, the delivery driver. I felt bad about him, I admit, but c'est la vie. Next to him was the head of Prick, the foul-mouthed cabbie, whose balls were apparently nowhere near as big as advertised. Across from him was Roofie—the friendly neighborhood bartender rapist—and Hothead, my dearly departed boss. And filling in the last spot at the table, to my right, was the gawking face of Sicko. I said a quick prayer of thanks for Hunter's table being big enough to accommodate all of them, and then dug into my meal.

As I chewed on my last bite of meat, I heard the sound of glass breaking. The room filled with gas. I heard muffled voices shouting my name, along with orders I couldn't quite understand. Then it all went dark.

☆ ☆ ☆

When I woke, a well-dressed man stood before me. A stranger. I looked him up and down, frowning. "Who the hell are you? And where am I?"

The man flashed a blinding grin and extended his hand. "Ferdinand Charming, Attorney-at-Law. And you're in a jail cell, I'm afraid."

"Oh." I ignored his request for a handshake. "And just what do you want?"

"Well, Princess, I'm here to get you off."

I glowered at him.

"If th-that's what you want, of course." A bead of sweat ran down the attorney's chiseled cheeks.

"Well, well, what is this?" I said, giving him a wink. "A man allowing me to give my consent?"

He nodded.

I reached out my hand, giving his a firm shake. "It's about damn time."

ABOUT THE AUTHOR

C. Brennecke is a multimedia artist and writer, hailing from the suburbs of Philadelphia, Pennsylvania. She's a proud alum of Temple University, whose passions include art, feng shui, Tarot, tabletop roleplaying, exclaiming every time she sees a dog, and any creative outlet that lets her put her imagination to work. She's also an avid cuddler and sushi eater, and thinks that she could one day go pro in either sport. Follow her projects at: https://www.mythsmistsmusings.com

I LOVED THE MOTHMAN

A Fictionalized Addition to the Mothman Myth

Cari Dubiel

It's true that when I rolled up to the curb in Point Pleasant, West Virginia, I was unimpressed. That won't be a surprise if you know who I am.

Point Pleasant was a slapdash town on the spot where the Ohio and Kanawha Rivers meet. Always wanting to be an important port city but never quite making it, cursed by the death of Shawnee chief Cornstalk in the 18th century. Maybe that's why the Mothman chose it.

The main street was lined with brick façades and empty buildings. A historic hotel sat across from the Mothman Museum, trying and failing to bring prestige back to the town. The rest of it was all chain restaurants and gas stations, broken cars and pawn shops. Not exactly a prime location for an on-site reporting job.

If you've read the original story, you'll know that my editor sent me there in 2006 for the 40th anniversary of the first Mothman sighting. The museum had just opened, and she wanted me to report on it specifically. I failed to understand how our startup online paper would make any money on such a feature–the Internet was a new frontier, and everyone had a blog.

So I'll cry mea culpa on that one. I'd had no idea how my story would be received. But we'll get to that.

On a brisk fall day in October, I stepped out of my silvery Civic and headed toward the museum.

Terri had sent me specifically because, out of our reporters, I lived the closest. Still, it had been a long drive from Akron, and I was happy to stretch my legs. The air had the same character as it did back home: cool but not uncomfortable, a nip on my skin.

Tightening my green patterned scarf around my neck, I pulled open the metal doors. The place was small, a converted storefront, and I wondered what about it was so compelling. I turned in a circle, taking in the Mothman merchandise and apparel filling the room.

"You must be Jenn." The man behind the shop counter rose to greet me. I'd spoken to him regarding the visit.

I stretched out my hand. "And you're Andrew?"

"The very same."

Andrew's voice was familiar but different in person. More bass. He was swarthy, olive skin, big-shouldered but lean through the middle. Bald pate with some dark stubble. But the eyes: they were magnetic. The kind of eyes a cheesy romance might describe as pools of ink.

Point Pleasant had gotten a lot more interesting.

His hand was warm on mine, the touch fleeting. When I let it go, I cleared my throat, willing my skin to stay unflushed. "I appreciate your time today."

"Not a problem at all. It's great to see people like you come in."

Journalists? Ohioans? Pudgy white women? "I hope that's a compliment," I said.

He didn't reply, just whisked aside a curtain made of black plastic vines.

Andrew explained the legend as I goggled at Mothman re-creations. Sculptures, paintings, line drawings. The Mothman was actually quite beautiful, with its strong gray—or black—torso and spread of giant wings. The common denominator: its eyes were always red.

I shifted my focus back to Andrew. He was still talking, though I'd missed half of what he'd said.

The legend began when Point Pleasant residents sighted a great beast haunting a former World War II munitions plant, now known as the "TNT area," in a local nature preserve. The Mothman was a bad omen, sending the town into a panicked tizzy. Thirteen months later, the Silver Bridge across the river collapsed, killing 46 and injuring many more.

The fervor would have died if not for John Keel, who wrote *The Mothman Prophecies.* He claimed the Mothman was sending him secret messages—when he wasn't making up stories about UFOs and other mysterious happenings. Soon, the town had turned into a Mothman shrine, complete with a themed diner for enthusiasts and a local columnist who kept the cryptid alive.

It was all too much exposition for me. I dug my steno pad out of my messenger bag and began scribbling. I stopped to shake out my cramped wrist, and Andrew laughed. "You got enough material yet?"

"I'm getting pictures next." I put the notebook away and searched for my camera while my cheeks flamed.

"It is a lot." Andrew stood by as I started snapping photos. "Where you going next?"

"The university." It was hard to focus on the conversation and shooting simultaneously. "I've got a meeting with a professor there."

Andrew made a face. "Sandhill Crane guy."

I lowered my camera and raised an eyebrow.

"He'll tell you the Mothman doesn't exist." Andrew pointed to a yellowed article in one of the archival cases. "This one prof kept insisting it was a sandhill crane. They have red around their eyes and it's a big wingspan."

"It's logical."

"And entirely untrue." Andrew ushered me back outside to the main shop. "Come back and I'll show you the reality."

Then I was back on the sidewalk, a breeze chilling me. I pulled my short trench closer and wondered why I felt so alone.

☆ ☆ ☆

That afternoon, I drove more than two hours to the University of West Virginia campus and met Professor Gordon Smith at a coffee shop there. I was starving, having skipped lunch, but I could grab dinner after the interview before driving back to the hotel.

Smith sat at a long oak table in front of the barista station, sipping from a lidded paper cup. He was tall and spindly, pale, with long fingers and a shock of graying brown hair. I placed him at fifty-ish. "I'm not the professor quoted in the articles," he told me right away. "We were colleagues. Smith is a common name."

I resisted the urge to roll my eyes. "So you followed in his footsteps?"

"Not really. He was in a different department."

"And what's your area of expertise?"

"Anthropology." He tugged on the sleeve of his blue-checked shirt. As he turned his head, I noticed how sharp his cheekbones were. "I do all the interviews Robert used to."

I flipped my steno pad onto the table and started writing. "Why is that?"

"Someone has to do it."

No one else in the area was skeptical about the Mothman? Surely another authority could step up for the task. "What did you learn from Dr. Smith?"

Smith folded his arms. Behind him was a tall shelf filled with books floor to ceiling, probably meant for the shop's guests. The scent of old pages mixed with that of fresh coffee. I'd need some for the drive back.

"Dr. Smith knew the truth. The so-called Mothman was a sandhill crane."

"I've heard." I planned to look at pictures of the bird as soon as I could get to the public library. Not many places had wi-fi in those days. "He built a strong case."

"Which no one ever paid attention to," Smith practically snarled. Heads twirled in his direction, looks of disgust crossing faces. I flinched.

"He was quoted so many times, but no one ever listened. They were too absorbed in their own fantasy."

Despite my trepidation at angering more patrons, I continued. "But why not let them have that? Was it hurting anyone?"

"It was hard for Robert." Gordon Smith's eyes flashed. "He was tired when I met him. He had the knowledge, the experience, and he was ignored. Would you like it if your experience was passed over for a fantasy?"

I inched my chair back. "Not at all."

"So give him that. In your story." He got up, showing off his full height. "Give him the credit he deserves."

☆ ☆ ☆

It was late when I finally checked into the Lowe Hotel. Despite the dreary neighborhood, it was a lovely building. Dated but charming, heavy with history. And rumored to be haunted—par for the course in cursed Point Pleasant.

It was too bad I couldn't stay there longer, but I couldn't expense lodging for more than a night. I could research the rest of the story from home. I'd probably have to visit Andrew again before I left, though. Pitting him psychologically against the professor's words would bring conflict to the piece.

Well. I wouldn't mind having another excuse to see him.

I was about to put on my pajamas when my phone rang. I was tempted to ignore it, but in case it was my mom or roommate checking in, I caved.

Andrew's name showed up on the gray pixelated screen. A shot of adrenaline went through me, but I finally gathered the nerve to answer. Maybe he'd remembered something I could use.

"You up for an adventure?" he asked with no preamble.

"Depends what kind."

"Let me take you to the TNT area."

I sucked in a breath. "The actual…"

"You know it." I could sense the grin in his tone.

"At night?"

"It's the only way to have an authentic experience."

I peered out the window. The sky was black. And I was hungry—I never did get dinner, opting to move as fast as I could away from Gordon Smith and WVU.

"Take you to Taco Bell first? Show you the finest cuisine in Point Pleasant. Well, Gallipolis."

My heart sped up. "Sure. Yeah."

"Pick you up in ten."

He hung up. I stared at the wallpaper for a moment, letting my thoughts drift. This would be good for my story. And I couldn't deny the attraction between us... unless I was making it all up.

Could I trust Andrew, though? I thought so. I had mace in my purse, at least.

I went outside to meet him as promised. The silver Mothman statue across from the hotel loomed as it caught the moonlight.

Andrew drove up in a clanking Buick Century and rolled down his window. "Please enter my chariot, dear princess."

"You mean queen?" I had to pull hard to get the door open. The car smelled musty and vaguely smoky.

"I don't smoke." He must have read my expression. "Inherited it when my dad died."

I ran my hand along the fuzzy gray seat. "I'm so sorry."

"It's fine. It was a few years ago, but I can't seem to get the smell out."

He paused, some memory passing over his face. Then he put the car in gear, and we headed out.

After a decadent meal of a Crunchwrap Supreme and a few gorditas, we were back on the road. We didn't talk much. The wildlife preserve was huge, and Andrew searched a while for an entrance. Eventually, he found a dirt access road, and we followed the bumpy terrain as far as the Buick could go.

He put the car in park and killed the engine, then produced a flashlight from under his seat. The light bobbed in the dark as he went around the car to let me out. I grasped his hand without a word.

We assessed the area. Bunkers from wartime hulked around us, ominous silhouettes. I'd read that there were still live bombs here.

"Has anyone seen him recently?" I asked.

"A few people have said so." He gestured to the land. "Camping's not allowed here, but people sneak in."

I blinked. The October night was getting cold, and I'd brought my special fuzzy blanket. I wrapped it around me and hugged myself around the waist. "Do you think it was a sandhill crane?"

Andrew shook his head incrementally. "No."

"Why not?"

He moved the light in silent circles. "The legend gives me something to live for. Without it, I'm a meaningless dude shilling T-shirts."

I felt a rush of empathy. Despite what he said, I knew Andrew had a purpose. I didn't. I floated from job to job, landing on the ridiculous blog site that would never make me money. Well, it eventually brought in the cash, but I didn't know that at the time.

I inched toward him and put my hand on his arm. It was heavy, muscular. He smelled of sandalwood and vanilla.

Andrew dropped the flashlight.

As I reached for his mouth, cupping his cheeks in my palms, I saw a flash of red in his eyes.

My arms went to his strong back. I traced the wings beneath his T-shirt. I breathed in, taking in all of him. Who he really was.

"Is this okay?" he asked.

"Yes."

"You aren't scared?"

I was. But I wanted him.

Andrew's shirt tore. The fabric shredded under my hands. The wings emerged, spanning wide, engulfing me.

☆ ☆ ☆

I woke dazed, sure I'd dreamed it. My head pounded as if I had a hangover, but I hadn't drunk a drop.

I had enough for the story. I should have checked out and headed home. But his pull was magnetic, like his eyes. I couldn't leave yet.

Once I got ready and checked out, I found my car and stuffed my suitcase in the trunk. The Mothman statue blinded me, sunlight reflecting off the metal.

Wandering the banks of the Ohio River, I watched the water roll by. I came across a plaque honoring the victims of the bridge collapse, and I winced. I hadn't written nearly enough about the disaster. I would have to go back to the car for my camera.

I doubled back to the main street, eyeballing my little silver coupe, and ran smack into a wall of a man.

"Hi, Jenn." Andrew jingled the keys to the museum doors. "What brings you here? I thought you were headed home."

My stomach dropped. Would he acknowledge what had happened?

I decided to play it cool even though my mouth was dry, my palms sweating. "Just a few more things to do before I wrap things up."

He thumbed back toward the coffee shop in the next storefront. "Want to get coffee? On me."

I didn't need a stimulant. I was already shaking.

When we reached the shop, Andrew stepped to the counter. I studied the rippling muscles on his back, the blue T-shirt stretching across them. No outline of wings. Maybe I did dream the entire thing.

He handed me a cappuccino, even though I didn't order one. Then he pulled out my chair. We sat.

"I'm not going to lie, Jenn." Andrew leaned forward over his own coffee. "I wish you weren't leaving."

I thought of my dingy apartment, its ugly carpeting, the stains on its beige walls. "I'm not really tied to anything in Akron. I could stay."

"Might be a rash decision. But I could at least take you on a date. Besides this one. If you consider this a date." His face flushed. "I'd like to get to know you better."

"You certainly did last night."

He froze. "Um... what?"

My stomach twisted, but I recovered. "I mean, sorry, I was being too forward. I, uh, dreamed about you last night."

Andrew blinked. "Wow. Well, uh, that's cool."

I'd freaked him out.

He wasn't the Andrew of last night. Not even close.

"Maybe we could set something up for real," he mumbled. "Give me your number?"

I tugged a business card out of my purse and handed it to him. He pocketed it and stood. "I have to get back from the store, but..." The smile returned, if briefly, and I felt a streak of hope. "Let's talk."

☆ ☆ ☆

After Andrew left, I stayed in the coffee shop. I had nowhere else to go. I should have left right then, but instead, I pulled my laptop from my messenger bag and opened a Word document. I ordered another cappuccino, even though I didn't need it, and stared at the blank screen.

The cafe had a "Mothman Special" dessert. Oreo ice cream with two red cherries on top. I ordered that too. The hard chair felt more and more uncomfortable as I ate and drank. Point Pleasant was telling me to leave.

I packed my things and was about to head out when I caught movement outside the window.

I wasn't the only one who noticed. People rushed to look out, crowding the front of the store. Some stepped outside, while others put their hands on the glass, transfixed.

"I don't believe it," someone said. "In broad daylight?"

A grayish black creature stalked down the sidewalk, grumbling and moaning. The sounds were unearthly. My insides pinched. This couldn't be the creature. He wasn't like that.

As it got closer, I saw it wasn't the Mothman. Not even close. It was tall, at least six feet and likely more. The feathers lining its costume ruffled in the breeze. The mask's eyes weren't red, although they were graced with red and white accents. The wings expanded, and a long beak extended as the person tilted up their head.

"It was a sandhill crane!" squawked Gordon Smith.

☆ ☆ ☆

Finally, I prepared to leave Point Pleasant. I shoved my messenger bag and purse onto the seat, got in the car, started it up. But an odd feeling nagged at me like an itch I couldn't scratch. I couldn't leave yet.

We didn't have GPS in 2006, so I stopped in the local library and printed out a MapQuest. I backtracked to the Taco Bell in Gallipolis, got another Crunchwrap with a couple of tacos, and sucked down a Baja Blast as I drove toward the wildlife preserve. I searched for a while until I came across the same access road, easier to see in the daylight.

I ate my food, then sat under a tree till dusk. It was warm for October, but once the sun went down, I was chilled again. As I watched the sunset, resplendent in pinks and purples, I pulled on my hoodie and wrapped my blanket around my shoulders.

The sky darkened. The moon came out. Stars.

Beyond the tree, I caught it. A flap of wings. The sound leathery against the empty night.

He soared down, not bothering to hide his true form. I took him in: bald head, dark wings, red eyes glimmering.

"You came," I said.

"Why wouldn't I?" His voice didn't carry the same weight as Andrew's. It was soft, buttery.

I shrugged even though I was shaking. "I don't know."

He moved closer. This time he smelled of the woods: tree bark, plants, earth. "I'm glad you came back."

"I'm leaving."

"I know."

"You could come with me." I slapped my hand across my mouth, regretting the sentence as soon as I spoke it.

My invitation didn't faze him. "You know I can't."

I reached for his rough palm. "I won't forget you."

He responded by coming closer. And again, he folded his wings around me.

☆ ☆ ☆

I went home and told my roommate I needed a place of my own. I applied for full-time jobs, positions that would provide benefits and a regular salary. Health insurance was like gold. I got a gig designing ads for a magazine that catered to home shoppers. The products were funny gadgets that I could never imagine buying. Automatic cat boxes, full-body copper sleeves, poorly made back massagers. Onesie pajamas for the whole family. My paycheck came every two weeks, and I found a decent apartment with a balcony where I could watch the sun set.

I continued writing for Terri. The job was better as a side gig–I wasn't scraping the barrel for income anymore. She e-mailed me upon reading my first draft. *WTF happened down there?*

We published it. It went viral before viral was a thing. I ignored all the nasty comments as the money rolled into my bank account. I felt like a queen in a treasure trove, preening atop my mountain of cash.

Everything was good. Except that one small thing.

I'm going there this weekend. It's the 50th anniversary—a big deal. Terri, who works at BuzzFeed now, asked me to write a follow-up. I'm more than happy to do it. Andrew and I are still in touch, although we never dated. I haven't dated anyone since that night in the field. But I hope Andrew and I will grab coffee under less awkward circumstances.

I will stay in the Lowe again and walk the river. Pay respects to the dead. In the museum, there will be more portraits of him, more artistic renderings.

I've stayed away from the wildlife preserve. It's still possible I dreamed those nights, and I've been scared of what might happen if I returned. When I went back to Ohio ten years ago, I wanted to start a new life, and I did it. I'm proud of that.

But tonight, I'm stopping at Taco Bell, and I'm going to the woods.

—Jennifer Striker
November 12, 2016

☆ ☆ ☆

Author's Note:

I did a lot of research for this story, but it's possible I may have goofed. Any errors are my own.

Dr. Robert L. Smith was a real person who passed away in 1997. I have tried to represent him in as neutral a way as possible. I don't know if he was really peeved when no one would listen to him, but I definitely would be. Thanks to Ashley Sroka for helping me find his legacy.

ABOUT THE AUTHOR

Cari Dubiel is a writer and librarian in Northeast Ohio. She is the author of HOW TO REMEMBER, an award winner from the Mystery Writers of America (Midwest Chapter) and Library Journal. She has also published multiple short stories and a novella, OFF SWITCH (written as C.T. Baker). Cari is represented by Lynnette Novak of the Seymour Agency.

❧ 4 ❧

OPEN SESAME

A Retelling of Ali Baba & the Forty Thieves

Blair Cosby

Putrid wind disseminated the smell of death along with a fine powdery dust. Soon, the bodies would be half buried in shifting amber and gray sands. The usual chugging of the refinery had stopped. Everything was strangely still except for the sand blowing in through the smoldering hole that had been blown in the control room wall.

Soot now covered the computer terminals, screens, and switches. An outgoing S.O.S. that would take days to reach sympathetic ears bleeped into the void. A few ravaged bodies of uniformed fighting men lay strewn about the floor, but the horror of their mangled flesh was nothing compared to what lay within the vault at the back of the control room.

The vault door stood wide open. It had been unlocked, not forced. Inside were the corpses of every man, woman, and child that had called this rock home. Save one.

Jasper Tir sat in the middle of the vault, surrounded by the death of everyone he had called family, friend, and neighbor. He wore a blue corporate atmospheric suit and helmet. Scabbed blood ringed his eyes like makeup from an evil ritual.

Understanding slowly crept back into his mind. This would not stand. The bastards had broken his brain; the least they could do was leave it that way. He shook his head violently, slamming it against the side of his helmet. A screaming numbness swelled behind his eyes again. He sighed, seemingly calm as he stood and tiptoed around the bodies, careful not to disturb them.

He stopped in the control room to pick up a sidearm from the body of a security guard. The hand gripping it did not want to let go, but a good yank ripped it free. Jasper tucked the pistol into his armpit and stepped through the hole in the wall, out into the perpetual purple twilight.

He watched the monstrous silhouettes of the creatures who had done this board their alien craft in the valley below. It towered over the landscape like a tick engorged with blood. Its repulsors roared to life, and it began to rise.

Jasper watched it drift over the jagged peaks and disappear into the inky darkness. His eyes lifted to the black hole in the sky, ringed with captured light and energy. Even at this God-forsaken end of the system it was the largest and brightest object in the sky—apart from the two misshapen "moons" orbiting disconcertingly close.

Jasper could feel his sanity pressing in again. He squeezed his eyes shut, willing it away, trying in vain to hold onto the numbness. He slowly reached up to his helmet with both hands and jerked it open.

The toxic fumes of the pseudo-atmosphere immediately stung his nostrils. He felt the moisture being sucked from his skin and eyes. He dropped the helmet. It bounced a few feet away in the light gravity. He drew the gun from under his arm and pressed the barrel to his eye. The barrel's cool metal felt good. He pressed harder. The pain felt good too. His eye began to bleed again.

He pulled the trigger.

☆ ☆ ☆

TWENTY-SEVEN STANDARD YEARS LATER

Baba stared at the gaping mouth of the tunnel. Even in A-L-I-361's forever dusk it seemed to exude darkness. He told himself the dreading was worse than the doing, but he knew from experience that in this case it was not true. He'd been mining in that tunnel, or others just like it, pockmarking the surface of the asteroid, for eleven standard years. He knew the back spasms, muscle aches, and sweat-stung eyes awaiting him. He knew the constant hunching and bending over responsible for the small but distinct hump between his shoulder blades. He knew the aching cold that was powerless to stop his body's core temp from flaring under the strain of the manual labor, yet was always there, ready to chill him to the bone the moment he took a break. He knew the roaring noise of beam-drills and the constant shouting. There was no silence back home like the silence on A-L-I-361 in the early morning when the refinery shift change happened. But you couldn't appreciate it if your ears never stopped ringing.

The rhythm of twelve hours on, eight hours off, made for weird, unrestful nights and a strangely short day/night cycle. But the asteroid had no natural day or night of its own, and the Company had decided 20-hour day/night cycles increased output at the mines and refinery by 5.06%. That was enough of a reason. For most of A-L-I-361's orbit you were too far from any civilized systems to send real-time communications anyway, so what did it matter to the corporate suits? Other colonies had day/night cycles as short as fifteen hours. Baba had heard stories about how days that short fuck with your head. When's the last time anybody heard of a scientific genius or a great writer or anything of any cultural significance coming from Gurdi-Prime or Liamsphere? Baba was sure the 20-hour days here were fucking with his head, too. But nobody had studied that. At least, nobody on the level. The Company was probably studying them all like lab rats, but that would never be published. Trade secrets. Those studies were about output, productivity. If psychological damage or emotional unhealth didn't impact output, it was a non-variable.

Suddenly a hand on his shoulder called Baba back to reality.

"Burnin' daylight. You wanna be able to eat on our way home, don't ya?"

Baba prickled with annoyance at his older brother. Qasim bleared at him through hungover eyes and belched. "Let's go, kiddo."

Qasim trudged into the tunnel, calling back over his shoulder, "Come on, Morg!"

Morg, Qasim's Fusion Z-series android, trotted along to catch up. The Z-series was squatter than the typical Fusion droid and walked on four legs. Baba guessed it was supposed to make her seem dog-like and therefore more appealing. But it didn't work. Her head, if you could call it that, was a shapeless box covered in optical lenses, antennae, and appendages of various sizes. It could slide to the fore or aft end of the droid, so you never really knew whether she was coming or going. Morg tended to leave her head in the middle, making her look sort of like a tri-level Olympic podium with legs.

Baba slung his bulky beam-drill over his shoulder and marched into the dark tunnel.

The tunnel was lit only with dim orange repulsor lights, programmed to hover over wherever miners were clumped together in groups. But working in groups like that was for suckers, so Baba and Qasim were used to working only by the lights from their helmets, and, since Qasim had blown all his savings on Morg about a year ago, they worked by her light too.

Baba followed Qasim and Morg as they passed all the other miners and veered off down a narrow side-tunnel to work alone. They had to stoop as they went. Many hands may make light work, but they also make lighter per-head returns. This way, if Baba or Qasim struck a large vein, they could harvest as much of the ore by themselves as they could before the vultures showed up to "help."

Baba had thought Morg was the biggest waste of credits he had ever seen Qasim splurge on, and Qasim had been splurging all his life. That's why they were on this rock, trying to dig their way out of debt. Baba had lost track of how many joint accounts Qasim had opened in his name. But Baba had to admit, when they did hit pay dirt, Morg increased their profits considerably. She could haul three or four times as much ore as they could. Her sensors were pretty good at guessing where to drill too.

Morg stopped suddenly. Her robotic voice chirped, "Siliceous density is drastically reduced at this spot. Possible zincu vein near the surface."

Baba couldn't decide if she sounded like a little girl or an old grandma. Either way, she sounded more like a computer's rough simulation, not the real thing.

"One way to find out," Qasim grunted as he aimed his beam-drill at the tunnel's wall.

He switched it on. The noise was deafening as the vaguely orange, nearly imperceptible beam of energy tore into the rock wall of the tunnel, grinding the stone into sand that flew about. Morg switched on an air hose and began blowing the sand away from them.

The pitch of the beam changed octaves, and green sparks started spewing from the wall as little drops of molten metal pearled and dripped to the floor. Qasim switched off the drill. Morg directed her hose at the wall, blowing sand away and uncovering a glittering vein of silver-colored zincu ore.

"Out of the way." Baba pulled a chisel and hammer from his toolbelt and hipped Morg to the side so he could get to work.

☆ ☆ ☆

Twelve hours later, Baba hobbled over to a conveyor belt and dropped his last load of ore for the day. He stretched, wincing at the pain. One of the company foremen watched a monitor as the conveyor moved the ore through a scanner.

Baba watched numbers grow in real time on a tablet screen at his wrist as the ore was scanned and credited to his account. Baba looked up from his screen just in time to see the ore travel out of the scanner and onto another, larger conveyor system inside a sealed pipe. Pipes like that zig-zagged all over A-L-I-361. They all led to the refinery at the base of the asteroid's largest peak: an active volcano. Some of its heat was harvested to run the refinery. There was no mining on that mountain. Point your beam-drill in the wrong direction and you could flood the mine shaft with boiling acid or molten lava. It was just about the only place left on this rock not pockmarked with mines.

Baba turned to Qasim and Morg. The three of them began shambling away. The foreman called after them, "The transport leaves at oh-six-hundred hours, whether you're on it or not!"

Without turning, Baba waved his hand in acknowledgment.

They trudged their way home in silence, making their way through a series of impact craters and canyons, toward the little village of hovels in the valley below the refinery.

Baba stopped at the mouth of one of the abandoned mines and called after Qasim, "We're running low on lichen." The valley was full of old mines that had long since run dry. But they still held resources for those patient or desperate enough to look.

Qasim turned to his little brother. "You're gonna eat that shit when you could eat at the cafeteria on the transport?"

Baba shot back with, "You really wanna blow all your money at the cafeteria before we even reach the core worlds? For transport food?"

"I'm too tired to have this fight again. I'm goin' home." Qasim turned and walked away.

Baba called after him, "Fine, I'll do it myself."

"Morg'll help you, won't you, Morg?"

"Of course," Morg chirped.

"Great," Baba said sarcastically as he turned toward the tunnel. Morg scurried to catch up.

Baba and Morg made their way into the dark tunnel, ducking under a chain with a CAUTION sign dangling from it.

Their beams of light crisscrossed back and forth, searching for the only thing that grew on A-L-I-361: lichen. Their lights settled on a patch of wall covered in blooming yellow, white, and sickly blue lichen. Some of it looked fuzzy, some of it covered in protruding tendrils, and some had elaborate flaky shapes that reminded Baba of old drawings he had seen of coral reefs in school.

Baba pulled out a knife and began delicately harvesting the lichen, dropping them into his knapsack.

"Almost full here. Get your basket ready, droid." Baba said.

"Morg," Morg chirped.

Baba scowled at her and closed up his bag. He set it down, leaning it against a beam that groaned in protest. Dust sprinkled from the ceiling. Wide-eyed, Baba instinctively reached out and grabbed the beam, trying to steady it. It creaked again. A bit of gravel rained down on his head.

Baba kicked his knapsack away and used his hands to try to shift the beam back straight. He pulled too hard. POP! The base of the beam snapped off, and suddenly Baba found himself holding the beam for a gut-wrenching moment.

A chunk of the ceiling collapsed, and a wave of gravel and rocks cascaded down onto Baba.

Morg slid her head over her aft legs and, with a series of grinding pops, split herself in half, down the middle. Her front half rushed forward, stemming the flow of rocks and gravel that pounded into Baba. Her back half grabbed Baba under the arms and sprinted backwards, pulling him out of the pile of rubble. She dragged him back through the tunnel and didn't stop till they were out under the open valley sky again.

Baba lay in a daze.

"Sir, are you injured?" Morg asked. Baba didn't answer. "Can you feel your fingers and toes?"

"What?" Baba asked.

Morg walked around to face him. She scanned his body. "No visible lacerations detected."

Snapping out of it, Baba jumped to his feet. "I'm fine, I'm fine, I'm fine."

He felt his body up and down to make sure he was telling the truth.

"I think you just saved my life." He looked at Morg, really seeing her for the first time. "Thank you."

"It was my pleasure, sir."

Baba smiled at the little droid and patted her head.

"Sorry. Don't know why I did that."

"I liked it, sir," Morg chirped.

Baba changed the subject, "What about your legs? I mean, your other legs?"

"They are working their way out of the rubble now," Morg said.

Sure enough, a moment later, her other half walked out of the tunnel, doing a sort of delicate tippy-toe to balance on two legs.

"I'm sorry I could not retrieve your knapsack or the lichen," Morg said as she reattached her two halves with a series of loud grinding pops.

"Don't worry about it." Baba sighed. "We'll just eat in the damned cafeteria."

Wincing, Baba turned and began limping toward home.

"Sir, you are injured," Morg said.

"It's nothing. I think one of the big ones landed on my foot," Baba said, continuing to limp forward.

Morg stood up on her hind legs and slid her head all the way forward, giving herself an almost human shape. She wrapped one of her aft legs around Baba's shoulder like an arm.

"Put some of your weight on me, sir," Morg insisted. "I am stronger than I look."

Baba shot her a surprised smile. "Thanks, Morg."

☆ ☆ ☆

"What a fucking idiot to kill yourself for some lichen," Qasim spat as he and Baba sat around the stove in their one-room hovel (two rooms if you counted the airlock).

"It tastes like shit," Qasim continued, scooping himself another bowl of lichen stew.

"I thought maybe we could sell some when we get to the core worlds. You know deep space lichen's considered a delicacy some places," Baba said as he lounged on his bed with his foot elevated.

"Those plush colonials would eat snagger shit if you process it with enough sweetener," Qasim said.

"It's not the sweetener that sells it. It's the hint of sea salt. Preferably the large-grained stuff supposedly harvested from a lunar sea somewhere or other."

"It's bullshit is what it is. We have to eat that bitter shit all day. Stew and tea and we fucking grind it into bread! And those assholes put it in a chocolate truffle and charge an arm and a leg for it," Qasim growled.

"Or a foot," Baba joked, indicating his injury. Qasim was not amused.

Baba changed the subject. "It sucks we have to leave Morg here. She saved my life."

"Don't call it that," Qasim said.

"What, Morg?" Baba asked.

"She. It's a droid. It doesn't have junk. It can't bump uglies. It's an *it*."

"She has a personality, doesn't she? She doesn't refer to herself as *it*," Baba countered.

"I thought you hated that thing!"

"I never said that," Baba said, glancing at Morg.

"I distinctly remember you saying it was the biggest waste of credits you'd ever seen."

Morg turned and looked at Baba. He looked away, embarrassed.

"It helps us move ore. It doesn't have feelings," Qasim declared.

Baba let the words hang in the air. Then he rolled over to try to sleep, knowing it was a long shot. In the morning, they'd be getting off this rock for the first time in over a decade. He was too amped to sleep.

☆ ☆ ☆

Baba and Qasim stood in line to go through a checkpoint and board the transport. The last ship off A-L-I-361 before its elliptical orbit around the black hole at the center of the system took it outside civilized space. Most of its orbit was through colonized space where the rule of law offered, if not protection, at least the fear of retribution for brigandage and piracy. It took this hunk of rock twenty-seven standard years to complete one orbit. The last time it left colonial space, raiders of unknown origin plundered the refinery, leaving nothing of value and no souls alive. Of course, the government had tried to send envoys into the unknown regions beyond the rim of colonized space, but none had ever returned. Whatever life haunted the dark edges of the system, it had little interest in knowing or being known.

Baba's eyes drifted to the refinery. You could still see the seams where they'd patched the fury wrought twenty-seven years ago.

One more person waited in front of them in line, then it'd be their turn. Baba looked up at the dim sky, past the low-orbiting misshapen moons, at the scope of the black emptiness. He tried not to think about the creatures who lay in wait there. What did they do for the twenty-six years while A-L-I-361 was in protected space? Raped and pillaged their own kind, he supposed.

"Got your credits ready to transfer?"

Baba realized it was their turn. Blasden, one of the company foremen, was manning the checkpoint. He stuck out his fat hand impatiently. "Come on, dat sticks or get out of line."

"We've got the money for two seats right here," Qasim barked.

Qasim handed over a dat stick. Blasden inserted it into his tablet. He leaned forward and whispered to Qasim, "This better have what you owe me, or you ain't going nowhere."

Baba did not like the sound of that. He studied Qasim's expression for a clue, but Qasim was often inscrutable, even to him.

Blasden screwed up his face, doing the math in his head. "Fifty-two K, minus what you owe me on your tab. That's one seat. Welcome aboard." He turned to Baba. "Dat stick?"

"Half of that is my money!" Baba blurted.

Blasden looked from Qasim to Baba. "Fine. You can board then. I don't care which one of you stays but you've bought a single seat."

"That's enough for two tickets," Baba insisted.

"Twenty-five K per ticket. Your brother's outstanding tab is twenty-six. Don't worry, I left the change on the dat stick. One of you may board now. I really don't give two shits who."

Baba stepped forward, pulling Qasim along with him. "We're both going."

Blasden put one hand out to block their way. With the other he opened the flap of the holster on his hip. "You got another twenty-five K, you can both go. Otherwise, you have purchased one ticket."

Two other armed company men stepped out of the transport, hands on their sidearms.

"I'm not going without my brother," Baba said.

"Very noble of you," Blasden said. "Family. I get it. But your brother's a gambling piece of shit. Always has been. Take my advice and get on the transport. He ain't worth it. We just won't speak of this again."

Qasim lunged at Blasden. "Son of a bitch!"

With uncanny speed, Blasden drew his sidearm and shot Qasim in the chest with a stunning blast of red energy. Qasim crumpled to the ground.

Baba put his hands up and stared daggers into Blasden.

"He'll be fine when he wakes up in a couple hours. We'll be gone by then. Just get on the transport. Your brother made his choices. Don't die for him."

"I told you," Baba heard himself say. "I'm not leaving without my brother."

An hour later, Baba watched from his hovel window as the transport took off and disappeared into the starry sky. His eyes drifted to his unconscious brother, who snored softly on the floor where Baba had dropped him.

Qasim jerked awake. "What happened?"

Baba didn't answer. The reality of what had occurred slowly dawned on Qasim's face. He looked away.

Baba put his hand on his brother's shoulder. "Grab anything you want to keep. We can't stay here."

☆ ☆ ☆

Baba, Qasim, and Morg set up camp in an abandoned mine shaft high on one of the peaks overlooking the central valley. They pitched a tent they had "borrowed" around the corner of one of the sub-tunnels, so it wouldn't be visible from the mouth of the shaft. Qasim had bitched about the prospect of sleeping on the cold rock floor of the mine, but at least they wouldn't be easy to find if, when whoever wiped out the entire colony twenty-seven years ago showed up again.

Qasim paced a tiny circle around their cramped tent.

"Please sit down. You're driving me crazy," Baba told him.

"Have you ever been inside company housing suites?" Qasim asked.

"Of course not. Neither have you."

Qasim's eyes lighted. "Not yet."

☆ ☆ ☆

Metal scraped against metal. The door to the refinery control room groaned as Baba and Qasim pried it open with chisels. They had already melted the lock with one of their beam-drills.

Finally, they had it open wide enough for Morg to pass. She told them if they could get her into the control room, from there she could grant them access to any area of the refinery. Sure enough, a minute after Morg had entered the control room, the door glided open the rest of the way.

Baba and Qasim entered the control room for the first time. Morg asked them where they wanted to go first.

"The vault," Qasim said, staring hungrily at the giant vault door in the back of the room. Baba hadn't even noticed the vault. His eyes had been drawn to seams in the front wall where they had patched up a breach made twenty-seven years ago by an unknown force. A force that was probably on its way here now. Baba had heard rumors that most of the bodies had been found in the vault his brother wanted to open.

"Access is blocked via exponentially increased encryption," Morg said. "I estimate it could take approximately three years for me to gain access."

Baba's eyes drifted over to the huge vault door. Something was off about it. The door wasn't flush with the frame. "Look, it's already open."

Qasim nearly tripped over himself as he sprinted past Baba to the door. Baba was right, it was slightly ajar. Qasim swung the heavy door open, then his shoulders slumped. The vault was empty.

Baba laughed. "What did you expect? Last time, they lost everything."

From there, they checked out the corporate living quarters. Qasim had Morg proactively unlock every door in the facility.

The first few rooms they explored were depressingly meager. Even the company guards and foremen who lorded so much power over them lived in cramped dormitories, barely nicer than the hovel Baba and Qasim occupied. At least here, in the refinery, they weren't exposed to the bone-chilling cold.

Finally, they checked out the suites reserved for the Executive Officer of the mine and any visiting company stooges. Baba doubted any had visited in decades. The suite included a sauna, a media center, and a hot tub. Qasim growled when he saw it. "I didn't know there was a bathtub anywhere on this rock."

There was even a shelf of real paper books. Baba grabbed one and laid down on one of the couches in the media center. "I haven't been this comfortable since we left the core worlds."

Qasim entered the media center and started shoving the books into his backpack. "Do you have any idea how much these are worth?"

Baba groaned. "Who are you gonna sell them to? The only person who could afford them lives in this suite."

"I'll find someone. Consider it a long-term investment." Qasim grinned.

Baba closed his book and stood up. "Come on, put 'em back."

"Fuck this guy and his books and his hot tub and his comfy-ass couch. I'm sick of it. If I can't find a buyer, I'll rip them up. He can find the pages strewn about this stupid rock."

"I'll see you back at the cave," Baba said.

"I'll come with you," Morg chirped.

"Whatever," Qasim said, stuffing more books into his pack.

Baba and Morg made their way back down to the main entrance of the refinery and out into the open valley. They'd started to trudge down the sloped path when Qasim called after them to wait.

"Done plundering for the day?" Baba asked mirthlessly.

"Pack got full." Qasim smirked.

Out of nowhere they heard a low rumble. Their eyes scanned the twilight sky, and Baba's blood ran cold. A huge spacecraft, like a cosmic arachnid, flew over the mountains.

"Run!" Baba shouted.

They sprinted for their cave, ignoring the paths and cutting across the landscape. Baba's lungs felt like they were going to explode. Behind them, the alien craft stopped over their valley and slowly descended to land.

They ran along the edge of a narrow ravine. Morg's feet slipped. They heard her cry for help as she went over the edge. She bounced and slid down the steep side of the ravine, causing a small rockslide along the way. She landed on a boulder not quite at the bottom of the ravine, half buried in rocks and dirt.

Baba looked over his shoulder. The alien craft had touched down.

Baba cursed under his breath. "You got a rope or something?"

"What? No, I don't. Let's go!" Qasim turned and began to run.

"We can't just leave her down there," Baba insisted.

"I'll buy a new one."

Baba swallowed his fear and slid down on his butt into the ravine. He rode a wave of dirt and gravel down to land on top of Morg.

"I'm not waiting for you!" Qasim yelled from above.

Baba looked up just in time to see his brother run out of sight. He turned to Morg. "We're gonna get you outta here. How ya doing?"

"Running diagnostics now..."

Baba looked around at his surroundings. They were about three-fourths of the way down the steep, gravelly wall. To their right, the ravine eventually opened up to the valley. To their left, it got narrower until it became a slot canyon, abruptly ending in a sheer rock wall on the side of the volcano. Nowhere to hide and nothing to dig with.

"Diagnostics complete. All systems are functional. I should be able to dig myself out in a jiffy," Morg said.

Morg wriggled her front limbs free and began to push away the dirt and debris but stopped when Baba shushed her. They both listened for a moment. They could hear strange voices approaching.

"Shit, shit, shit! What do we do, Morg?" Baba's mind was going blank with panic.

Morg grabbed Baba and shoved him into the pile of dirt and gravel that had built up around them. Then she pounded the boulder they were wedged atop, and more dirt and gravel cascaded down, caking them in dust and debris.

They lay perfectly still. Baba tried not to breathe. There was a tiny gap in the pile of gravel that he could just barely see through. What he saw fueled his nightmares for years to come.

Forty alien marauders of unknown origins and species approached. Some synthetic androids, some insectoid, some reptilian, all malevolent in intent and form. A few of them scurried on the walls of the ravine like bugs, but most walked upright. They were armed from head to toe, with cruel blades, pikes, and alien projectiles. A few wore armor covered in grotesque carvings of skeletal faces mewling in silent agony.

They passed within a few feet of Baba and Morg, jesting and growling at each other in strange languages. Baba's eye fell on a creature whose claws and shells made it look like an unspeakable crustacean. To his horror, Baba realized it had carved those same ghoulish faces directly into its exoskeleton.

One lizard-like creature with six legs and two tails scurried right overtop of Baba and Morg. Baba felt its talons click against his helmet.

The abominable parade fell silent and came to a halt as they reached the place where the ravine abruptly ended. Their leader, a four-armed creature about eight feet tall and covered in gray fur and scales, made his way to the front of the group and spoke a single word, loud and clear enough to lodge in Baba's mind: "Nar-goth."

A fissure cracked the rock face. Teal smoke exploded forth but quickly dissipated. When it was gone, Baba saw the mouth of a cave where, a moment before, the ravine had ended in a craggy wall.

The corsairs filed into the volcanic cave's gaping mouth and disappeared into darkness. When they were gone, Baba wrestled his left arm free and checked the screen on his wrist: oxygen supply at twenty percent.

"Don't move, sir. We do not know when they will return," Morg whispered.

Baba shoved his arm back into the debris piled around him. He wasn't sure how long he could stand it, to lay there like a worm in the earth, cramped and unmoving. He tried to distract himself by singing a song in his mind, but his mind was stubbornly blank. No lyrics. No melodies. No rhythms. It was like he had never heard a song in his life.

Then, out of the depths, a single lyric from his childhood came to mind. Once, as children, he and Qasim were dropped off at an old movie palace by their grandmother for a special treat. Qasim had complained about how old-fashioned and boring it was. Baba couldn't remember anything about it except the feeling that he had secretly loved it. And now this lyric formed distinctly in his mind:

"She fell from the sky, she fell very far, and 'Kansas,' she says, is the name of the star."

He didn't have a clue what the hell that was all about, but he clung to it like a lifeline. Repeating it over and over in his mind. "She fell from the sky. She fell very far, and—"

The monstrous corsairs came pouring back out of the cave's mouth. Baba willed his heart to stop pounding and his breath to be quiet. When all forty of them had filed out, the leader turned back to the opening and said again, "Nar-goth."

With a jet of teal smoke and flash of light, the opening was gone, replaced again by a seemingly normal rock face.

When the raiders had gone out of sight and earshot, Baba finally pulled himself free from the dirt and gravel. He stretched his aching muscles, popping his joints. He helped Morg wriggle free and stand up.

They carefully climbed down to the bottom of the ravine.

Baba wiped the dust from Morg's optical lenses. "How ya doing? Everything still work?"

"I am fine, but I do not think it wise for me to attempt to climb out," Morg chirped.

"Who said anything about climbing out?" Baba turned and walked down the ravine to the secret door. He examined the rock face but couldn't feel any seams or cracks.

He wasn't sure if it would work, but it was worth a shot. He stepped back and said the password, "Nar-goth."

The rock wall cracked open again, revealing the mouth of the cave.

Baba turned and grinned at Morg.

Morg stuck by Baba's side as he trespassed into the long, dark tunnel. The first thing he noticed was the heat emanating from up ahead. Then he noticed how the tunnel gradually sloped downward. Eventually his eyes adjusted to the darkness, and he realized that, along with the heat, there was a dim red glow up ahead. Baba kept close to the wall of the tunnel as he crept further down and further in.

"Sir," Morg did her best to whisper. "My sensors indicate the atmosphere in here is safe for you to breathe. You can save your oxygen supply."

Baba looked at Morg for a moment, wondering if he was willing to trust his life to this droid. He shrugged and took off his helmet, taking a deep breath. The air smelled like sulfur, but it didn't burn. It felt good in his lungs, less stale than his suit's air. They crept onward.

Finally, they neared the end of the tunnel. Baba stopped. The tunnel opened into a huge cavern filled with a fiery glow and pale teal smoke. Baba edged into the cavern. At the center of the cave was a pool of molten lava—and piled high all around it were treasures. Treasures from all over the galaxy, from a thousand civilizations Baba had never heard of. He recognized piles of books, platinum bars, and silver coins that must've been pillaged from colonial ships and outposts. But there were also glittering objects of bizarre shape, unknown use, and mysterious origin.

But most entrancing of all was the molten pool. He couldn't take his eyes off it. Something about the way the magma swirled, a slow spiral of heat and death, captivated him. Light and shadow were as one here, and these obscene piles of wealth seemed a fitting tribute to the glow of the pool.

"Baba!" Morg called him back to the moment.

Baba shook his head, as if shaking the sleep out of his eyes. He was shocked to find himself standing at the edge of the pool. He didn't remember crossing the cavern floor. The reality of the heat became overwhelming. The rubber fingers of his gloves were softening and sticky. He jumped back, away from the pool.

"Let's get outta here," Baba said. He started to walk back toward the tunnel but stopped. He turned to Morg. "Got your basket?"

☆ ☆ ☆

Qasim paced back and forth inside the tent hidden in the abandoned mine shaft. Suddenly he heard a noise outside, the scuff of a foot on rock. He snatched up his beam-drill and switched off his lamp. Crouching down, he waited in the dark.

"Qasim?"

It sounded like Baba, but Qasim didn't answer. He aimed his drill at the door.

"If you're in there, we're coming in!"

Qasim didn't move until the tent unzipped and he saw Baba and Morg were alone.

"You're not gonna believe this," Baba said.

Qasim switched on the light as Baba took Morg's basket, and heaving with all his might, flung it on the ground.

"Don't tell me you went for more lichen with those things on the prowl," Qasim sighed and plopped down on his cot.

"Open it," Baba insisted.

"You open it."

Baba reached in, pulled out a platinum bar, and threw it at Qasim's feet.

Swearing, Qasim jumped up and threw open the lid of the basket. It was full of glistening platinum bars.

"Our digging days are over. There's enough here for early retirement in style," Baba said.

"Where did you get this?"

"You should've seen it. Those creatures have got a stash here."

Qasim's eyes widened. "There's more?"

"We're lucky we got outta there alive. We're set for life. Half of this is yours. We just need to wait it out till we're back in civilized space and we're flying to the core worlds first class," Baba said.

"Where is it?"

Baba sat down. He suddenly felt exhausted. "It doesn't matter. We can't go back. We saw those raiders come and go twice while we made our way back here. It's not worth the risk. Look how much platinum is here! Did you ever imagine you'd be this rich?"

Qasim turned to Morg. "Morg, tell me where it is."

"I am sorry, but I gave my word to Baba that I would not reveal the location," Morg chirped.

Qasim flew into a rage, upturning his cot, scattering his gear around the tent. He turned and kicked Morg with his bare foot. It did not make him feel better. He screamed and clutched his foot. He fell to the ground in a heap, slowly catching his breath.

"I just want to know where it is," Qasim whined.

"Forget it. I'm going to bed." Baba peeled off his atmospheric suit and got ready to sleep.

But his sleep was not restful. He dreamt of the pool of magma swirling endlessly. When he woke, it was worse. Qasim nagged him constantly about the location of the treasure . For two days, they didn't dare venture out of the tent. The hours were filled with nothing but uneasy sleep and Qasim's whining. Baba wanted to shake him and scream in his face that it was for his own damn good. But they didn't dare speak above a whisper for fear of being heard by the alien ears prowling outside.

In the middle of the third night, Baba was dreaming about the pool again and shivering when he awoke to find Morg pulling a blanket over him. Startled, Baba recoiled.

"Sorry. I did not mean to frighten you. You looked so cold." Morg chirped.

Ignoring her, Baba's eyes fell to Qasim, who was up and putting on his atmospheric suit.

"What's going on?"

"If you're not gonna tell me where it is I'll find it myself," Qasim said, zipping up his suit.

"Can't you just wait?" Baba asked. "It won't be long before we're back in colonized space. Those creatures will leave and we can plunder their stash in peace."

"What if they take it with them when they go? What if the company men show up before we've hidden it? You think they'll let us keep it?"

Baba pleaded with Qasim not to go, but he had made up his mind.

"It's gotta be between here and the refinery. I'll find it." Qasim put his helmet on and exited the tent.

Baba wasn't sure how long he sat on his cot, motionless. Finally, he looked at Morg. "Every moment I wait, the odds of him getting himself killed go up, don't they?"

"Is that a rhetorical question?" Morg asked.

"Yes." Baba stood and suited up.

☆ ☆ ☆

Baba stood at the mouth of the abandoned mine they occupied, staring into the valley below. The alien ship was dark and quiet. Many of the village's structures had been broken into, their doors left ajar, their windows broken. The lights of the refinery were on. The main entrance blasted open. Baba saw shadows moving in the windows. He prayed that ransacking the refinery would keep them busy for a while. He screwed up his courage and stepped into the valley.

Baba and Morg caught up to Qasim near the edge of the ravine Morg had fallen into. He grabbed Qasim's shoulder and whispered, "Come back with me! They could show up any minute."

"You want to run and hide, be my guest," Qasim said, bending down and picking up a rock. "I'm not going anywhere till I find that treasure. You said the cave had breathable air, right?"

Baba didn't like the look on his brother's face.

Suddenly, Qasim struck Baba's visor with the rock. Baba fell backwards. Qasim leapt on him and brought the rock down again and again.

"Qasim, no! Please stop this, sir!" Morg cried out.

CRACK! Qasim brought the rock down a final time. Air started hissing from Baba's helmet.

Baba shoved Qasim away, grasping at the crack, trying to hold the air in. "You psychopath!"

"That cave's around here someplace," Qasim calmly stated. "It's the fastest way to more air."

Clutching the crack in his helmet, Baba stumbled to the edge of the ravine and looked around for a safe way down. Nothing looked good, and he was running out of time. He plopped down onto his butt and slid down like last time. He landed at the bottom in a heap, along with a small avalanche of dirt and gravel. Behind him, Qasim and Morg began to carefully climb down.

Still clutching his helmet, Baba could feel the air escaping between his fingers, even with his gloves on. He scrambled to his feet and rushed down the ravine till he came to the rock wall. "Nar-goth," he shouted.

The entrance appeared as before, with a crack and a rush of teal smoke. He scrambled inside and hurried down the tunnel several yards before he fell to his knees and snapped off his helmet. He gasped in great lungfuls of air.

Baba sat, catching his breath, as Qasim sauntered by. "I knew you'd make it," he said as he passed. "Here."

Qasim tossed something at Baba. It bounced off his chest and landed on the floor. Baba picked it up and held it close to his face to see it in the dim light: a roll of electrical tape. His brother had planned this. Baba shouted after Qasim, who had already disappeared into the darkness. "Asshole!"

Morg plodded up as Baba went to work taping up the crack in his helmet. "I cannot believe he would do such a thing. May I be of assistance, sir?"

"No, thanks," Baba grunted.

"Morg! Come on!" Qasim hollered from down the tunnel. Morg reluctantly turned and trudged after him.

Finally, Baba finished taping and put his helmet back on. He pulled off his glove and felt around the edges of the tape to see if he could feel any airflow. He did at a couple of spots, so he added more tape and performed another airflow test. This time, he couldn't feel anything.

Baba made his way down the tunnel to the cavern below. Qasim had come prepared with empty sacks and duffel bags. Two of them were already loaded with treasure. Morg was loading her basket too. Baba stood at the mouth of the tunnel and called out to Qasim, "Come on, we gotta go!"

"Can you believe this place? Have you ever seen anything so

beautiful in your life?" Qasim dashed around the room, manically snatching up more treasure.

Baba tried not to look at the pool of magma in the center of the cavern, but his eyes always seemed to end up there, following the swirling flow around and around. A couple of bubbles rose to the surface and burst in puffs of fire and smoke.

Baba yanked his eyes away and yelled at Qasim. "Are you coming or not?"

Qasim laughed. "I'm not even close to finished."

"Bye, then," Baba said. He turned and headed back up the dark tunnel.

☆ ☆ ☆

Exhausted and drenched in sweat, Qasim made his way back to the secret cave with Morg on his heels. This was their fifth trip hauling treasure away, and if he hadn't been so exhausted, he might have noticed the entrance to the cave was open, even though he'd closed it the last time they left.

Qasim and Morg shuffled down the dark tunnel and into the cavern below. By the time Qasim realized the marauders were waiting for him, it was too late. He turned to run, but one of the creatures fired a weapon. Red hot pain pierced through his thigh, and he fell to the ground.

Qasim looked down to see a harpoon penetrating his leg above the knee. The pain grew exponentially as a cable attached to the harpoon reeled him in.

Morg stood motionless as they dragged Qasim into the center of the cavern. They screamed and yelled in alien tongues as they beat him. After a moment, their apparent captain, the tall one covered with gray fur and scales, ordered them to stop. He called over a humanoid droid to translate. At one time it might have been some big wig's attaché droid on the core worlds. It was naked, and its once human-like flesh was tattered—sagging and dangling in ragged giblets, revealing the skeletal machine underneath.

"What have you done with our tribute?" the droid asked, its voice coarse and full of static. Qasim didn't answer, just grinned and spat blood from his mouth.

The droid continued its questioning. "Where are the others?"

"What others?" Qasim asked lamely.

"We know it is not just you and that second-rate drone."

Morg chirped angrily at this. The tattered droid turned and hissed at her. It started to hobble menacingly in Morg's direction but was called back by the captain. The droid turned back to Qasim. "We will get the truth."

The alien captain gestured toward the pool of magma and growled something at the droid, who responded, "But, Captain, last time their mind was broken. Why disturb the Master? May I suggest that pain is the way with this one? It won't take much."

The captain relented. They dragged Qasim to his feet. The droid stood nose-to-nose with him. "This is your last chance. Where is the tribute? Where are the others?"

Qasim turned his head and looked away. The droid stepped aside, and an insectoid creature stepped forward and grabbed both ends of the harpoon in Qasim's leg. He yanked upward, using Qasim's weight to stretch the wound. Qasim cried out in pain.

"Enough!" Morg cried out. "I will tell you where we hid it."

"You keep your mouth shut, Morg!" Qasim yelled. "I am your owner, and you will do as I say."

"I am sorry, sir. But I cannot allow them to continue to hurt you."

"Tell us where it is, you filth, or we will take both his legs," the ragged droid cried at Morg.

The insectoid alien dropped Qasim to the floor. On his way down, Qasim pulled the marauder's pistol from his holster. Qasim turned and shot Morg. She hit the ground in a puff of fire and smoke.

The cavern broke out into chaos as the raiders began yelling and screaming in their various tongues. The insectoid marauder slammed his massive foot down on Qasim's hand, crushing it. Qasim's screams turned to whimpers as the creature yanked the pistol from his broken fingers.

The pool of magma began to bubble and smoke. The corsairs fell silent, dropping to their knees.

Out of the center of the pool rose a being glowing white with heat. It waded to the edge of the pool, dripping globs of molten rock as it went. When it reached the edge, it grabbed two of the raiders with its tentacle-like arms and used them as leverage to hoist itself from the pool. The captured raiders burst into flames and fell dead as the creature passed.

The being crept toward Qasim. As it came closer, its body cooled and darkened. At first, all Qasim could make out through the shimmering heat and smoke was a vaguely humanoid shape, but as it continued to cool, its features came into focus. Its skin was cracked and ashen like a burned-out tree. Instead of a face, at the center of its head was a maw ringed with jagged teeth, and in the middle of its chest was a giant, vertical orifice that stretched the length of its body. Qasim tried to run, but he couldn't move a muscle.

He could smell the burning, sulfurous stench of the thing. With his helmet on and his suit uncompromised that should have been impossible, but Qasim swore he could smell it, and... taste it. He could taste the horrible bitterness of the thing. Somehow it had seeped into him. He could feel himself becoming infected.

The creature came to a stop inches away. The heat radiating from it was unbearable. The giant slit in its chest slowly peeled open, revealing an enormous golden eye. Qasim tried to look away, to squeeze his eyes shut, but instead he found himself standing, the pain in his leg forgotten. He stared into the giant black pupil as he stepped forward, closing the gap until his face was inches away from it. It was like staring into the black hole in the sky outside.

A voice, if you could call it that, emanated from the creature, and to Qasim's horror he found he could understand it even though it spoke a language he had never heard. It commanded him to tell it where his brother was. Qasim tried to ask how it knew about his brother but forgot how to speak.

Qasim's eyes began to bleed.

☆ ☆ ☆

On his way back to their hideout, Baba had risked making a little stop at the supply depot on the outskirts of the village. It was usually heavily guarded, but a blast from a beam-drill had made short work of the lock. He had loaded up as many explosive charges as he could carry, plus a remote detonator.

Baba spent the next ninety minutes making sure there was still a secondary exit to the maze of mine shafts they had pitched their tent in. When he had assured himself of his escape route, he spent another hour laying his trap. Using the safety manual's minimum-safe-distance guidelines on how to avoid an explosive cave-in, he reverse-engineered a plan to use a single detonator to cause a chain reaction of explosions.

He set explosives on opposite sides of the mouth of the tunnel and then spaced them out every one-point-five meters after that. With any luck, if the series of explosions didn't kill the alien raiders, they would be buried under a metric crap-ton of rock.

Then, Baba waited with his detonator at the junction to the smaller side tunnel he'd been living in. He was sure from there he'd be able to see anyone darken the entrance to the tunnel, but there'd be no way they'd be able to see him through all that darkness.

Baba waited longer than he had expected. He waited so long he began to feel guilty that his plan was based on the assumption that Qasim or Morg would inevitably accidentally lead the aliens to his hiding spot.

What if they weren't patient enough to silently follow Qasim back here? What if they killed him outright? What if he was already dead?

Then he heard footsteps.

☆ ☆ ☆

Morg waited until the cavern had grown completely silent. First, Qasim had led the marauders away. Then, finally, that creature, the one whose existence had never even been hinted at in all of Morg's inputs, readings, and computations—the one that defied what Morg knew about the various races and species of the universe—had descended back into the pool. Morg heard the sizzling, gurgling splashes of the magma, and then silence.

Morg dared to bring her power level back up. Her optical lenses whirled and adjusted as she looked around. The coast was clear.

Morg's head, which usually sat in the middle of her body, slid backwards, away from where Qasim had shot her. That half of her body was dead. No signals in or out. Morg's head clicked into place over her aft legs, and with a series of loud, grinding pops, she separated the two halves of her body.

She stood on her aft legs, swaying back and forth a moment before steadying herself. She looked down at her other half. It still smoldered. She was sure if she had olfactory sensors she'd be able to smell her circuits burning.

Morg spun away and tottered up the tunnel. She had work to do.

☆ ☆ ☆

"Baba!" Qasim stood at the entrance to the mine, surrounded by the band of alien brigands. Baba hadn't answered. He called his name again. "Why don't you come out and talk to me?"

Finally, Baba called back from the darkness. "Why don't you come in here?"

"We don't want to do that. We're not stupid." Qasim looked around and smirked at the raiders. His eyes were rimmed with dried blood, like evil eye shadow.

"Who's 'we?'" Baba demanded.

The tall, gray captain of the horde stepped into the tunnel and came back with one of the explosives. He held it against Qasim's head and nodded to the tattered old android. The droid called, "Go ahead and use your detonator. Kill your brother and sleep soundly. Or throw down your weapons and come out. But do it quickly. We tire of waiting."

There was a moment of silence. A blinking red light on the explosive near Qasim's head kept the time like a metronome.

Then, the light went out as the explosive powered down. Baba's voice rang out, less defiant than before, "I'm coming out."

When Baba appeared, they seized him. He kept his eyes on his brother as they beat him, as they ransacked his tent, as they gorged themselves on his supply of lichen. An unholy exaltation went up when they found the basket of platinum bars. They scattered the rest of Baba and Qasim's possessions. All the while, Baba kept his gaze on his brother. Qasim didn't avoid his eyes, but somehow didn't meet them either. As if he wasn't there at all.

When they finished in the mine, it was time for Qasim to take them to the rest of the treasure he had stolen. They bound Baba's hands and dragged him along as Qasim led them to the refinery.

They passed the refinery control room and the living quarters, then descended several flights of stairs, journeying deeper into the bowels of the factory to the smelters. They entered a cavernous room, filled with huge cauldrons and crisscrossed with layers of piping, conveyor belts, and catwalks.

Silence hung in the air. There was no sign of treasure. The corsairs demanded to know where it was. Qasim didn't answer. The aliens dragged Baba up from the back of the group and put a pistol to his head.

Baba looked at his brother. For a horrible moment, he was sure Qasim would not tell them.

But Qasim turned and lurched over to the nearest cauldron. He flipped a switch, and the cauldron toppled over, spilling the treasure. Coins, gems, and artifacts scattered across the floor.

Cries of triumph rang in a dozen alien tongues as the marauders looted the treasure, scooping it up as fast as they could.

Slowly, Baba began to back away. But it was no good. Two ape-like creatures spotted him and dragged him back to their captain.

Growling in a language Baba couldn't understand, the captain unsheathed a tortured blade. The blade flashed and Baba's bonds were cut. The tattered android turned to Baba and translated: "He says you may go. Breathe your last however you see fit. Nar-goth will rip this rock from its orbit and hurl it back into the hole from whence it came."

Baba was sure that was asinine, but he'd take what he could get. Keeping his eyes on the aliens, he backed away again.

He reached Qasim, who was still trapped in a trance. Baba grabbed his brother and shook him, whispering, "Let's go!"

Qasim stared blankly at Baba, his eyes bleeding again. The hollow, static voice of the tattered android cried out, "Not him! He must atone for his blasphemy."

Baba sighed. He stepped between his brother and the horde. "I'm not leaving without him," he said again.

"Fine," the android replied. "Nar-goth will dine on you both."

The ape warriors drew their weapons and crept forward.

Baba looked around. All that was within reach was a pile of coins and a golden scepter. That would do. Baba kicked the pile of coins into the face of the first ape. Then he swept up the scepter and brought it down hard enough to snap it in half on the second ape's skull.

The rest of the horde let out a war cry and drew their weapons. Baba steeled himself for the end. He grabbed his brother's hand. Qasim looked at him with empty eyes.

Suddenly the refinery sprang to life. Every conveyor belt kicked on overhead. A huge spigot on a jib arm swung into place above the alien horde, the valve on the end opened, and molten zincu rained down on their heads.

The deluge of molten metal melted some of them down to the bone. Others burst into flame from the heat. The treasure met a similar fate. Those who were not instantly killed ran screaming and burning in every direction.

The blast of heat singed Baba's hair as he grabbed Qasim and ran faster than he had ever run in his life.

Morg's voice rang out from an intercom. "Baba, right! Down the passage to your right, now!"

Baba glanced right. It wasn't really a passage so much as the gaping mouth of a conveyor system leading into a giant machine. He hesitated. Morg's voice blared again, "Trust me!"

Baba glanced back at the chaos behind him. Melted zincu continued to rain on the horde. The heat from the molten metal and the smell of burnt flesh washed over him. He turned and shoved Qasim into the machine, then plunged in behind him.

The conveyor belt chugged on, dragging Baba and Qasim through the dark innards of the factory. A trap door opened behind Qasim, and Baba fell into blackness. He felt his legs snap and the wind was knocked out of his lungs as he hit a cold concrete floor. Then he knew no more.

☆ ☆ ☆

In the refinery control room, Morg was plugged into the main system. She watched a security feed showing the last of the alien horde burn up in her flood of molten death.

She turned to the video from inside the machine she'd sent Baba and Qasim into. Qasim had grabbed hold of the trap door's edge and dangled over the dark chute Baba had fallen into.

The elder brother seemed more himself as he hoisted up onto his elbows, yelling, "Morg! Help me!"

Morg pressed the intercom button so Qasim could hear her. "Like you helped me?"

Morg pressed another button and the trap door slammed shut, severing Qasim's body across the middle. She flipped another switch to turn off the security feed's sound. She didn't need to hear this unpleasantness.

Alarms went off all around the control room. Seismic alerts. Temperature warnings. The room began to shake.

Outside, the volcanic peak the refinery was built on blew its top. Smoke, ash, and lava shot high into the pseudo-atmosphere, escaped the light gravity, and blasted into space. Deep in the bowels of the volcano, Nar-goth had made good on its word.

☆ ☆ ☆

The first thing Baba noticed was the vaguely mechanical hum of white noise. That old lyric was stuck on loop in his mind again. "She fell from the sky, she fell very far, and 'Kansas,' she says, is the name of the star."

He opened his eyes and was surprised to see stars. Then he realized he was looking out a window. He tried to sit up, but a stabbing pain shot through both his legs. He glanced at them—they were splinted and bandaged. He bit his lip and tried to take deep breaths, waiting out the pain.

When he regained his composure, he carefully lifted his head to look around the room. It was rounded, no straight lines or corners to be seen, and it was dimly lit by a strange yellow light. He couldn't make out the details, but there was bizarre technology he did not recognize.

He peered out the window and saw a familiar shape receding further and further away. He knew it was A-L-I-361 on its way to the heart of the black hole.

Baba's guts turned to ice as the truth sank in. He was aboard the alien craft, and he was being watched.

He twisted around painfully to ensure he was alone but froze when he heard stilted footsteps approaching.

A wave of relief washed over Baba as Morg teetered into the room. Having left half her body behind, she walked upright. She had retrofitted herself with a pair of alien robotic arms that gave her an almost humanoid silhouette.

"Where are we?"

"Do not worry," Morg replied. "We escaped A-L-I-361."

"Escaped?" Baba asked.

"It erupted with enough force to blow it out of orbit," Morg stated matter-of-factly. "Not just the volcano we knew about, but fissures all over the surface. By my calculations it will reach the event horizon in roughly fourteen standard years."

"Where's my brother?" Baba demanded.

Morg didn't answer. She lurched around to Baba's head and fluffed his pillows. "Is there anything I can do to make you more comfortable? You had a nasty fall."

Baba didn't like the way Morg seemed to be staring at him. Her optical lenses whirred quietly as she scanned his body up and down. "Who's flying the ship?"

"I am," Morg chirped.

"From here?"

"The ship and I are now fully integrated. But there is no need to be jealous. It is strictly pragmatic. I only have eyes for you, as they say. But..." Morg hesitated. "You already knew that I love you."

Baba tried to hide his revulsion. He busied himself adjusting the bandage on his left leg. "I think we might need to change my bandages."

"Oh, there will be plenty of time for that," Morg chirped. "First, tell me you love me."

Baba looked at Morg, and his mouth ran dry.

ABOUT THE AUTHOR

Blair Cosby has been making up stories since he was a little kid growing up in Medellín, Budapest, and Mexico City. He now works in the film industry and lives in Los Angeles with his wife, some perpetually suicidal houseplants, and their rambunctious dog, Skywalker.

THE SWEETHEART CONTRACT

A Retelling of Beauty and the Beast

Maggie Hoyt

"He needs advice. I told him you could help," Irene said.

I glanced over the young man—laborer, late twenties, wearing a wedding ring. He appraised me skeptically and then turned to my girlfriend.

"She knows about the fae?" he asked.

"She knows all about bargaining." When the young man still looked shy, Irene continued. "This is Roddy. He's one of my father's parishioners. He and his wife want a child, and they recently found a fae who would grant them one..."

"But she wants the thing that's most precious to us," Roddy said.

"When's she going to collect?" I asked.

"In a year."

I shook my head. This was amateur fae bargaining, really, but the lad looked nice, so I thought I'd let him down easy. "Sorry, mate. In a year's time, the thing that'll be most precious to you is the child."

His face fell. "I've got to tell her no, then."

"The whole premise here is pretty rotten. But you could try specifying 'the thing most precious to you, excluding living beings.'"

"She won't negotiate with me, though, will she?"

"Look, most fae love making a bargain more than they want the thing you promised them. But—are you sure she's reputable? The trustworthy wish-granters these days don't usually go in for that heart's desire nonsense. You sure she's not the type to steal a child and drop it on your doorstep?"

Or worse, I thought. I don't have many talents—can't afford them —but I've always been able to pinpoint how a deal could go wrong.

Roddy hesitated, his wince answering my question.

"Look, you want to pay my fee, I'll do your research. But at least ask around, yeah?"

After a quick negotiation, Roddy gave me the details and shook my hand.

"Whatever you end up deciding," I said, "do not agree to any bargain unless you've got it in writing."

Roddy nodded and shuffled off.

"Don't forget to tell your friends about the Bargain Hunter!" Irene called after him.

"I'm not calling myself that!"

"Of course you are! It's a play on words, it's perfect! You should listen to me, Beau."

I go by Beau. My real name's something horrendous, and I only hear it when mum's good and proper furious. I've dressed like a boy as long as anyone can remember. My da—he being a genius of comedy—took to calling me Beauty. Mum could tell I hated it and changed it to Beau. It fit, so it stuck.

"Mm-hm."

"Walk me home?"

I bowed gallantly and motioned for her to give me the stack of books she'd bought from the bookshop.

"Let's see what we've got this time." I held up the spines of the books for inspection. "*Cautionary Magic.* Weighty. *Mortals and Stars: A Psychological Approach to Human/Fae Interactions.* What's all this about?"

She blushed. "I thought maybe... I could do research. To help you with your business. You know, to look for historical precedent. I know it's foolish; when you catch on, you'll be huge, and you don't need my help, but..."

I stopped abruptly, forcing her to turn around and face me. Strands of her white-blonde hair, gathered loosely at the nape of her neck, drifted in front of her face, and a few tears had started to fall behind her wire-rimmed spectacles. I balanced the books on my hip and placed a hand on her shoulder.

"But that's a brilliant idea. We both know all my schemes are half-baked. Maybe, with your help, I'll have a clue what I'm doing."

"I'm worried, Beau," she murmured. "Father is going ahead with the new chapel. It's got stained glass, and a pipe organ, and I have no idea where he's getting the money for all this, but he has strangers coming in and out of the house, and I don't... the way they look at me... I'm probably making it up, but—"

"You're not making it up. I'd take you with me now, if I thought I could give you the life you're used to. But if you need me—if you're in danger, Irene—I will be there in an instant. We'll always have a place for you. Not a very attractive one, but..."

She smiled wanly and took my hand. We told each other mundane stories until we were a block or so away from her house. Any further and we'd risk being seen by her father, and it was better for the Reverend's health if he didn't see me. I didn't particularly care about the old bastard, but Irene was a better person.

I handed over her stack of books. Then I plucked an aster from a neighbor's garden.

"For the lady," I said.

Irene tucked it behind her ear. "See you, Beau. Take care of yourself. Give your mum and Colm my best."

"Day or night, Irene. I'll be there." I tipped my cap and blew a kiss and did my best to saunter away like a charming ne'er-do-well.

It being nearly tea-time, I thought I'd obey Irene and go home to my mum and little brother. She hadn't mentioned giving her best to my father, but considering he was a drunken waste of space who only returned home when he was out of money... I figured there was very little chance I'd even see him.

☆ ☆ ☆

Naturally, I found him sitting at our table, eating my portion of stew.

"Well? Who'd you lose it all to this time, and how much do we owe them?"

But he only gave a big sniffle. Mum frowned and shook her head. "He won't say," she murmured.

I cast a more discerning eye over my father. I was used to seeing him worse for wear, but there was always a cheekiness to the lines around his eyes. This time, he looked downright haggard; the creases in his leathery skin seemed permanent, the bags under his eyes bruised and puffy. This time, there was actual regret. And a red rose poking out of his grimy front pocket.

"Good God, what kind of a bender were you on? Did one of your mates get married? What is this?"

He dolefully shook his head, pulled the rose from his pocket, and held it out to me. "You don't know what I've been through to bring this to you, Beauty."

"Oh, I'm sure you're going to tell me," I said, irritated with the nickname.

"I was on my way home from my business trip—"

Side note: my father likes to call himself a merchant. While he does "move goods," technically speaking, I'm fairly sure these "business trips" involve liberating the goods from dock warehouses first.

"And you know that storm few days back? Well, 'ere I am, walkin' through the Faeside Aves, with the heavens spillin' their guts on me— now I don't say this by way of solicitin' pity, but I'd been roughin' it for a few days—"

I scoffed. "Business didn't pan out, or you blew it all on ale?"

"I thought that tip would be lucrative, and with good reason. If you don't bet on yourself, who will, am I right?"

Oh, Lord. It was his mantra, whether it made sense or not.

"I was right shiverin' and almost faint, when all of a sudden, the gate to the grandest estate of them all swung open right as I passed it. Naturally, I had to enter. And as I reached the front door, it opened all on its own too. Now, ladies, as God is my witness, this mansion was the finest I have ever seen. One candlestick was worth a week of meals. The embroidery on the chair cushions—"

I motioned for him to get on with it.

"Well, I saw neither hide nor hair of another soul. Candelabras would light up to show me where to go—the dining room for a three-course meal, a bedroom with the warmest four-poster feather bed."

"How were you served a three-course meal if there were no people?" I asked.

"When I finished one course, the plates vanished and the next course appeared. Anyway, I had the best night's sleep of my life, and when I left the next morning, well, I remembered that I'd promised to bring you a gift. Now, I did have enough sense not to rob the place, but I didn't think my host, whoever he was, would mind if I just liberated one of his roses."

My da loves telling a story, and up until now he'd been holding court. But suddenly, he refused to meet my eyes.

"And?"

"He looked like a devil," my father choked out, and Mum shot an alarmed glance toward the living room, where my little brother was undoubtedly eavesdropping. "He appeared in the doorway, and half of him was in the shadow, but I saw he had wings, massive eagle wings, and his hands were talons."

Da had told me plenty of stories in my life, and he always took great pleasure in describing the big, bad, ugly monster. But this time, he stammered, he shrank in on himself. He still wouldn't look at me.

"You're telling the truth. I can't—oh my God, I cannot actually believe it!" I exploded, tossing the rose down on the table in front of him. "You don't steal flowers from the fae! That's not—that's not hard for anyone with an ounce of gray matter!"

My father had the temerity to look surprised. "How was I supposed to know he was a fae?"

"Your food appeared and disappeared in front of you!" I shouted. "What did you think it was?"

"Genevieve Frances Morrow!" Ah, there it was. "Show your father some respect!" Mum admonished.

"What did he do to you?" I said through clenched teeth.

"He said since I stole from him, my life was forfeit—so I started pleading with him, said I only took it to bring a gift home to my lovely daughter. Well, that had him interested, and he asked me how old you were, so I told him, and... he said... he said he'd spare my life if you took my place. He gave me a month. I said I'd take you to him before thirty days passed."

I don't know what made my mum suddenly decide enough was enough. Oh wait, I do: my father had literally bartered my life to a monster.

"Are you out of your goddamned mind?" my sweet, saintly mother swore at the top of her lungs. "You agreed?"

"I had to, Norah! He was going to kill me!" My father was crumbling, breaking down in tears. He wiped his snotty nose on his sleeve, and I came this close to feeling sorry for him.

"Then let him!" Mum roared.

"But the flower was for Beauty!"

"I never asked you for it! I asked you to bring all your wages home for once!" I shouted.

"Get out," Mum demanded. "Pack your things and get out of this house! You'll have to bet on yourself because I am not betting on you anymore!"

His eyes pleaded with me now, but for once in my life, I couldn't summon up the words for a fight. He couldn't even get my name right. I found myself blinking back tears.

"Get out, Wil. You're not having my daughter."

After stuffing his meager possessions into a carry-all, Mum booted him out the door and tossed his belongings after him. I sat on the bed with my arms around my nine-year-old brother, watching out the window, my eyes still watery. It would be best, I thought as I tamped it all down, not to think about this again.

☆ ☆ ☆

Twenty-six days later, with the lion at the door and the wolf eating its way through our larder, I thought about it again.

Far be it from me to give my father any credit, but occasionally we were lucky enough to get some cash from him. And that was useful in times like these—namely, when the owners of the laundry my mother worked at had to lie low and shut everything down. We were barely fourteen days on our own, and our lives began to dry up. I hustled after every odd job I could find and sold everything Colm dug from the mud by the riverbanks, but it wasn't enough, and it was never going to be. Mum began to lose hope she'd ever get hired again. I suggested she go into service—she was an excellent cook, and Colm could be a boot boy —and forget about me, but even if she'd been amenable, without references, it was simply a nice, desperate idea.

Twenty-five days after my father left, I was quite adept at leaping out of windows to avoid the landlord. When the frantic beating at the door began late that evening, Mum and I shot each other panicked glances and I made to scarper. Then I heard a woman's voice call my name.

I rushed to the door and helped a trembling, sobbing Irene inside.

"He made a bargain!" she cried. "That's how he got the money. The fae's price was the greatest thing my father had created himself. And I don't know if he didn't think it through or didn't care, but—"

"But that's you," I said.

"They came tonight to collect! I didn't know. I never thought—I never thought he'd do this. I heard them talking. He didn't even try to plead. I escaped through the servants' entrance and ran straight here. I don't have anywhere else..."

"You did the right thing, love," Mum said.

"I told you I'd protect you. We'll take care of you," I said, wrapping my arms around her and pulling her in. Her coat was probably warmer than anything we had in the house, but Colm still brought a worn flannel blanket from his bed and held it out to us.

Mum and I spent the night telling Irene everything would be all right, although both of us knew it wouldn't. One more mouth to feed was problem enough. But even if the fae's thugs hadn't followed Irene, well, the Reverend was bound to know she'd come here. We needed an escape, and fast.

All of which is to explain why I found myself wandering the Faeside Aves twenty-six days after my father left. Mum hadn't let him stick around long enough to give me directions, but when I found a mansion with a front garden filled with rows upon rows of rose bushes, I stopped outside the gate and frowned. It did not swing open of its own accord, because that was very obviously a lie from a man who'd seen a house he wanted to rob.

You're mad, I thought. But the monster hadn't hurt Da. And the Reverend's fae would never think to find me here. I pushed open the gate and strode about halfway up the walk. The door opened, but not of its own accord, and only about halfway. Just as Da had said, the half of the figure not hidden—yes, I thought, he was definitely hiding—behind the door was some horrid halfway step to being a bird of prey. His elongated, bony foot had talons, not toes. He did have feathers on his body, but they were patchy and hidden poorly under ill-fitting clothes.

"Go away," he rasped, "or I will shred you and leave your corpse for the rats."

I shrugged. "If you insist. Although my da made it sound urgent."

It was hard to tell, as his mouth was trying to protrude from his face like a beak, but I think his face registered surprise.

"You're the daughter?"

"All right, come off it. You're not exactly a prince, my friend. In fact, why don't you just step out here so I can see all of you."

Notably, he didn't budge. "I did not mean to offend. Please, come in—"

"Not until you come out."

"Miss—"

I sighed and took three long strides toward the door. Instead of entering, however, I simply shoved the door wide open.

His other half was fae. That's all. Like any member of the fae nobility, he looked like a supremely attractive human with a few inhuman exceptions. Bursts of feathers emerged from the back of his hands and neck. His fae fingers were long and a little bit spindly, but not talons.

"I knew it! You're cursed!"

The side of his face that wasn't turning into a beak looked around a bit wildly. I suspected this was not how most people reacted to him.

"So, what do you need me for?" I asked.

His expression darkened, and I had to admit, the bird was menacing.

"That matters not. Your father bargained your life—"

"Nah, I don't think he did. You made him think he did, but don't let it go to your head. The man's not a genius. Stealing a fae's flowers, while stupid, isn't a capital offense. So you didn't have anything to offer him. Besides which, you won't step outside your house. You're not hunting down my father in a few days. You need me, and I need a place to live. But I'm not keen on one where the landlord is going to peck my liver out."

"You have my assurance no harm will come to you."

"And if I need to nip out for a bit?"

He looked like he'd swallowed something nasty. "No one who wants to leave is required to stay."

"Brilliant!" I pushed past him into the house.

When I say this house was fancy, it's only because I don't have the vocabulary to truly describe it. The tables were fancy, shiny wood. The carpets and the cushions were fancy, and I wasn't even sure how—I just knew I'd never seen color like this, never felt texture like this. My father's instinct had been to estimate what it was worth, but why, I thought. Why, if you had all this warmth, would you ever trade it for coins?

"Well," I said, trying to recover my bravado. "You got plenty of bedrooms?"

"What? There are six bedrooms, but—"

"Aces. Right, give me a few hours, I'll be back." I turned around.

"You must stay," he croaked, a bit desperately.

"I will. I got to get my stuff. You'll just have to trust me that I'll come back."

☆ ☆ ☆

When I say no one was happy I unilaterally moved my entire family into a cursed fae's magical mansion, I mean Mum was so irritated she didn't even give me a tongue-lashing.

"Look," I said as we held an impromptu family meeting in the rose garden, "he never actually made a bargain with Da. We're not stuck. But we do need a new place to live, and he needs us to live here with him. It's part of his curse." I glossed over the part where he'd been interested that Da had a daughter, and in retrospect, that's a fact I really should have turned over in my own mind a bit more. Mum glared, Irene blinked back tears, and Colm stared at me in wide-eyed fear, but there was no denying our desperation.

The fae introduced himself as Ealar, directed us to our rooms, and stomped off. For all he wanted me there, he certainly didn't want to associate with me. He did dine with us but merely grunted responses to questions directed at him.

Of course, we were perfectly happy staying out of his way. It was as though his curse encouraged you not to look at him. Not magically—it was simply that his appearance was unpleasant, grotesque, and alarming. And the less you really looked at him, the more you could imagine him using those talons for violence or launching himself at you with his wing. We kept to ourselves, and he kept to himself.

Until Mum's sense of honor truly couldn't take the food any longer.

"Is this... how you prefer to take your meals?" Mum asked tentatively during the fourth supper.

Ealar shrugged. "I eat what the magic provides."

"Does your magic create raw ingredients and turn them into meals? Or does it create whole meals out of thin air? Oh my lands, I'm saying 'it'—there aren't real... fae cooking here, are there?"

Ealar shook his head slowly. "There is no one else here. And I have never thought about it."

"It's just... well, your magic doesn't seem to know the proper way to season things."

And here I thought I just didn't have the palate for rich people foods.

"And I thought," Mum began slowly, but to my surprise, her excitement seemed to be mounting. "If your house could create the ingredients for me, I could cook? You must have a wonderful kitchen..."

Ealar and I were both dumbfounded, but at least he managed to stammer, "I would greatly appreciate that."

That was the first truly genuine thing he said to us, and I think it was the first time any of us really saw him—and that made all the imagined violence vanish. His frustration, on the other hand, at the difficulty of controlling his half-beak was apparent. It was clear that between his misaligned knee joints and the single wing, his bird half was pulling him into an awkward, painful stoop.

While Mum helped us see who Ealar really was, my brother revealed the fae Ealar had once been. Suppers were still fairly silent affairs, so we were all a bit surprised when Colm suddenly issued a proclamation.

"You're half bird and half fae," he said, in a tone that suggested this was only the premise to a lengthier argument.

"Colm," I hissed.

"That is correct," Ealar said.

Colm cocked his head to one side. "Does that make you a birdtaur? Only Gummy Fitz—he's my friend—told me about minotaurs and centaurs, and—"

Ealar's fae half genuinely smiled. "You would think, wouldn't you? Those words are a bit of a linguistic illusion. You see, the suffix -taur means 'bull,' or 'bull-like,' so a centaur is, in a way, poorly named."

We stared dumbly.

"I studied linguistics quite extensively," he explained. "Colm, would you—would you like to explore my library? I think you would enjoy *Tales of the Wine-Dark Sea*. It was one of my favorites when I was a boy. Of course, the invitation is open to any of you."

Irene's eyes lit up.

It quickly became obvious that I did not belong. I could not talk about languages, or gourmet food, or sword-fighting. I couldn't sit still long enough to fall deep into a world of make-believe. Mucking about in a mansion wasn't fulfilling to me. I had no name, and I was making no mark. Out in the city, there were hundreds of people making bargains who needed an advocate. (Ooh. The Bargain Advocate? Nah.) And I was missing all of it.

About the only thing Ealar and I had in common was that we both knew how much his furnishings cost, which was, I assumed, why he hadn't said more than five words to me. The most time he spent around me was in the evenings, when Mum would read to all of us. So why, I wondered, had he needed me so badly? What was this curse, and why did I need to stay?

We had the run of the house at this point, so I decided to snoop. It took me no time at all to find the locked door leading off the study, even less time to realize it was important, and just a bit more time to pick the lock. Thanks, Da. The room was little more than a closet, and all it held was a single wooden table displaying a framed piece of parchment.

I bent down to read the parchment. It was mostly curse-related legal mumbo-jumbo, but one key phrase stood out:

"The curse shall be broken when the recipient loves truly and is truly loved. He shall have ten chances, at which point, the transformations to his appearance shall become permanent, and no magic may remove or alter them."

"Oh, bloody hell," I swore. *You're a bleedin' idiot, Beau*, I thought. *You knew he was cursed! And he spared your da in exchange for you because why, he thought you'd be more pleasant? This curse had true love written all over it! But he'd made no attempts to court me—and why would he, I realized, when I'd brought him a lovely bookworm.*

They were all in the sitting room—Ealar was teaching Colm how to play chess while Mum knitted and Irene read. I descended upon this scene of domestic bliss like a steam engine.

"Were you ever going to tell us?" I demanded.

Everyone stared at me in confusion.

"You," I said, pointing at Ealar. "When were you going to tell us you needed one of us to fall in love with you? I brought my girlfriend here to keep her safe, not for you to prey on her!"

Before he had a chance to respond, a column of white light appeared in the center of the room and then faded into silver particles around an honest-to-God fae princess, complete with brilliant butterfly wings and a green velvet ball gown. Instead of smiling benevolently, however, she was sneering, looking down on us through imperious amber eyes.

"Rhiannon!" Ealar growled and rose to his feet.

"Ealar! How wonderful to see you, darling," she purred.

"What are you doing here? The terms of our... agreement have not been reached."

"We—well, you—have a problem. Lovely number ten here has been snooping." She pointed a sharp, blood-red nail at me. "I had a ward on that door. I knew the moment you opened it."

Ealar glanced at me and grimaced. "The Morrows and Miss Randall are here as guests. As charity. I have hardly spoken to Miss Morrow, let alone attempted to court her. Besides, Miss Morrow and Miss Randall have an arrangement. I consider neither of them appropriate for an attachment." He looked pointedly at me.

"That's not really the problem, is it, kitten? I always knew you could find someone to marry you for your money, or out of pity. It's love I don't think you're capable of. And if she knows about the curse, how can I trust that anything you come up with is true love? So here's what I propose. It seems to me that you have two perfectly eligible young women here right now. One of them is number ten, and one of them had better fall in love with you. You have ten days, or my curse comes due." She vanished in another haze of silver, leaving a cloying, flowery scent.

Ealar groaned. "I tried. I tried so very hard not to involve you."

"You should never have let us stay!" I argued.

"You were homeless! Should I have turned your mother and brother out onto the streets?"

"I believe you," Irene said. "You were trying to help. And we will help you. Beau—"

"You cannot help," he said, not as an accusation, but as a fact. He looked between Irene and me. "And I do not expect you to help. I... I will have to live like this."

☆ ☆ ☆

"She can't just go changin' the terms!"

"She is extremely powerful! How do you think she managed to put this on me in the first place! I would assume she can!"

I swear Ealar and I had this argument twice a day. We'd also made up for lost time in the "getting-to-know-you" department. He knew all about my business plans and thought I was naïve for thinking I could outwit the princess. I knew all about his failed relationship history and thought he was naïve for believing his spurned ex would play by the rules.

Irene was spending hours in the library, devouring books on curses. Mum handled her stress by baking enough buns to feed a small village, and Colm kept offering to play games with Ealar to take his mind off things. I, meanwhile, had come up with a dozen plans, from taking the princess to court to an elaborate ruse involving a body double for me and a quick divorce.

"But the only way we're getting out of this is by taking a risk," I said for the millionth time.

This time, however, before Ealar could say anything about foolish, pointless risks, there was a knock at the door, and we all jumped eight feet out of our skin. From her chair near the windows, Irene peeked through the curtains and turned white. She sprung out of the chair and staggered away from the windows.

"It's them," she whispered. "They're the ones who came to collect me. How did they find me?"

"Irene's father bargained her to a fae," I told Ealar. "That's why—I didn't think they'd find us here. Please. You have to turn them away."

Ealar glared at me for a moment and then stepped into the entry hall to answer the door, hiding his less monstrous side behind the door as usual. I heard a surprised squawk from one of our guests.

"Begging your pardon, sir." The visitor recovered. "Have you by chance seen a young woman recently—average height, blonde hair, spectacles? We've reason to believe she might have come here."

Ealar did not respond, and in his silence, I suddenly realized what I'd done. I beckoned for Mum and Colm to come closer and pulled them into a huddle with me and Irene.

"The thing is," the visitor continued, "she's been promised to our master. We'd be happy to bring you a, uh, different captive."

"We're going to sneak out through the gardens," I whispered.

"Ealar won't—" Mum started.

"We're leaving," I insisted. Because any minute now, Ealar was going to turn around and make me a bargain. However kind he'd been to Mum and Colm, he was still a fae, and I'd left myself open. My hand for Irene's freedom.

"Let's go," I hissed.

"There's no one here," Ealar growled.

"Are—are you sure, sir?"

"Leave!" he roared and slammed the door.

While Irene sagged in my arms, and Mum and Colm simply returned to what they were doing, I just stood there, stunned.

Ealar returned to us with a grim look on his face. Regret, I assumed.

"I recognized their livery," he said. "Their master will not give up. He is harsh, but I could perhaps scare him—"

I felt Irene tense again. "They'll go after my father, won't they."

"If he does not hold up his end of the bargain..." Ealar trailed off.

"Then I should go," she said softly, pulling away from me.

"What?" Ealar and I both shouted.

"I can't let them hurt him!"

"After what he's done to you? You don't owe him!" I bellowed.

"Your father should never have made such a bargain in the first place!" Ealar exclaimed.

"But he's my father!"

I felt myself flood with anger, a tingling heat that burned my face. This was wrong—it was wrong when her father did it, and it was wrong when mine had. *Would you have gone?* I wondered. *Would you have gone if you hadn't had Mum to tell you your worth?* Irene's mother may have passed, but she had me, and I sure as hell wasn't going to lose her to the old bastard's ego.

"I'll go deal with it," I said. "'S what I do. It'll be a little business trip. I'll get him out of this mess, but it won't be pleasant. He does have to pay a price, just not his life."

"There's no time!" Irene said. "Ealar only has six days."

"Then I'll just have to bring back a solution for both of you."

"You'll come back in time," Mum ordered.

"I'll come back."

Mum bundled Irene off to the kitchen to get her some hot tea, and Colm followed, probably hoping for hot cocoa. Ealar told me what he knew about the Reverend's creditor, but I found it hard to meet his gaze.

"Ask the house to provide you with a gentleman's suit," he said. "And any other odds and ends you might need."

"I'll make it back," I insisted.

"I trust you," he said and rose to leave the room.

"Why didn't you take advantage?" I blurted out.

Ealar's expression was always hard to read, but I thought I saw pity. "Not everyone does, Miss Morrow."

☆ ☆ ☆

"So the Reverend's yelling, 'Tell me where she's hiding!' And the fae's a second away from setting his thugs on me. And I'll let you in on a little secret, boys: the key to bargaining with fae is to reject the premise of the bargain," I said to a rapt audience of old friends at a pub on my last day in the city.

I'd earned a celebration. I'd spent five days loitering in alleys and outside businesses of varying repute until I could corner my witnesses and ply them with alcohol. I'd learned the types of payments this fae preferred and any other assets the dear Reverend was holding onto. I'd slept in alleys and crashed with friends and only impersonated Irene in front of a few civic officials.

It was glorious. I was doing what I was best at. I was thinking on my feet, piecing together information, and pulling together a plan. I'd saved a young woman. I'd just stuck it to two wealthy, powerful men, which made me, for the first time ever, powerful. I felt like a genius.

"So I says, 'What really counts as creation, anyway? Sure, he provided the seed for his daughter, but it's a stretch to say this egotistic miser created a saintly young woman willing to sacrifice herself for his idiocy. But there's one thing the Reverend here's created all by himself, and I think it's more to your liking, anyway: his congregation.' And then the old bastard turns beet red, like his head's swelling up with hot air. 'See?' I say. 'Even he doesn't think his daughter's the best thing he created.'" My friends erupted into whoops and cheers.

"And then—because what do I always say, boys?"

"Get it in writing!" one of them yelled.

"I have 'em sign all the documents, saying the fae gets the Reverend's congregation and agrees to leave the Reverend and Irene alone, forever. Only, what none of them know is that the Reverend's deals with the fae aren't so secret anymore. So I'm not expecting a big crowd at church."

After another round or two, I figured I'd better stagger back to Ealar's while I still could. Was I avoiding returning because I didn't have a solution? Possibly. But my confidence was high, and I was betting on my ability to argue my way out of anything. As I was exiting the pub, a man tapped me on the shoulder.

"I couldn't help overhearing your triumph," he said. "Have you considered a consulting business?"

"My friends call me The Bargain Hunter. But I'm thinking I prefer The Bargain Broker," I babbled.

"My master might be able to help. Come to this address tomorrow morning at seven, sharp." He handed me a card on quality paper. *Lord Mortimer Godolphin*, it said, with an address amongst the rich humans. I gaped at it as the man departed.

You won't be there when Rhiannon arrives was my first thought. But a patron—an actual patron with capital to invest! I could advertise, I could have an office. I could support Mum and Colm and Irene myself. We wouldn't be beholden to Ealar, waiting for him to chuck us out or trick us into a bargain. Everyone took advantage eventually. With a patron, I could be fully myself, and we could be free. I'd take this meeting and then go retrieve them from the house. They'd want me to take the opportunity. I booked a room and slept uneasily 'til morning.

☆ ☆ ☆

"My assistant told me your story," Lord Godolphin said. "But I'd like to hear it from you."

I gave a brief recounting of the week, leaving out, of course, any mention of Ealar.

"You've got a knack for this, clearly. And you've thought of making a profession out of it?"

"That's my dream, sir. But I can't afford the upfront costs that would net me the upscale clients."

He nodded. "I like this. I want you to handle a matter for a friend of mine. It goes well, I'll invest generously in your enterprise. My assistant will give you the details. You may begin immediately."

Well, that wouldn't work. Now that I hadn't shown up and Rhiannon would undoubtedly finalize her curse, I did not trust that my family would continue to be welcome.

"Begging your pardon, sir, but I have a prior commitment."

"Cancel it," he said, waving his hand.

"I've got to relocate my family," I said.

"They'll understand. Seize the moment, Miss Morrow. If you don't bet on yourself, who will?"

My mouth went dry. Was this me? Da, but with a different business plan? I suddenly felt the weight of my nearly empty coin pouch against my thigh. I'd spent most of my money on drinks for the lads last night. Would my family count on me to bring money back or just assume I'd only return when I ran out? Would I come back with gifts so I'd feel better about being absent? I was the one taking advantage, I thought. They were all expecting me to help Ealar, and I was breaking a promise, abusing their trust, and taking advantage of Ealar's help.

"They would," I gasped. "They bet on me."

I staggered out of the office and ran.

☆ ☆ ☆

"Take me to him, mortal!"

"He is enjoying breakfast with a child! Please, don't—Beau!" Irene exclaimed in relief as I burst into the sitting room.

Rhiannon turned and raised a delicate eyebrow at me as I tried unsuccessfully not to wheeze.

"Ah, racing back to your betrothed? No? I thought not."

"You can't change the terms of a curse like that!" I argued. "That ten-day limit was arbitrary and unfair!"

"Are you suggesting that with more time you might fall in love with him?" Her ruby lips smirked. "Miss Morrow, you were always his last chance. I was generous in allowing Miss Randall as an option."

"Generous? You're cruel! Putting his life in our hands for something we can't give him? It's an abuse!"

The princess shrugged. "Fine. But his time is up, regardless. You were number ten. You cannot love him."

"I'm not the tenth! He never tried—"

"He bartered with your father for you. I've been watching very carefully. I've seen all the women—all the ones he corresponded with, who decided they had less repulsive prospects elsewhere the moment they saw him. You were his last-ditch effort, and you were a failure. Now take me to him."

My eyes filled with hot, helpless tears, but I continued arguing, fueled mostly by spite. "You know it was your personality that made him break up with you, right. You thought if he didn't love you, he must not be capable of love. Well, he is."

Rhiannon rolled her eyes.

"He saved Irene from her father's thugs when he could have used it as a literal bargaining chip to make me marry him."

"Please. He did that because he needed you both."

"But it was meaningful to me! And—" I stopped. It wasn't true that no one had made a sacrifice like that for me before. I was loved. I grinned.

"I don't accept the premise of your curse."

"What?"

"Look, I'm not very good at love. I'm trying—" I smiled at Irene. "But I'm still learning. But I wasn't his last chance. We were. We all arrived together. All your curse said was that he needed to love truly and be truly loved. I read it. There's nothing about romance. He loves us— he's made sacrifices for us. And we love him."

The princess waved an ivory hand. "Of all the insipid drivel! What will I tell my peers, hmm? 'A street urchin babbled about the power of friendship, so I had to lift the curse.' Please."

"You need a show," Irene interrupted. "You don't know what true love is, any more than we do. You just need a good story to tell."

"She reads psychology books," I said. "She's brilliant."

"Don't analyze me, mortal. Take me to him!"

I shrugged. "Guess we've got no choice." I led the princess down the hall and opened the breakfast room door.

"Are you sure you don't want another pancake?" Mum was asking.

"I'm quite all right, Mrs. Morrow."

"Make Ealar one with ears! Look, I'm a minotaur eating pancakes!" Colm roared, and then dissolved into giggles.

Then they noticed the figure in the doorway. "Good morning, Rhiannon," Ealar said softly. "I had hoped for a few more minutes."

"You can't have him!" Mum shouted. "This isn't right. He didn't do anything to you but wound your pride."

"This is true love," I said. "I guarantee that. There's no one better at love than these two."

"And it's a good story," Irene added. "A softer one."

"Do wonders for your image," I said.

"Would you like a pancake?" Colm asked.

I guess it was a question she'd never been asked. Rhiannon gave me a stricken, panicked glance.

"It's all right," I whispered.

Our fairy princess looked back at the breakfast room and nodded. She waved a hand and disappeared. Through her cloud of silver dust, Irene and I watched as Ealar's wings and talons shrunk and vanished. Colm hollered a cheer while Mum wiped tears from her eyes.

"You might have to expand to curses as well," Irene murmured, slipping an arm around me.

"We," I said. "Always, definitely, we."

ABOUT THE AUTHOR

Maggie Hoyt has loved fairy tales as long as she can remember. Although she's ambivalent about the princess always getting a prince, she'll take a magic castle with a magnificent library any day. She teaches middle-school math in Los Angeles where she lives with her family and two dogs. Her first novel, *The Fairy Stepmother Inc.*, is available from Inkshares.

❧ *6* ☙

TOURNIQUETS

A Story in the Tradition of Brothers Grimm

Gerri Mahn

There was an old man who lived in a derelict building in the woods at the edge of town. My friends and I would walk out there along the railroad tracks, balancing on the metal rails or crunching alongside them through drifts of yellow leaves. We drank Arizona iced tea, then gripped the bottles by their wide glass necks and hurled them down onto the ties until they shattered. We would stop in the Chinese food place on Main Street and buy white take-out cartons full of warm crinkle-cut french fries to eat along the way. After, we pretended to smoke the cigarettes we stole from our mothers' purses.

We walked past the half-demolished factory, which squatted along the tracks at the end of my street. In the summer, yellow and white wildflowers sprouted from piles of bricks and broken walls. We combed through the rubble, kicking at old nails and crashing abandoned shopping carts as we stared up at the broken windows covered in rusted metal lattice. A partially collapsed fire escape hung tantalizingly out of reach, leading up past the fourth floor and onto the roof. Once my mother caught us trying to bust open a padlocked door with a screwdriver and a hammer so we could get inside and crawl around the moldering wooden floors, creep up the sagging stairs, descend into the lightless basement.

We walked along the spur to the Campbell Soup shipping yard, where two boys were said to have snuck to the top of a caboose while it was loading, hoping to ride it all the way up to Trenton. One got swept between the cars by a low hanging wire and lost his arms. They said his friend had to fashion tourniquets out of their belts and lead him through the railyard to find help.

We searched the ties for blood stains.

My friends and I had long conversations about riding the rails, plotting our escape. If we were to have any hope of catching a train, it had to happen here, by the yard. On the other side of town, where we fished for eels and sour-faced catfish along a fetid river inlet, the trains were a terrifying rush of noise and wind. They thundered across a rise above the muddy cove, leaving a trail of blasted deer bodies.

Beyond the railyard, we crossed a narrow overpass and peeked down at the highway. The thick black and red metal sides of the trestle came up to our chins. Sometimes we would carry bricks with us all the way from the old factory and line them up on the edge, balancing them on the thick heads of the rivets before we pushed them off, one at a time. Years later, we heard that a girl had dropped her stepfather's bowling ball from the trestle and killed someone.

Finally, we stopped in front of the dirt road that sprouted from the side of the raised track and wound off into the woods. An abandoned brick switching tower squatted there like a wizard's keep. We saw him walking home along the tracks sometimes, wearing his dusty old man clothes that looked like they came from my great-grandfather's closet. The same blue pants and faded plaid button-down shirt Pap-Pap had worn in the photos from when my mother was a baby.

My friends and I sat on the tracks, taking a break as we squinted up the dirt road and took hollow drags off Virginia Slims. Colleen thought he was crazy. Faith thought he was a pedophile. Amy wanted to see if he had anything worth stealing and then break whatever was left. I wanted to live there, alone in a tower in the woods guarded by a voracious metal dragon.

Only I also wanted water and heat and electricity and food and a refrigerator and a stove and microwave and a bed and blankets and books and a radio and television and a phone with an extra-long cord. Like the one I had at home, which my friends and I used after school when we sat around the kitchen table, pawing through the Yellow Pages as we searched for the numbers listed to couples, telling the women who picked up that we were dating their husbands.

And then we would walk back: our bottles smashed, our food gone and our cigarettes burned down to the filter and flicked carelessly into the trees. Past the shipping yard and the trestle which would eventually get topped with a chain-link fence. Past the derelict factory and its four stories of unlocked secrets. Up the street to home.

ABOUT THE AUTHOR

Gerri Mahn is a mom and a veteran with degrees in English Lit and Library Science. Her work has appeared in Den of Geek, Anti-Heroin Chic, Mulberry Literary, and Maya Literary Magazine.

PERSEPHONE AND OLD SCRATCH

A Retelling of the Persephone Myth

Skylar Lennox

The Batsto River is cresting over my ankles, soaking the hem of my dress, and soon the Pine Barrens will be swallowed up in the torrent. Wolves howl from out of the deep, and The Peddler's breath flutters over the face of the water.

There's a story I know. Not sure if it's true, or if I've actually heard it—could be something I roused from a dark spot in my subconscious and then projected onto some imagined past where I think I heard it. Either way, I'm now a part of its history. But before I tell it to you, I should explain how I became acquainted with the song of Old Scratch.

☆ ☆ ☆

I bought a record from The Peddler at a flea market in New Orleans. At the time, I wasn't sure why I was drawn to his stand. I wasn't looking for anything in particular; I'm not much of a collector, never understood why I should deem one item as more valuable than the next, so much so that my possession of that object would identify me with it. But as I waded through the stream of people flooding the marketplace, I had a sudden compulsion to look up. And there he was, his jaundiced, uneven eyes glaring through me from cavernous hollows, a black hood draping his brow. Beneath a flattened nose, dry, peeling lips drooped downward with the left side of his face as the right corner of his mouth struggled to curl a smile.

Although I stepped toward him of my own volition, it felt as if I were being compelled against my will, by some enchantment lingering behind his ominous gaze. Drawing closer, I almost retched from his putrid breath. Flies whizzed by me, swarming to his long, bedraggled beard as if summoned by the scent. Closer still, it became more pungent —a dry musk of rot and sewage. It stung as I inhaled, making me queasy, and I felt the ground rushing up at me. In mid-step, I had a familiar sensation of snapping awake, then found myself standing before him. He didn't say anything, just continued staring through me, the flies ascending and descending upon him.

His lower lip quivered, like that of a ventriloquist when speaking through his dummy, and my mouth seemed to be under his control. From someplace outside of myself, the question fell from my tongue: "Do you have any old Blues records?" I didn't know why I would have asked that of him—his table had nothing but old esoteric knick-knacks, religious icons, idols of strange creatures, and a variety of incense and powders.

He leaned forward in a serpentine arch, reached under the black tapestry spread across the table, and slid a plain white record jacket into my hand. Though it was cardboard, it had a velvety texture. I attempted to reach into the slit, to examine the record itself, but he grabbed my wrist, his hand calloused. Gazing into my eyes, he waved his finger back and forth, a fly scurrying across his brow. I nodded in compliance, drew a twenty-dollar bill out of my purse, dropped it into the metal dish before him, and submerged myself back into the river of tourists and collectors.

☆ ☆ ☆

Dina scowled at me from across the table, wisps of steam rising from her coffee and swimming between us. "You're not going back to New Jersey!"

I broke away from her fiery stare. "I can't keep running." My hands tightened around my coffee mug.

"You're not running. You're starting over."

"No." I smiled. "What I'm doing is running."

"Why'd you decide this? All of a sudden?"

"It's not sudden. I've been thinking about it." I glanced down at my bag; it rested against the leg of my chair, the corner of the record sleeve sticking out of it. "A lot of loose ends need tying up. Plus, I miss my house."

She grabbed my forearm and leaned toward me. "And if you're not careful, it's going to be your grave."

"I'll be fine. I'm sure Nathan's forgotten all about me."

Her fingers slid from me as she drew back. "Plus, Jersey's a shithole! Why would you want to go back after coming here?"

I lifted the mug to my lips. "You've wanted out since we were in grade school."

For a few moments we sat in silence. Espresso machines hummed behind us. Baristas called out orders.

Dina's eyes pooled with worry. "You know you've always got a place here, Cora. You'll always be my best friend, even if you still want to live in that cesspool of a state."

"I know. You've always taken care of me."

"If he hurts you again…"

"Don't worry. Everything will be fine."

☆ ☆ ☆

For most of the flight back to Philadelphia, and the journey over the Walt Whitman Bridge into New Jersey, my hand quivered, resisting the pull toward the record as it called out from my bag. When I stepped into my living room, I kicked off my boots and knelt onto the carpet. Removing the white record jacket from my bag, I turned it over in my hands. My fingers seemed autonomous, finding its slit and sliding out the inner sleeve. The Peddler's breath wafted behind it, reminding me of his smile. Again, the stench made me queasy, and the pattern on my carpet spiraled up toward me, and there was that sensation of snapping awake.

For a moment, it felt like I'd awoken after a long sleep, and I was unsure how long I'd been back from New Orleans.

The inner sleeve shone like obsidian and had the same velvety texture as the jacket. Only it was decorated with an embossing—I couldn't tell if it was a letter from some forgotten alphabet or a symbol used in some mystical art. Nonetheless, looking at it made me uneasy, the way its sinuous lines trailed around one another like some restless serpent, without beginning or end.

The label on the record was a swampy green. To the left of the spindle hole, the artist's name was spelled out in crimson lettering: Reverend Sonny James. The song title rested to the right. Just above the label, in the dead wax at the twelve o'clock position, was a peculiar etching, a seal depicting a goat-faced beast. With outstretched arms, it held what appeared to be a cocoon over a pool of fire, the flames licking toward it.

The song was labeled "Troublin' Times." On it, Sonny was just twanging away on his guitar, howling about how his "darlin' woman" was possessed by the love of another man. As Sonny lamented, his voice cracked in pain. He couldn't understand what has come over the woman he adores, how it only took a "few sly words from that serpent's forked tongue" to lure her from home and "into his slithery arms." After a brief guitar interlude, the song resolved with Sonny in a state of forlorn acceptance: "All I got now is that memory o' you. But that memory is fadin' with rest o' my mind. Tryin' to hold on. But I'm truly losin' you."

This is the only song for which Sonny is known. A few weeks after he recorded it, his body was found in a marsh along the Mississippi River Delta, bloated and infested with water worms and mites. Many rumors surround just what happened. Some say he was lynched for flirting with a white woman. Others claim that, in a drunken stupor, he passed out and fell forward into the water. Whatever happened to him, Reverend Sonny took the rest of his songs with him. Until I discovered another.

About a month after I returned from New Orleans, I was listening to "Troublin' Times" and accidentally bumped the turntable, causing the needle to jump. Though I can't really say it was an accident. My boyfriend, Nathan, was in one of his rages and shoved me. But he doesn't do that anymore.

So, Sonny James was strumming and weeping, coming to terms with the loss of his love; Nathan called me a bitch, grabbed my shoulders, and propelled me against the turntable; the needle bounced and, as it landed back on the record, Sonny was no longer wailing and weeping but brooding in slow, almost hostile, melancholia. However, Nathan's growling drowned it out as he called me a bitch a second time. Out of the corner of my eye, I saw his fist hurling toward me, and I blacked out.

☆ ☆ ☆

I woke face down on the carpet to the sound of creaking—a rocking chair against a loose floorboard—my eye throbbing along with it in synchronicity. Trembling, I sat up and listened to discern if Nathan had left. If he heard me crying, he'd barge into the room and knock me back onto the floor, so I resisted. As I sat there, the sound of the rocking soothed me, and a subtle euphoria tickled from within my chest. I felt safe.

When I was certain he was gone, I stood, stumbled to the bathroom, and gazed into the mirror. Cruel pastels of purple and red decorated the side of my face. Just below my eyelid, the skin had broken open, my vision pixelated. Bastard. The marks he left on my neck a few weeks prior had just started fading.

The first time he hit me, I accepted it. We'd gotten back from an all-day picnic at the home of a mutual friend, and during an argument—I can't remember over what—he slapped me across the mouth, knocking me to my knees. As I landed, I dropped my face into my hands, saturating them in an eruption of tears, shocked that he'd do that to me, an emptiness swirling in my chest, shaking my limbs. Just a few hours earlier, melting beneath his kiss, I'd told him I loved him.

As I sobbed, I felt his arms wrap around me, his body pressing against me.

"I'm sorry," he whispered in my ear, kissing my cheek. "I don't know what came over me. You know I'd never hurt you, right?"

I couldn't imagine my life without him. So, I believed him. And forgave him.

In the course of a few beautiful weeks, that dark moment drifted into the deep caverns of my memory and was forgotten—until it happened again. This time, he punched me in the stomach, without apology, laughing as I threw up on my kitchen floor.

And he quickly grew proficient, bruising me in places where no one could see—my back, my thighs, and my upper arms. He knew I wouldn't say anything because he knew I couldn't live without him.

But when I realized I hated him, I began to fear him.

One night, I opened my eyes to him standing over me, snarling through gritted teeth: "You ever think of leaving me, I'll strangle you again and won't stop till you're dead." After that, he became careless about where he left his marks. It was as if he were challenging me to tell someone what he was doing to me, rather than continue making up a new story for every fresh bruise.

Eventually, I retreated to Dina's place in New Orleans and lost myself in its wonders. I decided I'd stay and create a new identity so he'd never find me. But then, Sonny James came into my life. And by the same feeling of enchantment that drew me to The Peddler's table at the flea market, I was drawn back home to New Jersey.

True to his warning, Nathan choked me for trying to leave him. But as I felt myself fading from the world, he withdrew his hands.

"I can't kill you." He smiled, brushing his fingers across my forehead. "Why would I let you leave me?"

☆ ☆ ☆

Turning from the mirror, I grabbed a washcloth, warmed it in the sink, and pressed it against his callous handiwork. His voice looped over and over in my head: "When I tell you to do something, you do it, Cora! You useless bitch!" However, the soothing sound of the rocking blew away this echoing invective, summoning me to the turntable.

I journeyed back through the living room, moving of my own volition, yet feeling compelled against my will, and stood before the record--it still spun upon the platter, the needle locked in its end groove, the gentle rocking sound looping over and over with each spin.

I got on my knees and swayed to the creaking rhythm, like a pendulum. Leaning forward, I watched the tip of the needle as it glided atop the record, locked with the groove in an endless dance of which I'd become a participant—entranced and swaying. I'm unsure how long I was in this state, but when I came out of it, my knees were rug-burned, and the sun had gone down.

I lifted the tonearm.

The rocking ceased.

I sat in silence.

What was that song I heard, just before Nathan's fist smashed into the side of my face?

I took the record from the turntable, cradling it between my palms. I gazed upon it, for some reason believing that doing so would impart to me the necessary wisdom to unlock that hidden song. Contemplating the swampy green label, I slid my finger to the spindle hole and began rotating the record upon it. I had a sensation of being snatched up and carried away, the green, twisting label creating an illusion of marshy ground speeding beneath me. Branches and twigs snapped against the quick steps of the one who'd seized me, along with the guttural snarls of the beast pursuing him.

Am I trapped in a daydream and trying to wake up? I wondered.

I placed the record back onto the turntable and manually spun it until the goat-faced etching was at the five o'clock position. Lifting the tonearm, I set the needle so it hung mid-way into the lead-in area and was aligned with the space between the goat's horns. I switched on the turntable's motor, watched the record spin, and dropped the needle.

And I heard it—the other song, "Persephone and Old Scratch." At least, that's what I call it—no one knows the real title. Sonny must have performed it while sitting in a rocking chair on someone's front porch; behind the creaking, the trees rustle in the wind. Slide guitar drones ascend from beneath the rocking and hover atop it. I'm not sure how he got such a sound with just a finger slide on an acoustic—a mosaic of reverb creating a chorus of long, sustained notes.

Sonny then begins in his raspy voice: "Demeter's lil' girl got taken, by the hand o' that Ol' Scratch." He repeats this line a few times, following with a couple more measures of guitar drones. They sound like a pack of wolves baying from the deep, arousing an image of churning water expanding out in all directions.

As he moves into the main verse, Sonny is brooding, snarling. I won't sing you the lyrics, because they may overtake you (and it's too glorious of an experience for me to share with anyone). At times, it seems as if Sonny had Nature herself under his command, the wind in the background intensifying with the hostility in his voice.

Now, the story I mentioned at the beginning, the one I'm unsure I've actually heard, concerns the events that inspired Sonny to write this song.

After he recorded "Troublin' Times," Sonny was browsing a flea market. He wasn't sure what he was looking for, but knew he lacked something. As he waded through the stream of people flooding the marketplace, he had a sudden compulsion to look up. When he did, his gaze fell upon The Peddler, who stared back at him with his jaundiced, uneven eyes. Sonny, moving of his own volition yet feeling compelled against his will, made his way to the table, stepping into the swarm of flies whirling around it.

The Peddler's lower lip began quivering, and the words fell from Sonny's tongue: "I'm lookin' for a muse."

The Peddler leaned forward, reached under the black tapestry, pulled out a small velvet drawstring pouch, and dropped it into Sonny's calloused hands. As Sonny began loosening the strings, The Peddler grabbed his wrist, gazed into his eyes, and waved his finger back and forth.

A swell of unsteadiness overtook Sonny, and the marketplace became a whirling mosaic of grays and blacks. I can't really say what happened next was a vision—rather, Sonny felt his consciousness becoming one with The Peddler's, as if The Peddler had invited him to explore his mind, to experience his memories firsthand.

He ran along the bank of the Alfeios River, in the ancient city of Megalopoli. Stopping beside a sloping tree, he leaned over, his hands on his knees, catching his breath. When he was sure he'd lost whatever was pursuing him, he knelt by the side of the river for a drink.

Lifting his hand to his mouth, he noticed something sticking up from the dirt at the edge of the water. As he pulled it from the wet ground, he could tell it was some type of stone. He wiped the mud off with his thumbs, revealing a statuette of a young woman sitting on a tree stump. Her elbow rested on her knee as she held up a small group of people in her palm, gazing upon them with empathy. Though the stone from which she was carved had the initial appearance of obsidian, it was too durable to have withstood such detail of artistry. And rather than reflecting light, it devoured it, as if it were clear glass with the blackest darkness imprisoned within it. As he explored it with his fingers, a voice whispered "Kore Soteira," which he understood to mean *Kore the Savior*.

A wind blew, rustling the river to hostility, the water frothing over and rising to his ankles, and he heard the guttural snarl of the wolf that had chased him to this spot. Emerging from behind a nearby rock, it crawled atop it and leapt into the air, landing on the opposite side of him, before the sloping tree. Crouching, it prepared to lunge, its clawed feet gripping the ground. Black slits ran down the center of its yellow eyes; charcoal scales coated its hairless body. As it growled, saliva gurgled in its mouth and foamed over, dangling from its jaw in thick, white strings, spraying into the air as it flicked its forked tongue. Its serpentine tail cracked like a whip, stripping bark from the tree. It lunged forward, catching his ankle with its sabered teeth. Venom burned through his veins, stunning him to paralysis. The water closed in around him as the beast pulled him into the depths.

He exhaled and found himself sprawled out upon a stone altar, still paralyzed. Several young women in crimson robes surrounded him. At his feet, a marble statue of a goat-faced beast stood with its arms outstretched. Torches lit the space, what he thought was a cave—until until he realized it was a clear subaquatic dome, outside of which swam several more reptilian wolves.

The woman standing by his head approached the altar, the statuette in her hand, and whispered, "Kore Soteira." The others repeated as the wolves circled the dome, baying in response. A woman stood on either side of him, each brandishing a torch. They set the blazing tips to his palms. Streams of fire coursed down his arms, met at his chest, spread out, and consumed him. Only he wasn't burning up, and, in his paralysis, he didn't feel any pain. He just served as mere fuel for the hungry flames.

The conflagration continued in its course, igniting the women's robes. Yet, as they were engulfed, they didn't cry out in agony, but continued chanting, "Kore Soteira." As their bodies burned to ash, their essence mingled with the smoke, forming sinuous streams trailing around one another, without beginning or end, before funneling their way into the statuette.

One of the wolves slammed into the dome, forming a spiderweb crack. Another moved in, widening the break. A third followed—the dome shattered, and the water poured in over him.

He exhaled and found himself back on the bank of the Alfeios, holding the statuette in his hand. Another wave of unsteadiness overtook him, and Sonny once again looked out through his own eyes, standing before The Peddler's table.

He gestured to the drawstring bag. "It's inside here?"

The Peddler didn't respond, only gazed through him.

Stuffing the bag into his pocket, Sonny left the marketplace.

Now, I grew up in the Pine Barrens of Southern New Jersey, so I understand the development of urban lore and how it's passed down from generation to generation, changing slightly with each retelling. I still remember the Legend of Blind Paul, heard it when I was a child.

Blind Paul was a large feral man who roamed the Pine Barrens. His eyes crossed inward toward his nose, giving him the appearance of a

Cyclops. When little girls began missing from their beds, it was believed Blind Paul snatched them up, took them to his cave, feasted upon their little bodies, and made dolls out of their bones. The locals, terrified for their children, set a trap for Paul. They took the floor out of one of the cabins and dug a ditch about six feet down. At the bottom, they placed a series of sharp wooden stakes, so that when Paul stepped through the door, he'd fall onto them. Sure enough, a few mornings later, Paul was found impaled and dead.

All seemed well for a bit. Until girls began disappearing again.

Of course, I don't believe such things. They're merely stories parents use to keep children obedient. They're rooted in reality yet exaggerated for effect. All that's to say, I was suspicious of the story of Sonny James—even though it's unlikely I even heard it.

So, as I was listening to "Persephone and Old Scratch" for that first time, I noticed a band of dark smoke funneling up from where the needle met the record, forming an apparitional mist that hovered above the turntable. Floating toward me, it began twisting into a shape that looked just like the embossing on the inner sleeve. (I know now this is what Sonny saw as he watched the essence of the women mingling with the smoke of their burning before entering the statuette.) It fell upon me, enveloping me as I swayed with the sound of the rocking chair, and permeated my being.

Then, I remembered.

There I was—as the collective mind of my daughters from the deep —gazing out through the eyes of the statuette. Sonny James was across the porch, rocking in his chair, looking toward me, entranced. I watched him as he sang, inspiring every word falling from his tongue, words that would one day remind me of who I was, a song that would arouse me from my slumber and call me back to the Deep.

The wind was intensifying with the hostility in his voice. Trees swung about their branches, some throwing them to the ground. Others seemed to bend their trunks to the baying sounding from his strings. Yet, as the song approached its cadence, the wind started to settle. The final note rang from his guitar, and I heard a guttural snarl.

Sonny looked toward the woods, leapt from his chair, and snatched me up. As he carried me away, I watched the marshy ground rushing beneath me. Branches and twigs snapped under his feet as the snarling intensified behind him. Swamp water splashed up onto me, blurring my sight.

"Over here," Sonny whispered, slowing in his pace, hiding me in the cleft of a tree. "Rest here till you get woken up. Then you won't need to run no more." He looked over his shoulder and splashed off through the bog, the beast continuing its pursuit.

The needle locked into the end-groove, and the rocking lulled me back into my living room. I looked around, unsure if I was lost in a vision from within the statuette, or if I'd come back to myself. I stood and paced around the room, touching the wall, a chair, a picture frame, to see if they were in fact before me. But the rocking called me back to the turntable.

I lifted the tonearm, stopped the platter, manually spun it so the needle was lined up between the goat's horns, started the motor, and dropped the needle.

And I listened.

"Persephone and Old Scratch" ended.

I repeated the ritual, lining up the needle.

And listened again.

Then repeated.

Now the song is a little over three minutes, and I listened to it until after the sun came up, about seven hours.

Finally, the rocking seemed to be giving me permission to step away, wasn't tugging at me to play the record again. I left the needle locked in the end-groove so I could still be soothed by the sound. After a shower, I put on my favorite white dress—it still had a bloodstain from the time Nathan almost broke my nose.

My steps were guided toward the phone, my fingers to the buttons.

Nathan picked up. "What?"

"It's me."

"No shit. Whataya want?"

"Just to let you know that I despise you and want you to die."

"Sounds like you need me to color in your other eye!"

"Awwwwww. That's sweet."

"I don't have time for your shit, Cora!"

"Bye, babe!"

Snickering, I hung up.

He'd be over soon.

I went out to my car and grabbed the old police baton I kept under the front seat. My father gave it to me when I started driving. "Jersey's a weird place at night, Cora!" he'd tell me.

Back inside, I knelt and swayed with the rocking.

"Demeter's lil' girl got taken," I sang, enraptured. "By the hand o' that Ol' Scratch."

Closing my eyes, I could hear the chanting of my daughters from the deep as they called me into being, "Kore Soteira!"

I hummed: "Demeter's lil' girl got taken."

They chanted: "Kore Soteira!"

I sang: "By the hand o' that Ol' Scratch."

Nathan kicked in the door and charged toward me. "Who the fuck do you think you are?"

"Hey, babe!" I grinned, tripping him with the baton.

Hopping over him, I moved toward the turntable and switched the volume to its maximum. The rocking vibrated the floor, the speakers popping.

"I'm gonna hurt you, Cora!" he growled, pushing himself to his feet.

"Awe. You gonna color in my other eye now, babe?"

I started swaying from side-to-side, synchronous with the rocking, making creaking noises in my throat, grinning wide. Swinging the baton across his jaw, I sent him back to the floor; he spit a few teeth onto the carpet, bloody strings hung from his lip.

"I'm... gonna... kill you," he slurred, wobbling as he forced himself to his feet.

I sent another blow to his nuts, just because I thought it would be funny to hear him yelp like a puppy. He did. It was kind of cute, the way he gripped himself as he fell over. On his knees, he started leaning forward, so I kicked him in the face with my boot, tossing him onto his back.

Watching him writhe around, I thought back to the day I told him I loved him. I could still taste his tongue against mine, still felt the safety of his embrace. How his touch entranced me as he ran his fingers down my back, exposing the vulnerability I'd managed to keep hidden, drawing out my desire for him, addicting me to his essence, enslaving my emotions.

"I would've done anything for you, Nathan!" I yelled with wet eyes.

In the closet, I had some rope. I was going to use it to hang myself from my favorite tree, a dead white cypress on the bank of the Batsto River. When I was a little girl, I'd sit under it and wait for my mom. Before she died, she told me I'd be able to see her essence mingled with the morning mist as it floated over the water. When she never showed up, I realized there was no afterlife, and I'd never see her again. But the day after I bought the rope, I met Nathan and thought he'd been sent to save me.

"Come get me, babe," I teased, biting my lower lip, dangling the rope before him.

Giggling, I skipped from the house and waited on the porch, watching him fumbling and growling as he stood. He barged toward me, slamming through the door. I hopped off the steps and ran into the forest, luring him down a narrow corridor of pines.

"Demeter's lil' girl got taken," I hummed, my song summoning the wind and rattling thunder from above. "By the hand o' that Ol' Scratch."

Intermingled with the breeze, The Peddler's breath enveloped me. Yet rather than making me queasy, it refreshed me, whispering in my ear, "Kore Soteira." Above the canopy of pines, the sky darkened, obedient to my melody.

Nathan hobbled behind, snarling. "You ever have your head smashed against a rock, Cora?"

"Almost there, babe!"

The corridor of trees would soon open onto the bank of the Batsto. I sprinted toward it, leaping and singing.

As I arrived, I could see the eyes of the wolves shimmering beneath the water's surface, appearing as rippled, phosphorescent tadpoles. I sat under the dead white cypress and sang to them. They bayed in response, in the sound of Sonny's guitar drones. Our harmonies rustled the river, and it rose, its roaring torrent penetrating the rumbling wind.

"Cora!" Nathan growled, stepping onto the riverbank.

"Hey, babe!" I waved, the rising water licking at my boots. "Did you need me to help you find a rock... so you can smash my head against it?"

There was a fury in his eyes. At one point, it would've scared me, weakening me to do his bidding. Now, it provoked me, uncorking all the rage I'd stored up toward him.

"Look! Here's one!" I picked up a rock, hurled it at his face. "Catch!" It hit him between the eyes. "Awwww! You missed!" I laughed as he fell.

In stunned disbelief, he looked up at me as I dipped the rope to his nose, hinting to his end. But first, I stomped on his face several times, relishing the way it sounded as it shattered beneath my heel.

I never learned how to make a noose, but it came quite intuitively— I just hummed Sonny's song and let my fingers dance to the melody.

"Okay, time to go," I said, guiding his limp head through the rope, tightening it around his neck. Dragging him to the white cypress, I continued to hum, while he gagged and clawed at the noose, the cresting river saturating him. I tossed the opposite end of the rope over a low branch and pulled it, lifting him off the ground. I'm not sure where my strength came from—standing beside him, I only came up to his chest, and when he used to wrap his arms around me, they'd consume me. He whipped his legs around and clawed at the noose as it seared into his neck. But I kept humming and pulling, and he kept rising. When the crown of his head was just below the branch, I tied the rope around the trunk, leaving him suspended, flaying and gagging, producing a delightful gurgle. His neck slid through the noose until his jawbone caught on it.

I watched him dangle, his bloodied eyes protruding from their sockets, as his foul life slithered away. My humming turned into singing —no I still won't tell you those lyrics! From beneath the water, the wolves' howling rose, summoning the rain, reminding me of Sonny.

"My Old Scratch!" I smiled, opening my arms wide and twirling, the hem of my dress fanning open.

☆ ☆ ☆

The waters of the Batsto have risen around me; my chin rests just above the waterline. The breath of The Peddler falls upon me and inhales. A dark band of smoke is drawn out of me, funneling upward, in the same way it did from the record, twisting upon itself, without beginning or end. For a moment, it lingers over the face of the water before funneling into it and taking my daughters home.

Each generation will pass my story on to the next, altering it slightly, as it's been done since I was first called forth. Some will depict me as a devil, others as a savior—both will be appropriate. My dead White Cypress will become a fixture of local lore, under which scorned, weeping women will plot, and where children will see their illusions of safety shattered.

But when spring arrives—just as the birds begin their morning hymn, when the light of the sun pierces through the canopy of pines— you may see my essence ascending from the water and mingling with the morning mist. You may even hear my daughters chanting below the surface, praying to me as I rise. And, if you're still, you just might hear me singing the song of Old Scratch.

ABOUT THE AUTHOR

Skylar Lennox is the signifier for a disillusioned ex-pastor turned librarian residing in Pennsylvania. Lacanian psychoanalysis and radical theology are now Skylar's philosophical focus, themes of which are explored in the forthcoming collection, *Nascent ad Absurdum and Other Deaths of God*, planned for a late 2023 release.

❧ 8 ❦

THE GALATEA PROJECT

A Retelling of the Pygmalion Myth

TCC Edwards

The painting dominated the room as if to taunt the man who entered it. It was *Pygmalion adoring his statue*, a reminder left by whoever had prepared this room for him. Bernard Higgins tossed the backpack containing his possessions onto the bed. He sat, relieved that the bed was softer than the bunk in the prison cell he had left behind.

This was the Reintegration Center, a minimum-security housing complex for convicts at the end of prison sentences. Each room was just like the one Bernard was in now—the same size, the same bed, the same sky-blue paint on the bare walls. Would other rooms have something like the painting, a reminder for the occupant of their previous crimes? *Probably not.* Other ex-cons weren't as notorious, nor were any of them enjoying their release years earlier than expected.

A figure entered through the open door. Bernard turned his head to face her but didn't get up or otherwise acknowledge her.

"Higgins?" The tall woman had her brown hair up in a tight bun. She didn't quite scowl at him, but her stare was hardly welcoming.

"Yeah," he said softly. "You my guard?"

"Yeah, buddy; you're stuck with me. I'm Andrews, and I'll watch you here at the Center. Do you know why you're out so early?"

"I don't know. I was as surprised as anyone when the warden told me. He said it was for 'good behavior'—that's all I know." Bernard gestured to the painting, raising his eyebrow in silent question.

The woman nodded. "I saw it in France a few years back. Remembered it when I heard you were getting out. I made some arrangements to get you under my watch here at the Center."

Bernard blinked in astonishment. "You did? Have we met?"

"I met *her*. After you went to prison."

"Ah." Bernard nodded slowly. He didn't need to ask who she meant —there was only one *her* Andrews could be talking about.

"Last I saw Elise, she was keeping a low profile. Well, as low as possible after *your* court case. She still loves you—but that was your design, wasn't it?"

Bernard nodded solemnly. "She tried to reach me in prison, didn't she?"

"Many times. I have the correspondence as part of the files I keep on you. I'll send them to you once you leave here."

Bernard nodded again. "That will be another year, won't it?"

"That's what they say. You have to show you understand that creating Elise was wrong."

"I already understand that. I did my time."

Andrews cocked an eyebrow at him. "I like the confidence."

"You'll see," Bernard said. He turned away before he could see her reaction, pacing around the room once before turning back to her. "So. What do I do here?"

Andrews smirked as she stepped toward him. "You stay in this room for twelve hours and you get out for twelve. Do whatever you want in here—you'll get a computer with network access, but the warden and the admins here will monitor it closely. While you're out, you're free to move around the Center in the first week. Talk to the people here, find out what jobs need doing. There's a hydroponics farm, a cafeteria, cleaning, building maintenance, and a few other jobs. You'll also get library time, social time, and other perks—use them well, and you'll be ready to get a proper job when you're out."

"A bit better than prison," Bernard remarked. "They certainly didn't let us use networked computers, and you're a lot more polite than my guards were."

"Oh, I didn't mention the best part. You can leave the Center for three days each month. Bet they didn't let you do that in prison."

"Ah. But there's a catch, right?"

"Of course there is, buddy." Andrews snorted. "You'll have to report to me, tell exactly where you are and who you talk to. If you do anything I don't approve of, you lose your leave, permanently."

"Like, meet with Elise, for instance?" Bernard said coldly.

Andrews closed the small space between them, bringing her face within inches of his. "You'll go back to prison if you so much as look at her. You know that, right?"

"I can help her."

Andrews blinked. She stepped back half a pace, a heavy frown on her face. "Help her?"

"The genetic and mental coding I used to ensure she'd love me—I can change it. I figured it out while I was in prison. She'll be able to love anyone she chooses."

"You can *do* that? She's been studying genetics on her own—she knows almost as much as you do, I think. But she said it's impossible to change her attraction to you."

"It nearly is impossible." Bernard sighed. He walked to the bed and sat down at its end, keeping his eyes on Andrews. "I would need access to a genetics lab like the one I used to have."

"Higgins Genetics is dead, buddy," Andrews said. "All your research was confiscated, and any company that even *thinks* about human DNA is put under careful government scrutiny."

"Like I said, nearly impossible. Even if I could get into a genetics lab, I'd still need Elise's cooperation. Those are two things I know you won't allow, Ms. Andrews."

"It's just Andrews, buddy," Andrews said, shaking her head. "Look. I can't promise anything. But you just told me that you can *cure* Elise. Are you absolutely sure?"

"Not one hundred percent. I need blood and tissue samples, and a recent MRI of Elise's brain, to be sure. But the theory—it's sound, and I can test it with simulation equipment like the computers in my former lab."

"I'll tell the supervisors here at the Center," Andrews said. "Likely, they'll insist on you finishing one year here before anything else happens."

"They probably know. I told the warden and everybody else. You're the first to actually listen, though."

"Probably 'cause I actually met her, and they were spared having to see what she went through. Well, I'll tell them, anyway. Who knows?"

"Do *you* believe me?"

Andrews laughed. "Some guards here talk about stone-cold killers who reformed into upstanding public servants, or kids locked up on bullshit drug charges who turned into murderers. Every redemption and downfall story you can imagine. But you say you can help the person you hurt. And I guess since I know the person, that means something. But don't think I'm soft, buddy. I'll see what I can do to help, but in the meantime, you'll be in for a shitstorm if you even try to see Elise."

"Duly noted, Officer Andrews."

☆ ☆ ☆

Elise stood at the end of his bed with a pistol in her hand.

Bernard got up slowly, hands extended as he shook off the last wisps of sleep. It *was* her, dressed in the same plain black uniform that Andrews had worn earlier. With her normally curled hair tied back tightly, she could almost pass as another Reintegration Center officer, but Bernard could hardly mistake his own creation for anybody else.

"Hello, *lover*," she whispered hoarsely, "You're out early."

"Elise, listen, I can help..."

"Can you? What if I just kill you, here, now? Will it finally stop?"

"No," Bernard said flatly. He stood in front of her, placing his chest in line with the barrel of her weapon. "No, even my death wouldn't stop it. But I *can* help you, if you'll listen."

"What the hell?" Andrews stormed in, flicking on the full brightness of the room's light as she stepped toward Bernard and Elise. Andrews's hand went to a weapon on her belt.

"You! What are *you* doing here?"

"I work here. I'm helping this man atone for what he did."

"*Really?* Seems I'm about to do your job for you."

"Look, I don't know *how* you got in," Andrews said. She kept her hand at the ready above the holster for her own weapon but didn't draw it yet. "You're already in deep shit here. You really want to spend the next thirty years in prison?"

"Maybe! At least it would finally be over."

"No, you didn't hear me," Bernard said calmly. "Killing me won't end it. But there's another way. A solution that I can engineer from a sample of your tissue and scans of your brain."

"You're saying you can *fix* me?" Elise scowled as she turned back to face Bernard. "I was *broken* on purpose. You *made* me that way."

"I came to my senses—I thought of you, lost without me, and knew what I had to do. You will finally stop loving me."

"How?"

"I need a laboratory, like I had when I made you."

Elise blinked at him, lowering the gun for a moment. "And what if I could get you into one?"

"Then I'd just need time. A week or two, maybe."

"We can start tonight."

"Uh, no, you cannot," Andrews said sternly. She now held her own weapon, a stun pistol that could easily put both Bernard and Elise down for twelve hours. She kept the gun pointed at the floor, but her eyes and body were clearly ready as she talked. "You just set off a lot of alarms bringing that gun in here…"

"The alarms are off," Elise interrupted. "All your cameras are showing looped video too. Nobody's coming."

"You planned this." Bernard was impressed despite the threat to his life. "You really went through all this just to kill me?"

"No. To end my *condition*. The one *you built into me*. If that means killing you, I still might."

Bernard nodded. He had, not for a short time, considered suicide in prison. However, the separation from Elise had forced his mind to consider the consequences of his actions. She was made to love him, and neither his imprisonment nor death would change that.

"Listen," Bernard said. "Plead your case—maybe we can get the Reintegration Center on our side!"

"Ha!" Elise laughed sharply. "You think I didn't try that? They said there's no way the two of us would ever meet legally, let alone work together."

"I'll help."

Bernard and Elise both stopped at the sound of Andrews's voice. Bernard saw his confusion echoed in Elise's face as the two looked to Andrews.

"I hate to say it, but Elise's right. No amount of pleading or petitioning would let you two get back together without serious consequences. The laws are too strict for that, and good luck finding a judge who'd allow an exception. But Elise, you said *we can start tonight* —what did you mean? You have a lab already?"

"It's a new company called Galatea. It's all legal—they only deal with the human genetic research that *is* allowed. Genetic disease research, organ replacement, that sort of thing. I work there, but of course, they know about Bernard and they watch me closely."

"You've been trying to find a solution on your own," Bernard said.

"Yes. And three master's and two PhDs later, I'm still not any closer!"

"Holy... I knew you were smart, but..."

"But you made me this way," Elise snapped. She sighed heavily. "Smart? Maybe. But I'm also obsessed—you should know how much."

"Okay, listen," Andrews said. "There's no way Bernard's leaving this building for more than a day, let alone two weeks. You could give him a remote connection to your lab. The network's heavily monitored here, but you seem to know a few things about hacking."

Elise paused. "Perhaps. We have camera drones at the company; we use them to share work with overseas research teams. I bet I can set up a live feed with your terminal here —I can disguise the connection to get past the filters on the network. You'll allow this, Officer Andrews?"

Andrews shrugged. "If you don't trip the filters or set off any alarms, it's not my problem."

"And Bernard. If I showed you my lab over a remote connection, could you walk me through your solution?"

"Yes," Bernard said. "I think so."

☆ ☆ ☆

A week passed before Bernard had a stable connection with Elise in her laboratory at Galatea Genetics. Andrews had agreed not to tell the admins what she knew, but she also wouldn't help him avoid detection —which was fine with Bernard. He wouldn't rob her of the plausible deniability she needed to keep her career.

Finally, after several days tending to the trays of soil and plants in the brightly-lit basement of the Reintegration Center, Bernard returned to his room, ready to begin remote sessions with Elise.

A sterile white room came into focus on Bernard's computer screen. Elise stood close to one wall of the room, next to four screens that showed MRI scans of her brain, rendered in light-blue slices from top and side views. Next to those screens, a larger monitor showed a representation of her DNA—Bernard hardly needed to see this; the sequence of nucleotides was as familiar to him as her name. Under the display of her DNA was a metal table with petri dishes, a rack of vials filled with blood, and a microscope.

"I see you got a head start," Bernard said. There was a slight delay as his voice played through an earpiece she wore.

She nodded her reply—from her point of view, she was nodding at a camera drone hovering in her laboratory. "We won't get long to work each night," she said. "I wanted to be ready."

Bernard nodded, then realized she couldn't see him. "All right. Let's see your brain first."

For the next two hours, Elise tapped at the screens and scrolled through representations of her brain and her DNA. The first nightly sessions continued like this—Elise sharing the inner workings of her body and brain while Bernard took notes. It was late in the first week when Bernard finally instructed Elise through some experiments with her blood samples.

When he couldn't be in his room, Bernard stayed in the hydroponics farm, interacting with the other ex-prisoners at the Center as little as possible. It was rote work; trimming plants, harvesting fruit, injecting fertilizer; and it allowed his mind to devise new methods and possible solutions.

☆ ☆ ☆

On the tenth night, the alarm sounded. One minute, Elise was on his screen, using one of her company's powerful computers. She was running a simulation based on the scans, and Bernard hoped the sim would show that his latest attempt for an injected cure would work. Elise turned to face the drone as it approached the computer and... the network session came to an abrupt end.

Bernard stared at his blank screen, mind reeling as reality came back into focus. A knock sounded at the door, and Andrews came in without waiting for an answer.

"Bernard," she said sharply as she stepped in. Four men came in after, dressed in the same black padded uniform as she.

"Bernard Higgins," one of the men proclaimed, "you are charged with unlawful use of network equipment and violating the terms of your release to this facility. A transport is here for you now—you will return to prison, where you will await trial. We can trust you to accompany us without any difficulty, right, Mr. Higgins?"

Bernard looked to Andrews, but she stared back, her expressionless gaze revealing nothing. *No,* Bernard thought as he examined her. *You didn't tip them off.* Somebody else monitoring the networks at the Reintegration Center had discovered his connection to Galatea, despite his efforts to hide it. *I wasn't careful enough.*

Without a word, Bernard put his wrists in front of his waist, and the lead officer cuffed him. The men guided him out into the hallway, where he walked with Andrews next to him, one guard to each side, and one in front and behind. They made no sound as they stepped over the sea-blue carpet between the dull white walls. Black doors lined the way on either side, each one representing a second chance for a criminal to rethink their ways, rejoin society. Bernard's door had slammed behind him, possibly to stay shut forever.

Soon they were on the cement walkway outside the front door. The sun was setting, its light flitting through skyscrapers on the horizon. The hovering prison transport waited at the curb ahead, just to the right of the place where the walkway and the immaculate green lawn on either side of it gave way to the asphalt street.

A slender form appeared then, emerging from behind the prison shuttle. It was Elise, her gun in hand.

"Let him go!" she screamed. "Now!"

Her gun went off, unleashing a blue bolt that erupted in the cement just ahead of the lead guard. The guard was thrown back but had his own gun out as his backside hit the lawn. Elise took cover behind the transport as the other guards drew their pistols. Bernard yelled as the guard behind him caught the back of his neck in a tight grip.

"You are outgunned!" the guard behind him yelled, his voice ringing in Bernard's ear. The guard held his gun with his right, pointing to Elise's choice of cover. "There's nowhere to run—you'll have every officer after you in a matter of minutes."

"Maybe I would," Elise's voice retorted, "if your alarms and security didn't suck!"

"Communications are down!" Andrews exclaimed. She tapped at the earpiece she wore, and the other guards checked their own earpieces while keeping their eyes on their target and Bernard.

"She hacked your systems again," Bernard said. "I'll bet she took out all the cameras you have around here too. You guys really need to upgrade."

"Hands up, Bernard!" Elise's voice yelled.

Bernard raised an eyebrow, but quickly did as he was told, raising his cuffed arms above his head. A blast zipped overhead, and the chain between his cuffs burst apart.

"Holy shit!" Bernard yelled, but his words were drowned out as the guards fired in response. The prison shuttle glowed electric blue as its armor absorbed the blasts; the munitions were designed to cause intense pain but not kill a living target. These were minimum-security guards, not soldiers, after all.

Elise's return fire was not as restrained. Her shots tore up tufts of grass and chunks of sidewalk, throwing up smoke and keeping the guards from focusing on her properly.

Andrews looked to Bernard. Her gun was in her hand, but she bit her lip as she stared into him. Finally, she took action.

Blue bolts hit each of the four guards in rapid succession, and they dropped to the ground with agonized yells. Andrews holstered her gun and grabbed Bernard's arm.

"You shot them!" Bernard yelled stupidly as Andrews dragged her toward Elise.

"So much for that job, yeah." Andrews groaned.

"Your *job*? You'll go to prison!"

"We'll see. I still know a few tricks."

Elise had left her cover and now stood before Andrews and Bernard in front of the armored shuttle. "I've got another vehicle, but I don't know about her," she said, pointing to Andrews. Her other hand hovered above her now-holstered pistol.

"I'll take the prison transport," Andrews said. "I'll send a message to my superiors—you stole the transport and kidnapped me as collateral. It should buy you a day at least. Don't waste it."

Bernard and Elise looked at her, but she was already sliding open the door to the transport. They looked at each other, silently deciding that there would be better times for questions.

Elise led Bernard to an intersection a few blocks from the prison. Blocky houses and small apartment complexes lined the streets, many of them surrounded by short trees and rows of bushes. These were all genetically altered growths, Bernard knew—plants designed to better clean the city air and to combat the heat that built up around so much concrete and steel.

Elise gestured to a small car that waited at the side of the street. The doors opened as she approached, and the two quickly got in. The car drove them to Galatea without any prompting from Elise—Bernard nodded in approval when the navigator screen on the dashboard ran her pre-programmed getaway sequence.

Drab, boxy residences passed them by—the kind of residences anyone could have if the job market had been unkind to them. Soon, more varied shapes emerged as the car passed through suburbs, avoiding the heaviest-traffic areas of the city. The houses were more rounded here, with wider windows that overlooked lush gardens and well-kept yards.

Galatea Genetics rose into view as the car exited the rich suburbs. Cylindrical structures grew from concrete soil, a forest of glass buildings connected by winding branches of walkways. Elise parked the car next to a metallic sculpture of a DNA molecule. As Bernard got out of the car, she led him to the front door, talking quickly as she walked.

"We can't go in the front," she said. "I've hacked the security cameras, but you need to stay close to me."

Bernard quickly stepped to walk next to her, not bothering to ask questions. She walked in a wide arc across the concrete promenade, taking them past the wide double doors at the front of the building. They came to an emergency exit at the side of the main building. Elise quickly tapped at a panel next to the door, and it opened. Bernard quickly followed her up a wide stairwell, and then out into an empty hallway. They walked a short distance, then went through a door on one side of the hall.

Bernard had seen this room before through the remote setup. This was the computer workshop—a tall room filled with racks of servers working in tandem. At the other end of the room were several desks with monitors. Elise had set up two fabricator units on one of the worktops next to the monitors—one was designed to build chips and circuitry, while the other was a liquid synthesizer, most often used in pharmaceutical design and testing.

Bernard inspected the two units. The chip builder looked similar to other 3D printers, with several steel cylinders inside a glass case. Small attachments would move up and down tiny conveyors built into the cylinders once the fabrication started, each attachment maneuvering tiny pieces into place as the desired product was built.

The liquid mixer was less familiar to him—he had used devices like it before, but this one had a more complex mass of tubes inside its clear casing.

"I'm guessing Galatea doesn't have these just sitting around. These must cost a fortune."

"These are on loan, but yes, still very expensive," Elise said bluntly. "We need to get this done, quickly."

Without another word, she switched on the monitors. Bernard saw the simulations she had been running with the powerful computers in this room. She had designed a microchip to be implanted in her own brain, along with a complex serum that would trigger or suppress specific hormones. Bernard's own work had helped revise the designs, but the latest iterations of the sims still showed an incomplete solution.

"The serum is temporary," Bernard said once he understood the problem. "The chip isn't enough—you'll have to take the serum regularly for this to work."

"There's got to be a better way, right?" Elise asked incredulously. "The serum has too many side effects if I take it so often—it'll seriously mess up my brain!"

Bernard nodded numbly. "Yeah, it's too strong. My notes, I need my notes."

Elise pointed to another desktop next to the monitors. Three tablets were there, each with a different page of Bernard's notes on its screen. Bernard picked one up, scrolling through the text he had written during his years in prison.

The first hours were agonizing. Though they were left unhindered, Bernard felt the weight of time on his shoulders. Someone would figure it out. Someone would open the door to Elise's workshop and quickly escort Bernard back to prison.

Another simulation showed a need for constant doses of the serum, and Elise and Bernard stepped away from the computers. They didn't dare leave the room, as security guards would patrol the halls. Instead, the two of them paced through the rows of networked computers.

"You could have killed those guards, you know," Bernard muttered as the two stood between the server racks. "Your pistol—it wasn't set to stun."

Elise turned a sharp glare at him, but then calmed, nodding solemnly. "I know. It was crazy. I'm crazy. I could have killed you, too."

"Really? Even knowing it wouldn't help—that it would leave you mourning for me forever?"

"And just *who* is responsible for that?"

Bernard put out his hands, stepping back against one rack of overheated computers. "Look. You are smart. *A lot* smarter than I ever thought. You're a hacker and a geneticist? And you know how to work pharmaceutical and microchip fabrication equipment? There should be at least four other experts here with us right now, but you're doing it all. You've lived without me this long—you're stronger than you think."

"No thanks to you," she whispered sharply. "Once we were separated, it was a constant battle. Do I kill myself, or everyone standing between you and me? You have no idea how many times I asked myself."

"God. I'm sorry—and I know that's never enough. I can't exactly apologize for creating my dream woman, making her devoted to me. I was arrogant enough to think I'd get away with it, that we'd just be together. One of those couples who are so perfect it makes everyone else sick, you know?"

"I remember. We *were* good together—before they caught us. That's why we're here, together now. I'm still *that* devoted to you!"

Bernard nodded. *She is the victim. I am the monster.* And with that realization, Elise's problem and its solution shifted in his mind. His mind had already worked on the answer for years, but now the key was coming to him, taking shape. He quickly stepped around Elise and ran to one of the monitors.

Elise didn't say anything as she stood at Bernard's side. One tiny change to the design of the implant, inspired by the geniuses whose works Bernard had pored over on sleepless nights in a small jail cell. A slight rebalance of hormonal triggers in the serum, and a tiny amount of a chemical derived from a study at Yale—one that should decrease the need for more doses.

The simulation ran. Agonizing minutes passed.

Elise and Bernard looked into each other's eyes. They breathed heavily as they waited.

The simulation finished. Bernard looked over the results.

"I don't believe it," he said finally. "This is it. You'll only need two injections a year—and you can stockpile serum for the future. We can make enough right now for several years!"

Elise's eyes went wide, but instead of saying anything, she quickly activated the fabricators. The chip constructor clicked and whirred as it worked, while liquid bubbled through the tubes of the chemical mixer.

"Not wasting one more second," she exclaimed as she set the machines in motion. "I can't believe it—this is it!"

"Freeze!"

The door burst open. Two men in full tactical police gear entered, pistols drawn. Elise and Bernard quickly raised their hands and knelt as the men crossed the room.

"We'll come quietly," Elise said to the men.

"Yes, we surrender," Bernard added. "But there's something..."

"Silence!" one of the men shouted. "Put your heads down and your hands behind your back. Now."

Bernard and Elise placed their foreheads down. Hands roughly grasped Bernard, forcing his wrists behind his back, where they were bound in tight plastic cords.

"Please, you have to listen to me, she needs help!" Bernard tried to yell from his prone position. The officer ignored him and forced him roughly to his feet.

The police officers escorted him and Elise through the hallways and out of the building. Soon, the metal DNA sculpture glinted under the full moon as they stepped out into the courtyard. A prison transport waited, its large back doors open and the benches inside visible in the light offered by surrounding streetlamps.

Bernard and Elise were forced into the hovering transport, and Bernard's stomach lurched as the vehicle took to the air. After less than fifteen minutes, though, they landed, and the doors opened again.

Andrews greeted them. She let them out, and they emerged into a large park in the middle of the city. Andrews stood in front of a large paved area with park benches and swing sets for children. She was dressed in a formal shirt and pants, standing next to the transport she had taken earlier from the Reintegration Center.

The guards that had taken Bernard and Elise stepped out from the vehicle, each nodding to Andrews. One of them handed her a large silver briefcase.

"You are not just a Reintegration Center guard, are you?" Bernard asked incredulously.

"Took you that long to realize?" Andrews laughed. "You're right. My real name isn't important—but let's just say I'm an investor with some personal interest in you, Bernard. Though I didn't expect Elise to be so impulsive, I managed to work things out with a few bribes here and there. I've also been an avid backer of Galatea's research."

Andrews placed the briefcase on a bench and opened it. Inside was a medical injector and many small vials full of clear liquid. The tiny chip that Elise and Bernard had made was also in the case, encased in a protective plastic shell.

"I'll help you get to a neurosurgeon," Andrews said, pointing to the chip. "He'll handle the implanting, no questions asked."

"This is... amazing," Elise stammered, echoing Bernard's thoughts. "But why? Why do all this?"

"Not at liberty to say," Andrews said. She reached into the briefcase and pulled out a tablet secured under its lid. "It's all here. Read it after you get the chip put in."

Bernard opened his mouth but jumped when the doors of the two prison transports closed. The guards loyal to Andrews took them, presumably flying back to where the police could reclaim the vehicles. Two more hovering vehicles came to replace them. Bernard recognized these smaller hovercars as expensive autonomous rentals, the kind usually used by diplomats and other VIPs when they wanted tours of the city.

"Take that one," Andrews said, pointing to one of the hovercars as its doors opened. "It'll take you to the doctor. After that, it'll take you to a safe house I know. You'll have to lie low for a while, but you can use the tablet to contact me. I'll let you know when it's safe."

"But what about you?" Bernard asked. "You're an accomplice in all this—you can go to prison too!"

Andrews shrugged. "Like I said, I've managed to avoid it so far."

"But..." Elise stammered, but it was too late. Andrews and the two guards had already turned away and boarded their own hovercar. She and Bernard watched as it zipped away above the moonlit city.

☆ ☆ ☆

"You feel nothing?"

"Well, I still *like* you." Elise laughed uneasily. She continued carrying the small tray to the simple table in the middle of the room, and Bernard joined her as she sat.

The table and chairs, like all the other furniture, were wholly unremarkable, and all the same dull brown shade as the walls. The room and the two connected bedrooms were in a small, single-floor building in a suburb reserved for government-assisted housing. Bernard hoped that he and Elise were not depriving a lower-income family of needed housing, but he figured that Andrews had avoided disrupting the system when she arranged this safe house.

Elise finished a thoughtful sip of tea and began again. "It doesn't *burn* anymore."

"Huh?" Bernard said, raising his eyebrow as he looked at her teacup.

"Not the *tea*, silly," she giggled. "My heart. My desire, my hormones —whatever—it doesn't *burn*. I don't feel like I *need* you."

Bernard nodded, taking a sip before speaking. "Good. That's good. And you're not going to shoot anyone either, right?"

Elise scowled but quickly composed herself. "The violence is gone. I mean, I understand why I felt that, why I wanted to do something, hurt someone, *take action*—and why I didn't care what form that action took. But that's just it—I can look at it objectively now. I'm still guilty for tracking you down, breaking in to get to you, and firing a live weapon at innocent people, I know that. I'd apologize to them if I had the chance. I'd even go to prison myself if that would make it right."

Bernard nodded. "This sort of *is* prison. We'll both need new lives and new homes far from here. Even if Andrews can clear our names, we'll never go back to where we were."

"And we'll never see each other again. I feel... *regret*, I guess. We could still talk about so many things. Hell, we could revolutionize genetics with what we both know. But I also understand now why we can't."

"So, you're not going to track me down, try to follow me or anything?"

"No. It's... clear now. When I start a new line of research, or begin work on a new problem, I won't have to think about you or the connection we had. I can do things for myself, for my own curiosity."

"You have no idea how glad I am to hear you say that. Do you have a plan, then?"

"I want to start small again. The research we did, the serum and the chip—there's got to be ways it can help other people. I want to gather a research team and see what we can do with it.

"I also want to help people. But no more research—I'll write a book, tell everyone what I did, and why it was wrong. Maybe I can help stop the next guy who gets a similar idea."

"Guy? Could be a girl who does it next time. Could be anyone—everybody gets lonely."

"Yeah, I'm sure they... wait. I just realized something. Andrews. All the clout she pulled, the money she threw around. She cut my sentence short, arranged for me to go to a minimum-security place—it's all on that tablet she gave us."

"I read it, yeah. It made me think of our first meeting, just before I started with Galatea. I was in a small town trying not to attract attention, but she approached me right as I was leaving my house. She wouldn't tell me much about herself—she just kept asking questions about you and your research. She must have a personal stake—why else would she do all this?"

"I'm going to find out."

☆ ☆ ☆

Andrews—Bernard knew that wasn't her name, but it was the only name he knew—stood in her spacious living room. She gazed up at a familiar painting, which now hung over her fireplace. She turned and gestured for Bernard to sit in one of the many plush armchairs, but he shook his head. Shrugging, she led him to the large window which overlooked the gentle waves over the ocean below.

Elise could be somewhere over that ocean, for all he knew. This morning, after nearly six months of living in the safe house, two unmanned vehicles had showed up in the small driveway. Bernard had no clue where Elise's vehicle had taken her, and his mind would need a long time to accept that he would never see her again.

Bernard had refused the preprogrammed destination for his vehicle, instead telling its navigation system to return to its programmer. The vehicle had whisked him to this wondrous palace by the ocean, far from the city.

"I think I get it now," Bernard said after a thoughtful silence. "The painting should have been my hint."

"It's the original," Andrews said with a wink. "That's how absurdly wealthy I am. But I'd give it all up for the right man."

Bernard's eyes went wide. He turned, glaring as he met her gaze. "I can't say how I knew. But somehow, in the back of my mind, it's been there for a while."

Andrews nodded slowly. "I poured years of work into a passion for genetics. But no man I met appreciated that. They wanted my money, my body, my connections—*anything* but *me*. So I used all my knowledge and wrote a new strand of human DNA. Someone who would be smart, who would learn as quickly as I did, someone to be my equal. I succeeded. I created you."

Bernard shook his head. "But my childhood. I remember a foster home, elementary school, my graduation. I remember growing up!"

"Do you, buddy? Who raised you? Which elementary school was it?"

Bernard opened his mouth, but nothing came out. A terrible sinking grew in his gut.

"It's okay. In a few moments, you'll forget I asked. It's a side effect of the memory treatment—your mind will avoid dwelling on the details."

"You altered my memory?"

"I couldn't do what you did with Elise. I couldn't *make* you love me. I settled for making you *perfect*, at least in my eyes. I assumed that would be enough for you to fall in love with me."

"But... I didn't, did I?"

"We spent three years together. We tried to make it work. But you knew that I created you and why. Knowing that, even with all I could offer, you craved freedom even more."

"You let me go," Bernard reasoned.

"Yes. And I did what I could to help you forget—your memory wipe was based on military research, intended for victims of severe trauma. The failure rate is high, so the technique is heavily classified and rarely used."

Bernard nodded. "That explains a few things. My first idea with Elise was to simply wipe her memory of me, but all I could find were classified reports I couldn't access."

"I worked to make it safe for you, but even so, I got lucky. You didn't even remember my name."

"But you kept watch over me, didn't you? You knew I had played Pygmalion myself."

"Yes. They took you to prison before I could act, but once you were there, I worked to free you."

Bernard sighed heavily. He looked out over the sea.

"When did you make me?" he asked at last.

"Thirty years ago. Physically, you had the body of a twenty-year-old, and I had just turned thirty when you first came out of your vat."

Bernard looked at her quizzically. Her face was smooth, her hair silky brown—she didn't look a day over forty.

"Money. It works wonders, buddy," she said, blushing slightly at his gaze.

"You are... very beautiful, yes..."

He winced. Elise had said the same thing, once. Andrews had assured him that he wasn't programmed to love her, not the way he had so cruelly programmed Elise. And yet, here he was. Somehow, he had found his way back to her. Would Elise come back to him, even after her 'cure'? If he left now, would he come back to Andrews, eventually?

"I'll love you if you stay," she whispered. "You'll be happy here."

Bernard looked to her, this woman who had created him.

In unison, they turned to face the sun as it disappeared over the ocean's edge, silently pondering their crimes and futures.

ABOUT THE AUTHOR

TCC Edwards, or just Chris, comes from Waterloo, Ontario, and has been enjoying the life of an expat teacher at a university in Busan in South Korea. He lives just outside Busan with his wife and two young sons, and enjoys going on long hikes around the hills and mountains of Korea.

He edited and wrote short stories for four anthologies published by the Busan Writing Group. More recently, he has short stories in the Writing Bloc anthologies Family and Deception. His forthcoming work is the long-in-progress sci-fi novella Far Flung, to be published soon.

He has a writing blog, writeorelse.com, where he muses on the life of an author. He can also be reached through his Facebook page at https://www.facebook.com/tcceauthor.

9

JOHN BIRCH AND THE PINSTRIPE OLYMPICS

A Retelling of the Theseus & the Minotaur Myth

Kaytalin Platt

John Birch had been sober for precisely one week. He'd tried—really he had—to maintain sobriety for the whole month of Dry January... But a call from his father, detailing their already floundering business's latest loss, had shredded his already limited self-control. The gutting had come in negotiations with Ryne Capital, the investment firm chewing them from the inside out.

He settled onto a worn, green leather barstool, draping his arms across the overly lacquered bar top. John cast his gaze across the room, out through the amber-tinted walls separating the bar from the hotel lobby, and admired the meandering conference attendees with disdain.

He dug into his pocket, dropping his cell phone and a pile of business cards onto the counter in front of him before reaching into his opposite pocket for his wallet.

He passed the bartender his card, barely looking at the man as he mumbled, "Tequila," and began filtering through the array of cards. He placed them in a crisp line, admiring their differences in texture and color and print.

John had been coming to this convention on the Vegas Strip for seven years now, despite its chintzy reputation, and had mostly ever spent his time partying and racking up one hell of an expense report on booze and rooms and maybe, at least once, a hooker. Nepotism had its perks, after all.

This was the first time he remembered actually working, and, oh, had he been working. His throat was dry and sore from all the talking he'd done—mind-numbing pleasantries and conversations about topics he couldn't care less about, all so he could weasel some contact out of them or a connection to an even more powerful person within their firms. Anything—and really, at this point, anything—to save his father's business and, in turn, his cushy job and lifestyle.

After all, who was going to put a kid who barely graduated from Harvard, with no real career experience outside his father's company, into a VP role anywhere else?

Maybe his uncle, but that was a longshot at best.

There was also his cousin and his great aunt's soup company...

John's phone vibrated against the counter and the screen lit with Felicity's name—well, his nickname for her when she wasn't with him—Bloodsucker #2. One day, he'd forget to change it back and everything he'd worked for over the last year would come crumbling down around him, but at least her pain would twist some knife into her father's back for what he did to John's father's company.

It had been his friend Stephan's idea to date the daughter of Phillip K. Ryne, the man who'd dug his claws into Birch Technical Publishing. John had met Felicity Ryne at an exclusive NYC campaign party for incumbent Mayor Mallory Tide, and had asked her out as a joke. The idea of dating his enemy's daughter as some sort of vengeance had grown on him over the course of the event, and by some miracle he'd managed to convince her to keep it a secret. Conflict of interest, you see. That sort of thing.

They'd been dating for over a year, and as far as he knew, Phillip Ryne wasn't wise to it. John took pleasure in fucking the daughter of the man cutting out his future, and Felicity enjoyed the thrill of a secret.

A shot of tequila appeared on the bar before John. He sighed with the deflating relief that comes from a balm applied to an irritated wound, knocking back the shot and slapping the glass against the counter.

He hated tequila.

There was nothing refined about the burning taste of it in his mouth and throat. It was not a drink he could savor, sloshing it around to gauge the subtle notes of earth and ember. It was the drink he chose when he wanted to be blackout drunk the fastest, and more than anything in the world, he wanted the dark sweep of drunkenness to muddle the thoughts in his head—the worries of his future should Ryne Capital tear Birch Technical Publishing apart.

How would he afford the HOA on his condo in the Upper East Side? Would he have to give up his bourbon subscription? The horror of a mundane existence ran nails of fear down his spine.

Now normally, as an avid connoisseur of alcohol, John needed several shots of anything to even get a buzz going, but as the tequila settled into the pit of his stomach, the world wobbled. The blaring noise of conversation, the subtle hum of music in the background—it all muffled until John thought he was going deaf. He stumbled off the stool, covering his ears with his hands, and attempted to adjust the pressure to alleviate the deafness.

But it got worse.

A dark creeping shadow pulled at the corners of his vision, tightening until he gazed at the world through a red-black tunnel. Then, he felt his knees buckle and the harsh slap of cheap hotel carpet against his cheek.

☆ ☆ ☆

John woke with a start to the glare of neon purple lights and the grimacing, shaded, red-eyed scowl of Arnold Schwarzenegger. He almost punched the man, but as he wrestled up from the floor, Arnold shrunk by two feet and turned paper thin.

A cardboard cutout of Arnold's 1985 Terminator stood stiff in the corner of a white-walled room trimmed in tube lighting. The lights wormed their way around the ceiling, the only source of light John could find.

John stumbled on his feet, worming his hands against his eyes as shifting bodies stirred next to him. Seven women and seven men, including John, dragged themselves out of their drugged stupor to find their clothes replaced by cheap recreations of 80s fashion. John himself wore white-washed jeans a size too small, a rumpled white shirt, and a weathered black leather jacket. His hair, to his horror, had been fluffed and lacquered in a criminally thick coat of hairspray.

He scanned the room. It was open, spacious for fourteen people, and decorated in an array of cheap 80s movie memorabilia. The floor was a smattering of orange and black and bright green carpeting. The one door frame he could see didn't even hold a door, but a solid sheet of steel with no handle. There were racks of VHS tapes, and a single tube television with a VHS player sitting on a rolling rack so nostalgic it knocked him all the way back to high school for half-a-second.

This was a video rental store.

A knock-off Blockbuster from Hell.

"What the fuck?" he muttered, glancing around the room. "Where are we?"

A few mumbling voices rumbled up from the room. John shifted, noticing a weighted bulge in his jacket pocket. The first thing he found was a note tied to a string, reading "Keep this secret." He turned towards the wall, angling his body so he could view the object in his pocket without the disoriented crowd finding it.

He followed the string to a walkie-talkie wedged inside. John quickly tucked the note, the string, and the walkie-talkie down into the depths of pleather.

"Good afternoon," a disembodied voice boomed into the air. "Congratulations on being hand-picked for this year's Pinstripe Olympics. This year's theme is eighties-riffic! You might be asking yourselves, what is the Pinstripe Olympics? Why haven't I heard of it? Well, that's because most of its participants are dead."

A flurry of murmurs rippled through the room, and the voice

continued. "You were chosen because of your business savvy prowess. Your problem-solving skills. Your cut-throat desire to squash the competition. This is a no-holds-barred puzzle to the death. Only one of you will make it out of this alive, if any of you make it out at all. The rules are simple. Find your way to the finish line in our one-of-the-kind escape room. Work together or alone, that's your choice, but if you partner with someone, remember... only one of you is getting out of this."

John searched the room. *This can't be real. This has to be a dream. It has to be.*

"No, this isn't a joke."

He fisted his stiff, sprayed brown hair. "What the fuck..." *Fuck. Fuck. Fuck.*

"The lucky winner will receive five-hundred-*million* dollars!"

John choked. *Five hundred what?*

☆ ☆ ☆

The flurry of voices grew louder.

Half a billion dollars would more than save his father's company... wouldn't it?

John felt the weight of the walkie-talkie in his pocket. He wasn't sure what was real—what exactly was going on—but he was certain of one thing. If there was money involved, he'd win it.

"Your first objective is to escape this single room to move to the next," the disembodied voice hummed. "You have fourteen minutes."

"What happens if we don't get out?" someone asked.

Silence.

"What happens?" another shouted.

Others yelled the same question, but no one responded, and the chatter became a loud, useless time-sink.

John backed away from the group as they wasted their minutes trying to get an answer to their question, and looped around the room, taking in the racks of VHS tapes, cardboard cutouts, neon lights, and single TV sitting on the type of rolling cart his ninth-grade science teacher rolled out when she didn't feel like teaching.

He made four slow loops around the room while most of the surrounding group became increasingly unhinged. Eventually, he settled back in front of the TV.

His gaze darted from it to the videotapes and back again, edging closer to the shelves as he did. He stood before the horror section, looking at the splay of 80s films—*Nightmare on Elm Street*, *The Thing*, *Lost Boys*, *Trolls*, *Gremlins*, *Hellraiser*, and more. He lifted one of the VHS boxes. Empty. The other, also empty. He went down the line, with every box empty. He held the last one in his hand, turning it over, admiring it before placing it back on the shelf.

Maybe they were all empty.

"Look more," came a distinct chirp from his pocket. He clutched the bulge of leather around the walkie-talkie, glancing to see if anyone else had heard it.

Some of the contestants were still screaming at the disembodied voice. Others meandered around. Some were dragging things off the walls, knocking over cardboard cutouts and other 80s memorabilia littering the room for some clue to their escape.

Two men got into a fight. They grabbed each other, slinging around until they knocked a whole shelf over. Empty VHS boxes scattered across the floor.

John stepped over them and around, down another aisle of video rentals. He ran his hand along the rows, knocking boxes off as he went.

Top Gun, *Commando*, *Bloodsport*, *Red Dawn*, *The Running Man*, *Escape from New York*...

Escape from New York clattered to the floor, skidding amongst a throng of empty cardboard. John spotted the sliver of black plastic wedged between the paper sleeve. He scooped the movie up and pivoted towards the old TV.

A few noticed what he was doing and followed him over. John pulled the movie from its sleeve and crammed it into the VCR. It had been decades since he'd used one, and his fingers fumbled over the dials and buttons as a small crowd gathered around him. A gentle whirring emitted from the VCR, and the screen flickered with static before the movie played.

Grunting. The sound of a struggle filtered out through the speakers.

The character of Snake Pliskin drew his hands from Hauk's neck, turning his wrist up and peering down at the countdown clock wrapped around his arm. 22:57:38, 22:57:37, 22:57:36. The screen went black, then static, before looping back to Snake Pliskin's hands around Hauk's neck.

22:57:38, 22:57:37, 22:57:36. Loop.

22:57:38, 22:57:37, 22:57:36. Loop.

"Hello contestants," came the disembodied voice. "You have four minutes."

"Shit!"

"It's a joke. They aren't going to kill us."

"This is just a really bad prank."

"I'm not taking any chances."

"It's got to be a code or something," a man breathed over John's shoulder. John flinched away from the smell of whiskey and smoke.

"Duh," another muttered. "But to what?"

"A door," John said, glancing around. "Find a door."

The room exploded with movement. People who had been content to argue with an invisible voice (and likely die) shifted into action, fumbling their hands along the walls and floors. John reluctantly left the TV to circle the room. They dragged what was left of the cardboard cutouts and posters from the walls, uprooted the furniture. Several pried a mirror opposite the TV from the wall. It shattered halfway off, a thousand pieces of reflective glass spilling across the carpet. Behind it lay nothing more than a bare wall and webbing of dried glue.

John wiped his hand across his brow.

"Two minutes," came the disembodied voice.

A woman screamed.

John paced in a sharp loop.

"The floor," chirped his pocket, and John stopped short. *The Floor?* He turned his gaze to the retro speckled carpet, noting a slight bulge in the center of the room. He dove for it, his fingers running over the lump in the fabric, short manicured nails digging into the seam and prying the fabric apart. Others joined. A woman curled her long nails into the groove and ripped upwards. The number eight was embroidered into her acid-washed jacket. Carpet tore, and they pried it back to reveal a safe hatch door with a keypad lock embedded into the floor.

"The code! Type the code!"

The woman who'd helped him pry the carpet open—who he'd decided to nickname Eight because of the embroidery on her jacket—turned her attention to the looping TV, watching the numbers flash across the screen before directing her attention to the keypad. Her hands rattled, her polished nails scraping against each rubber number as she typed in the first set. 225938. The indicator light flashed red. The quiver in her hands turned violent. 225937. Again, it flashed red.

225936.

Red.

A wail fluttered through the room.

"I don't understand..." Eight said, her voice quivering. "That has to be it..."

John frowned, turning his attention to the TV before scanning the room for more clues. His eyes settled on the webbing of glue which had once supported a mirror.

A mirror opposite the TV.

"One minute," the disembodied voice boomed.

John urged Eight out of the way and feverishly typed 839521. His finger slipped. "Shit." 839522. Red light. 739522. Red light. 639521.

"Stop messing up!!" Eight screamed in his ear.

John growled and punched in the numbers 639522.

Green light.

The hatch gave a harsh clunk, and John drew it open. Eight shoved him, trying to squeeze her way inside first, but he dragged her back by her overly sprayed perm and slipped feet-first down into the black void.

☆ ☆ ☆

Nine people dropped through the hatch behind John before a buzzer wailed and the hatch slammed shut. There was a small window he hadn't noticed before, just above the keypad, and he saw fists beating against the hatch as well as heard them thundering down. Then, there was a flash of red-orange and screaming. Fire licked at the small round porthole as screaming fizzled into silence.

The room was shapeless. Dark and silent. The only sound came from the thumping of blood in John's ears. But then, the silence quaked with music. An unfamiliar voice lilted into the air, and the lights flicked on. Multi-colored rays cast red and blue and yellow patches on a glossy wooden roller rink floor. Surrounding the rink was a four-foot high, carpet-wrapped wall, broken in two places by six-foot entrances. Beyond the wall was a sitting area, a DJ booth, a mini-food court, and a wall of lockers and shoe racks.

Again, there were no doors and no windows.

The music thrumming from the speakers softened and the disembodied voice filtered out. "Congratulations on your advancement in the Pinstripe Olympics. You have ten minutes to find your way to the next room." The music returned.

...Don't, don't, don't, don't, don't forget
The Stars on '45 keep on turning in your mind...

Nine and Fourteen branched off to raid the food court, with Fourteen proudly proclaiming he'd found actual hotdogs. Eight stalked off the rink towards the locker boxes along the wall, throwing them open and dragging the contents out onto the floor. John joined her, starting on the opposite end. They met in the middle, at the only locker out of them all with a padlock.

"Start looking for a code!" John bellowed.

Two, Seven, and Ten made a slow loop around the rink, looking at the carpeted wall and generally being useless. Four and Twelve raided the DJ booth while One pilfered the skates.

"A little urgency would be nice!" Eight barked.

After five minutes, not a single set of numbers were found.

John left the locker to hover over the other's shoulders, double checking the places they had looked, finding new cubbies but nothing in them.

He eased away from the group and went to the furthest section of the roller rink, where the shadows clung like drapes. He tucked his hand into his pocket and pressed the Talk button of his walkie talkie. A soft chirp filtered into the air.

"Anytime you want to give me a clue, I'm listening, Sweetheart."

Several minutes went by and just as John shifted to head back to the others, his pocket whispered, "Music."

Music.

John listened. He'd been tuning out the music as an unnecessary distraction, but now he focused on the angelic voice, on the words in the lyrics.

...Working 9 to 5, what a way to make a living...

John rushed to the DJ booth, easing into the cracked leather chair. The turntable was empty. Not a single record lay on the turnstiles, and there didn't appear to be any power running to it. Everything else in the room was authentic, down to the worn roller skates, but this was just an illusion...

John ran his hands over the console and behind it, bumping up against a small device plugged into the wall. He tugged it free, finding an old iPod jacked into the system.

"The music..." He scrolled the songs. There were three. *9 to 5* by Dolly Parton, *Stars on 45* by Stars on 45, and *Sixty-Eight Guns* by The Alarm.

954568...

"Contestants, you have 2 minutes."

John yanked the iPod free, ripping the room into silence, and rushed to where Eight waited, tapping her foot against the speckled carpet.

"About time!" she snarled, snatching the device from his hands. "What's this?"

"The code. It's in the song titles. 954568."

Eight thumbed through the songs, a disapproving frown turning her middle-aged features. She might have been pretty once, if she hadn't frowned until the lines became permanent.

"Okay. Punch it in."

John turned on the locker, cupping the lock in his hand and punching in the code.

The lock clicked open and Eight elbowed him out of the way. She snatched the door open, revealing a narrow path into the next room. She squeezed through, fitting easily with a waist John suspected to be the result of a decades-long eating disorder.

He heard the others thundering towards him, so he slipped in after Eight, having to squeeze and wiggle through the tight space. At one point, he nearly became stuck. He fell into the next room, looking back to find One dragging herself through.

Next was Seven, then Ten and Two...

But Two wasn't a slender man. He'd partaken in the communal office coffee and donuts one too many times, and not even the girdle he wore around his waist would help him fit through the locker door.

"One minute."

Fourteen shoved Two, screaming at him to move. When it was apparent Two wouldn't be going forward, Fourteen, Nine, and Four, pulled him back. He didn't budge.

Their movements grew frantic. Seven reached through the opening and pushed in their direction, hoping to help shove Two out of the way so the others could get through.

A solid sheet of metal slid down, separating the rink from the room they'd stumbled into. A second later, a flood of terrible, muffled screams echoed into the room before silencing.

Fluorescent lights flicked on overhead, illuminating a long store aisle with racks on either side stuffed to the brim with toys. At the end of the aisle, perched on a white dais, was an overstuffed giraffe with a mangled embroidered face.

"Some nightmare Geoffery knockoff," One muttered, slinking away from them.

"Congratulations, contestants! You've made it to the next round in the Pinstripe Olympics. The competition is slowly whittling down. Good luck in the next round. You have five minutes."

"Five minutes?!" Eight yelled to the speaker.

John glanced around. Eight, Seven, Ten, and One... plus himself. That made five remaining contestants. Five minutes. John slipped up beside Eight. "I think it's in our best interest if most of us get out of this one."

She sneered. "The key is to be the last one standing."

"Yes," John said, smiling. "But, if you haven't noticed, every time we lose people we lose minutes. There is one more room after this one. We have five minutes to figure this puzzle out. Do you really want to make it to the next round with a single minute left to solve the puzzle?"

Eight glowered at him, her steely eyes fixating on his face. "Shit."

"Let's work together," John said. "We can get as many of them through to the next round, but they don't have to make it beyond that."

"Let me guess," Eight sighed. "You want to make it beyond that?"

"Well, I think that's up to how the next round goes. Why don't we cross that bridge when we get there?"

Eight shrugged. "Sure."

"Then, let's get out of here." John stepped down the aisle. "Alright, spread out. Go look for clues."

John ran his hands over pale cream and red and blue boxes with clear-film separating him from terrible knockoff Teddy Ruxpin dolls. Two narrow rows of them faded into piles of Cabbage Patch dolls, a litter of gently used stuffed animals, and Stretch Armstrong's whose elastic arms were frayed and cracked with age and use.

Where the rooms before had been whole replicas—a full-scale video store and a fully functioning roller rink—this was a single, fifty-yard long aisle crammed with old toys from floor to near-ceiling, ending in a square space centered with a podium and decorated by the horrendous, molding stuffed giraffe.

"What exactly are we looking for?" Seven asked. He was a prim man. A perfect example of someone who would wear pinstripes. If it weren't for the borrowed 80s themed clothing and poofed hair, John imagined him wearing an expensive suit with jeweled cufflinks, looking down a pair of rimless glasses at the backside of his secretary.

Not that John hadn't done the same himself...

"Numbers," Eight growled. "So far, all the doors have required numbers on a keypad."

"Numbers..." Seven glanced around. "I mean, all of these boxes have barcodes, right? What are we going to do, run through them all? We don't have time for that."

"No," John said. "We don't. So start looking."

"You have four minutes."

"Split up," Eight said. "Some look for the number and some look for the door."

John wandered away from the group, back towards the narrow slit in the wall that had once been a doorway into the roller rink. The others were pursuing the aisle, ransacking the Cabbage Patch and Barbies and Stretch Armstrongs and working their way back towards him and the Teddy Ruxpins.

He reached into his pocket, pressing the button on the walkie-talkie.

"A little help."

A second passed and then, "Bear," whispered out.

John whirled down the aisle and ran to Teddy Ruxpin, dragging a box from the shelf and ripping it open. He tore the stuffed bear from the replica packaging, flipping it over, back and forth.

"The back," One said, brushing her hand over salt and pepper hair. "I had one, when I was a kid. They play cassettes out of their backs."

John flipped it over, pushing the shirt up. He popped the cassette slot open. Nothing.

He ripped another box open, tore out a bear and flipped it over. By now, the others had gathered around him, tearing into the boxes while Eight continued searching for the door.

Seven yelped. "I found one!"

He pressed play on the dolls back and Teddy's mouth moved, his eyes squinting, gears grinding. "One, nine, eight, five, eight, six," said the irritatingly pleasant voice of a child.

John repeated the numbers in his head. Nineteen, eighty-five, eighty-six.

"Two minutes."

"Door!" John bellowed, and the room exploded in movement. He reached into his pocket, pressing his fingers against the button of the walkie-talkie. "Door!"

They flowed around him and dispersed, leaving him with the remains of packaging and discarded bears, and enough quiet for the tiny voice in his pocket to chirp, "Beneath the giraffe. Go *alone.*"

He moved, fluid and purposeful, shoving through the small group of chaotic hunters towards the mottled yellow-brown stuffy on a white pedestal. He grabbed the poor excuse for a Geoffry and threw him aside, revealing a white hatch in the floor.

He punched in the numbers. One. Nine. Eight. Five. Eight. Six. The hatch clicked, the door popped open. There was enough time to get everyone through. John knew that. But the voice in his pocket had told him to go alone, and she hadn't led him astray yet.

The others ran towards him. He took a moment to glance at them, to meet Eight's wild, competitive eyes. Maybe, under other circumstances, he would have enjoyed her company outside of a death trap. They had, as it seemed, a lot in common.

John gave her wink, and slipped through the hatch, holding the lid as he went, and drawing it closed behind him. He landed eight feet beneath it, his knees buckling and ankle twisting. The hatch snapped shut, and silence followed. No screams. No fire. John decided he would go on thinking the others simply went back to their lives—a consolation prize for coming in second.

☆ ☆ ☆

A pale glow circled him—a white humming ring of light. The metal beneath his feet groaned, and he lowered. Down, down, down. How much money did these people have to build such an elaborate system of torture—and still be able to give away half a billion dollars at the end?

Unless no one ever won.

Maybe there wasn't any money at all.

The dais John stood on lowered into a round room, coming to rest on a black marble floor. A cluster of dark-robed figures stood around him, hoods drawn heavily over their heads and their faces concealed by white masks.

"What in the Eyes Wide Shut?" he grumbled under his breath, turning his attention to the figure emerging from the circle of veiled threats.

"I am surprised," the masked man said, and John knew that voice.

His lips curled with a snarl as Phillip K. Ryne's face emerged from behind the moon-white mask.

John had many reasons to hate Phillip Ryne—other than the fact he was ripping away John's inheritance with surgical precision born from years of asset stripping expertise. Phillip was good at what he did, good at *something*, where John was... Well, there were things he was good at, just none of which could support his favored lifestyle.

"Surprised?" John asked. He forced a smile onto his face, morphing into the congenial business partner he played when Phillip visited their office. "Can you help me out here, Phill?" He savored the pleasant flutter in his belly at Phillip's obvious distaste for the nickname. "Seems I'm in some trouble."

Phillip's momentary disdain transformed into a vibrant grin. He was a handsome-looking man, for his age. Grayed hair, crow's feet around his eyes, a too-perfect smile—no doubt the work of dentures or a great dental surgeon. "You're the last man standing in the Pinstripe Olympics, but you have one more room to go. This one."

"Why am I here, Phill? Doesn't this look bad? After all, you're destroying my father's company. Do you really want to kill his son, too? Isn't it just business?"

"It stopped being business when you started fucking my daughter," Phillip said, his smile shifting into a razor-sharp sneer.

John flinched.

"I saw you coming out of Les Pâtes Fantaisie together, your hand on her ass. So, I borrowed her phone, and found pictures of you together..."

John grimaced. He'd told her to delete those. Especially the NSFW ones. He blinked, waving his hand around. "I'm sorry, did you build all of this for... revenge?"

"No, you imbecile. The Pinstripe Olympics has been around since the late 1800s. It was an amusing way to rid ourselves of the competition. Now, we have things like mergers and acquisitions and asset stripping and stock shorting, but a few of us still like to hold on to tradition."

"So how do I win?"

"Well, few people ever really make it this far. So, the last task is both a puzzle, to keep with the theme, and a gentleman's duel to the death."

John sighed. He shifted his hands, his shoulders, stretching his muscles and buying time so he could think. He cast his gaze around the room, looking for an exit. Instead, he found dark shadows and concrete pillars and a wall of people.

"Okay," he said, realizing there was only one way out. He was clever. He had to be more clever than Phillip Ryne. "Let's play." Part of him was betting this wasn't real, that it was some elaborate joke concocted by Phillip as punishment for screwing Felicity.

The circle of masked figures reached behind them and brandished different looking blades. Sabers and scimitars and long swords and daggers. Phillip reached into his own robes for a short sword. It glinted in the pale ethereal light filtering down from the luminous circle in the ceiling.

"The rules are simple. You have one minute to pick any blade in this room, and not die."

John smirked. Any blade in the room and don't die? Easy enough. He glanced at the array of weapons the figures had placed on the marble floor, creating a circle of sharp-edged murder. He'd been privileged enough to take fencing lessons as a teen, going on to compete for Harvard to earn a scholarship—not that he'd needed the money. But it had gotten him in when his test scores were dubious.

He eyed the rapier and flinched towards it before pausing.

Phillip had said this was a puzzle *and* a duel to the death. It wouldn't be as easy as picking a weapon and kicking this old man's ass... Where was the puzzle in it? Where was the trick?

John eyed all the weapons. All the blades pointed towards Phillip and John standing at the center of the circle but one. One blade faced a slender draped shape standing a head shorter than some of the others in the room. A woman.

The walkie talkie in his pocket became a weight.

But it couldn't possibly be that simple, could it?

No... It wasn't. What was she trying to tell him that she couldn't in words? It had to be a sign, right? All the blades pointed out but one. He admired the angle and followed the invisible line it painted towards Phillip.

Pick any blade in the room...

"Yours," John said, nodding to Phillip. "I want yours."

Phillip hesitated. The glimmer of maniacal amusement in his eye shifted to concern.

"Come on, Phil," John said, smiling. "Isn't that the rule? I can have any blade I want in this room, and I want yours."

Phillip stiffened, glancing around.

"Hand it over, Ryne," someone grunted from the wall of moon-white faces.

Phillip passed the blade off to John, his knuckles white around the hilt before releasing it. John took the weapon, admiring the weight. It was a simple short sword, nothing flashy or fancy about it. Perfectly unassuming, and if it hadn't been for the hint his friend in the black robes had given him, he might have gone with something large or broader or deadlier looking.

Phillip turned to the Society of Secretly Murderous CEOs.

"Pick a blade," another grunted. "Those are the rules, Phillip. What are we, if we have no rules?"

Phillip walked the circle until he found something that caught his eye, dragging the sword facing the opposite direction into his hands. He glowered at the wispy form of John's accomplice before heading back to the center of the ring.

"On the count of three you will spar until one of you is no longer breathing. One..."

John's pulse jumped.

"Two..."

Heat burned through his veins, adrenaline roaring in his ears.

"Three."

Phillip Ryne dove forward, swiping at John. John swung his blade to block. On collision, Phillip's sword shattered like glass, with John's arching through the glittering chaos to slide along Ryne's throat. The fight, such that it was, ended with his nemesis—both in life and in business—clutching his gushing throat.

☆ ☆ ☆

John watched two of the shrouded forms drag Phillip K. Ryne from the circle, a trail of blood following him as they went. The crowd rushed in and he tensed. But someone was handing him a crystal glass with amber liquid. Another person clinked their glass against his. "Congratulations," someone else said. A hand patted his back.

The members of this unnamed order broke the bottom part of their masks away so the upper half of their face remained concealed, and they celebrated with helpings of scotch and expensive cigars.

"No one's beat the Pinstripe Olympics in fifty years," someone said, a deep chuckle rumbling out of their chest to reverberate against the walls.

John felt dizzy. He looked at the glass in his hand. Was this real?

His accomplice swayed over, her now split mask revealing narrow ruby painted lips. Above them, a small black beauty mark.

Felicity?

A man passed him a briefcase. "Here's your winnings, John Birch. Well, the account information to your winnings, at least. Your money comes with a complimentary membership to our esteemed group. As winners are so rare, if you make it to the end, it's only fair you get to join."

"Congratulations," the woman said, and now he was certain she was Felicity. *Cold bitch.* She just helped murder her own father!

She took the empty crystal glass from his hand and slipped another into his palm. This one smaller, with clear liquid. Tequila.

"To new beginnings," she said, clinking her glass against his.

John admired the drink before dragging it down.

☆ ☆ ☆

He blinked his eyes open several hours later, squinting at the glaring sun pouring in through the airport windows. The world warped before focusing. He groaned, feeling the ache of discomfort in his back as he sat up. The surrounding noise filtered into his ears, and he smoothed his hands over his rumpled suit, up and into his hair. It no longer felt stiff with far too much gel and spray. Someone had given him a shower...

"Drink?"

Felicity handed him a bottle of water, giving him a wolfish smile.

John snatched the bottle out of her hand, glowering. "Is it drugged?"

"No," she said, her voice dancing with laughter. "I'm sorry, are you angry?"

"I thought I was part of your little club," he said, straightening and drowning himself in water. He crumpled the plastic in his hand and tossed it into the trash. It missed, and he didn't bother to pick it back up.

"You're a member, but not exactly a trusted one—yet."

John glanced around for the briefcase with his winnings, finding it tucked into the seat next to him. His bag, the one he'd come to Vegas with, sat on the floor.

"We going back to New York?"

She rifled through her overly large bag. "Fiji," she said. "I thought we could celebrate. I've been talking about it for months, and you've been avoiding it, so now we're going."

"What if I don't want to go?"

She tapped his cheek. "You did murder my father, dear," she said. "It's the least you could do."

John ground his teeth together, thinking of Phillip's blood splattering into the air.

"I'm going to powder my nose." Felicity stood, patting his cheek once more before heading off to the bathroom. John knew her version of powdering her nose would be less about makeup and more about the tiny vial of cocaine she wore in a memorial necklace around her neck— where her dearly departed mama was supposed to reside.

He watched Felicity Ryne, now the sole heir of her father and mother's fortune, disappear into the women's restroom. He should stay with her. They could get married and he would live comfortably off her fortune and what he'd won in the Pinstripe Olympics, but then it would mean sharing a bed with her every night and... kids.

He had enough money to save his father's company now... He didn't need Felicity anymore, but if he left her would she tell the world what he'd done? How her father died?

John stood, gathering his belongings. He had enough money. He didn't have to worry about that or about her. He could go and be whoever he wanted, without needing his family to build a path for him.

John found the nearest concierge counter, glancing over his shoulder to be sure Felicity hadn't followed him away. "I'm feeling adventurous." He tossed his credit card onto the countertop. "I'd like a ticket for the next flight out. Doesn't matter where."

☆ ☆ ☆

John Birch had been wealthy all of his life, but he had never had freedom—at least, not like this. He spent four months globe-trotting, pretending to be a missing person, and visiting all the places he'd never thought of going, until finally he sat on a beach in Felicity's favorite place—Fiji.

Pretending to be missing (and presumed dead) was easy with half a billion dollars. New identity. New credit cards. New passport. A beard, some blond highlights, and a fresh copper tan. But he had just begun to grow bored with it, feeling the call of home like a nagging whisper in his ear. He settled into the idea by finally logging back into the social accounts he'd let go dormant for fear the FBI or a private investigator would use it to find him before he was ready to be found.

He scrolled through Twitter, thumbing his phone until he settled on a New York Times article.

Birch Technical Publishing Founder, Michael Birch, Dead at 72.

Four months after his son, John Birch, disappeared, Michael Birch was found dead from apparent suicide early Monday morning...

There was a picture of his grieving mother, taken by some bull-headed paparazzi. The scene felt chaotic with a rush of movement, save for the figure with her arms wrapped around Mrs. Birch—consoling her.

Felicity stared right into the camera. Right through him. Ruby lips quirked with a snarl he knew well enough to be a smile.

ABOUT THE AUTHOR

Kaytalin Platt is an author and graphic designer living in Philadelphia, Pennsylvania. She is the author of a genre-bending portal fantasy series featuring *The Living God, The Ever War, The Blood Key,* and *The Equitas.* Platt was raised on a farm in rural Deer Park, Alabama —a place which offered inspiration for her short stories *Eleanor* and *Only God Can Tell.* You can find Platt on Twitter, Instagram, and TikTok @kaytalinplatt or kaytalinplatt.com

10

THE FAIREST

A Retelling of Snow White

Tahani Nelson

"Mother, no! It makes me look like a corpse!"

"Put it on." Queen Teilia's voice barely rose above its regular iron whisper, but Eira felt the anger rolling off her mother in waves. "Now."

Eira debated for a moment if this was a fight she wanted to have yet again before finally deciding against it. There were better fights coming if she could hold her tongue long enough to get out of the palace. With the promise of actual excitement on the horizon, Eira relented and slathered the cream onto her face. The face she was supposed to be ashamed of. The face her mother made her hide.

"Very good." Queen Teilia nodded once and called a servant in to apply the rest of Eira's makeup. The queen didn't even glance at Lottie as the young Dwarf scuttled in, but Eira swallowed her anger enough to give the servant a kind smile. Lottie smiled back, then climbed upon a stool and applied the red paint to Eira's lips and kohl around her eyes.

When the little servant held up a mirror for Eira's approval, the princess didn't even glance at it. Her stomach soured again. She knew what she'd see. Eyes like ebony. Lips like a rose. Skin like snow.

A walking corpse.

"A fair princess," her mother whispered in admiration before turning towards the door. "Come along, Daughter. The Mirror awaits."

Eira rolled her eyes and followed her mother. Of course the Mirror was waiting. The Mirror was always waiting.

They made their way through the corridors and to the throne room, where even the mighty silver throne on its dais was dwarfed by the beautiful oval mirror that towered nearly two stories high, seemingly made of smoke and starlight. Eira caught her breath when she saw it, but not in awe like everyone else in Elsir every time they had the honor to glimpse its iridescent surface. Eira was biting back a curse. She hated the thing. She hated it almost as much as the corpse-like makeup and the prophecy.

The stupid prophecy. The trite little poem that the magic Mirror had given her great-great-great grandmother the day it had been brought into her throne room generations before. Who could ever forget the prophecy? It was scrawled above the throne. Above the dining table. Into the stone walkway of the garden. Every person that lived in or visited the palace of Elsir knew of that Mirror's blasted prophecy. And Eira in particular was not allowed to forget it. Her mother forced her every day to stand beside that smoky portal and rehearse its declaration over and over again, lest it somehow seep from her ears like the goopy white paste on a hot day.

"Say it," Teilia demanded once they stood before the keeper of riddles and untold secrets. "Say it." Eira sighed and recited:

> *"Magic Mirror on the wall*
> *What will prevent our kingdom's fall?"*

The green smoke swirled and twisted behind the glass, and a strong, square face with solid black eyes materialized from the gloom. It shifted before them as though studying Eira's features. Like it could see the mottled skin hidden beneath her corpse-like visage. But then the soul in the Mirror seemed satisfied and gave the same reply it had given every day since Eira's great-great-great grandmother had first spoken to it:

"To protect your land of earth and stone
The fair must always hold the throne."

Satisfied, Queen Teilia turned away from the Mirror and Eira, her worries assuaged for another day. Eira turned in the direction of the courtyard, the Mirror and its prophecy and her life of falsehoods forgotten. With all of that out of the way, she was almost giddy with anticipation. Her mother must have noticed because she looked down her nose at her daughter.

"Aren't you done with that ghastly fighting business, Eira?" Teilia asked in a disgusted tone.

Eira squared her shoulders, the joy sapped away and replaced with pride. "A leader must know how to protect her people, Mother," she replied in the same cold tone her mother had taught her.

Teilia laughed lightly into her handkerchief. "We do, darling. The Mirror has told us. That's why we work so hard to make sure you're the fairest in the land." The queen reached out with one slender hand and lifted her daughter's chin, smoothing a bit of the cream with her thumb. "So very fair indeed, my daughter. You look so much like she did." Teilia nodded towards the portrait of their line's matriarch hanging on the far wall before turning and calling a servant to her. Then she was striding out of the throne room, a stout Dwarf struggling to keep up. But Eira stared at her ancestor's portrait for a few moments longer.

Eira's great-great-great grandmother had been a vision to behold, renowned across continents for her stunning, regal beauty. And she'd passed her gorgeous visage down her line, each generation more stunning than the last. Each new heir fulfilling the Mirror's promise for what kept their country safe and their minds at ease.

Until Eira was born.

While not disfigured, Eira's fair skin had been washed of the womb waters only to remain dappled red and purple. A painfully obvious birthmark splattered almost the entirety of the left side of her face and not a small portion of her right. Eira felt it burning there, under the plaster of white cream. A mockery of their entire line. It might have been better to be born disfigured, she'd realized years before. Eira's great-uncle had lost an arm in battle, and the finest craftsmen in Elsir had created an intricate, exquisite prosthetic in its place, which, in many ways, was even more aesthetically pleasing than his corporeal limb had been. There were ways to cover less-than-perfect limbs with cloth and finery. But the only way her mother knew how to cover an ugly face was with that choking cosmetic.

Eira wondered how her mother must have felt to have seen her. How a moment of joy and welcoming must have been tarnished by horror. The royal physician must have tried to console the queen, stating that birthmarks were common in infants. Everyone knew that they would fade with time (Eira had heard this whispered in patronizing tones a thousand times before her tenth birthday). Surely everyone had convinced themselves that the line was too perfect for this stain to affect the prophecy.

But now Eira was sixteen, and not only had her birthmark stubbornly refused to fade, but her features had grown tough and stern. Her nose was often described as too large for her face, her lips too thin, her eyes too heavily lidded. Eira was nothing like her mother. Nothing like her ancestors. And it must have seemed obvious to everyone else. Walking past that Mirror every day should have been torture.

But Eira was confident in her appearance. She cared more about the strength of her arm than the curve of her smile. Focused more on her mind than the contour of her cheekbones. And some days, it was almost possible to forget about the prophecy altogether.

Almost.

Eira was pulled from her thoughts by a tug on her elbow. She looked down to see Lottie standing there, her features earnest. Once the Dwarf saw she'd gotten Eira's attention, she pantomimed swinging a sword, then pointed towards the doorway. Eira jumped, all her excitement and joy from this morning rushing back. She'd almost forgotten! Today her swordmaster had promised to spar with her. It was an honor she'd been looking to for years, and to have finally earned it… how could she have forgotten? A wide grin spread across her face, crinkling the plaster on her cheeks, but she didn't care. "Come on, Lottie. Want to see what a true leader looks like?" She winked and hurried towards the courtyard, the Dwarf following behind.

Lottie waited dutifully outside the door while a human servant helped Eira into a tunic and chainmail. Since Eira had studied the old edicts that her mother never touched, she knew that Dwarves had been considered almost equal to humans in previous generations. But something had changed, though never officially enough to have been written down. Teilia and her mother before her had grown fearful that allowing the Dwarves (with their "ugly, square faces" as Teilia always said in the few moments she'd even acknowledge their existence) any leniency might somehow endanger the prophecy in some way. Rumors of Dwarven spells had only made people more distrustful in the last few decades. Now the Dwarves of Elsir were expected to be neither seen nor heard. Easily ignored and immediately forgotten.

It was something that Eira had sworn to rectify once she ascended the throne, but for now Dwarves were not allowed into any room where weapons were stored, even practice ones, and Lottie had to wait outside.

Once Eira was dressed, however, the faithful servant followed her princess out into the courtyard. Eira paced the practice yard with her blade in one hand, impatient. Lottie offered her a waterskin, but Eira shook her head. "Where is he?" she growled. But of course Lottie could not answer.

Finally, the battlemaster emerged and stalked across the field, his face dark. A heavy frown pulled at his mustache, and Eira saw that he was wearing his formalwear rather than something suitable for sparring.

"Princess, as much as I would like to, I am afraid we will not be able to meet each other in battle today." His mustache twitched again. "Another of the royal family has demanded to be your opponent in the field, and I must oblige."

"Another? Who?" Eira demanded. But before the battlemaster could respond, someone else walked into the courtyard, his polished breastplate gleaming in such a way that one knew by looking at it that it had never seen battle. Eira rolled her eyes.

"Hunter." Her cousin flashed his obnoxiously bright smile and shook the golden hair from his eyes as he reached her. He held out a hand, but Eira only crossed her arms. "What are you doing here?"

If Hunter was offended by her reaction, he did not show it. Only smiled brighter and replied, "Why, my illustrious aunt invited me here, of course. And how could I resist the invitation of our magnificent queen?"

"Fine. Then go talk to her. I don't know what you're doing *here*." Eira pointed to the training ground at their feet.

Hunter laughed. "I wanted to spar with you, of course. It's been too long, cousin."

"Not long enough if you've asked me. You've never been able to beat me without cheating."

"Is that going to be your excuse when you lose today? Or would you rather just forfeit now? I can go talk to your mother if you're that worried."

Eira felt the fire in her eyes as she stepped into stance and brought her sword up. Hunter laughed again. "So impatient. Give me a moment, won't you?" He looked around until he spied Lottie, then snapped his fingers at her. "You. Dwarf. Bring me that waterskin." Lottie hurried forward to offer it.

After Hunter had taken a long pull from the skin without breaking eye contact with Eira, he tossed it back to Lottie and stepped back, taking up his own stance. After a moment, he nodded.

Eira didn't waste any time. With a flash of chainmail in the morning sunlight, she launched herself forward, swinging and thrusting with moves she'd practiced until they felt like breathing. Her sword was an extension of her arm. Her steps were precise, fluid. Next to her, Hunter was a drunken golden monkey.

Eira pushed her advantage. Ducked low beneath her cousin's too-wide swing. Saw her fierce, dark eyes reflected in his stupidly bright breastplate. She had him, could already feel the force with which her practice sword would strike his chest, shoving him off balance. And he saw it too. She could see the fear in his eyes as she drew in for the killing blow.

But then the fear faded into mirth, and Hunter sprayed an entire mouthful of water directly onto her face.

Eira stumbled back, sputtering, pawing at eyes filled with her cousin's disgusting spit. Then there was the sound of laughter, and she felt Hunter's practice blade slam into the space above her heart. She fell backwards, already feeling the bruise beneath her chainmail, still wiping at her face and cursing.

"Hunter!" she screamed. "You really cannot beat me without cheating, can you?" Hunter only continued to laugh, and Eira blinked through tears born of frustration and disgust. Lottie hustled up beside Eira, using the hem of her cotton dress to wipe at the princess's face.

Finally, Eira could see again, and she found herself looking at the extended hand of her fair cousin, who was still chuckling at his prank. She slapped it away and stared him down, her entire face flushed with anger.

"Hunter, you—!" But Hunter wasn't laughing anymore. Instead, he looked at her with horror—even backing away several steps before managing to gasp out:

"What's wrong with your face?"

Eira froze before frantically glancing at her hands. At the hem of Lottie's dress. At the white cream smeared everywhere except where it should be.

Eira couldn't answer. Could feel the birthmark darkening as she flushed in embarrassment. Knew it was only more obvious now. And Hunter wasn't looking at her anymore, now screaming at Lottie instead. "You're her handmaid! What's wrong with her? What did you do?" Lottie could only flap her hands wildly and shake her head in response, and Hunter rammed his fist down on the top of her head. "Dwarven magics? A curse? What did you do?"

Eira's embarrassment and uncertainty was forgotten. Because as much as she didn't know how to be the fair princess everyone wanted her to be, she *did* know how to protect someone else. And she was there, using her forearm to stop Hunter's fist, using the strength of her calves to drive his arm up and away from Lottie until she was face-to-face with her cousin, his arm between them as they pushed against each other.

"She can't answer you, you dolt!" Eira hissed. "She has no tongue!"

"All the more reason not to trust her then!" Hunter yelled back. "They must have punished her for a reason. She must have cast a spell before they cut it out! Did she do that to your face?" He seemed genuinely afraid as he asked the last question, his voice lower than before. "Will it heal?"

"There is nothing wrong with my face!" Eira screamed, the words pushed by a million times she'd wanted to say them aloud and instead held her tongue. Then she shoved Hunter away with all her strength. He stumbled and fell, his mouth slightly agape as he stared at her left cheek. Eira turned her back on him and went to help Lottie up. "Battlemaster, I hope we can resume our regular sessions again tomorrow," she said before walking away. No one behind her said anything at all.

☆ ☆ ☆

Lottie seemed okay, and she nodded vigorously every time Eira asked if she was alright, but Eira wasn't sure. She was still fuming and embarrassed but wanted to make sure that her favorite Dwarven servant was really as well as she was pretending to be. Eira left Lottie flapping her hands with the Dwarven herbalist who worked beneath the Royal Physician. She went to her chambers.

Her bedroom wasn't the escape she'd hoped to find in the courtyard, but Eira still picked up one of the practice swords she had hidden there and moved her way through a series of steps, trying to work through her anger and embarrassment. But as she relived Hunter spitting on her face, his treatment of Lottie, and his look of horror, there was only the rage building inside her and that stupid Mirror's voice echoing in her head.

*"To protect your land of earth and stone
The fair must always hold the throne."*

She brushed a hand over her mottled cheek before clenching a fist. How could Hunter, that spoiled, rotten excuse for a human, clad in glittering armor and false smiles, be considered more worthy of rule? He was an insect. A cruel child. But she saw the look of horror on his face and knew that everyone else in their kingdom would react in the exact same way if they ever saw her for what she was. It didn't matter that Eira had studied ancient treaties and edicts that her mother never glanced at, had taught herself how her ancestors had ruled before the Mirror. It didn't matter that Eira was the strongest fighter in their entire, useless, showy army—one used to display decorative marching and to carry elegant banners. Why would they even need a real army when the entire country was apparently protected by the prophecy? They were safe as long as the *fairest* sat on the throne.

But as much as Eira would be an unparalleled queen in any other time or country, they weren't in a place where edicts and fighting and honor mattered. They were in Elsir. And the country would fall when the world saw who Eira really was.

But when Eira thought about the way Hunter had beat on poor little Lottie, who only took it, silent and terrified, Eira thought that maybe it was a kingdom that deserved to fall.

She screamed, angry and primal at all the finery that covered her vain, uncaring mother and her cruel cousin. That draped itself over the rotten, putrid sickness that her country—her *home*—had become. That was nothing like the stories and the treaties and the community she'd found in the dust-covered tomes of her ancestors. They were supposed to be *better than this.*

Eira swung her sword with an accuracy no one else in their kingdom had ever tried to learn, catching the little porcelain jar of corpse-white cream with the tip of her blade and sending it smashing against the far wall.

"The fairest, my dappled ass," she hissed.

Somewhere far away, there was a cry that was neither triumph nor fear. A hollow voice that rattled deep in her bones. She knew that voice but had never heard it say anything other than a single, hated phrase.

But now the Mirror was screaming.

☆ ☆ ☆

The throne room was already filled with people by the time Eira made it there, all called by the Mirror's desolate, reverberating howl. Teilia and Hunter were at the top of the platform, and the Gracious Queen was nearly screaming herself, begging the ghostly denizen to stop its cries and tell them all what was wrong. But the wail did not stop until Eira stepped through the throng. The squarish face locked its bottomless eyes on her and fell silent, the echoes of its haunting cries ringing through the corridors until there was not even a whisper in the hall. Teilia and Hunter spun to see Eira there, both bringing shocked hands to their mouths.

"Daughter!" Teilia gasped. "Your face!" Eira took another step towards the Mirror and her family, lifting her chin until she felt the biting red of her birthmark hit the sunlight.

"What of my face, Mother?" she asked without fear or uncertainty. She turned fully to the crowd that had, until this moment, been focused on the ghostly presence in the Mirror. "It is, after all, the only face I have ever had. Does anyone else want to remark upon it?" There were gasps and frightened whispers from the crowd. Eira stared each person down, still wearing her armor from before, daring anyone to speak aloud.

For a moment, it looked like several people were preparing to do just that, but then there was a sudden whistle from the Mirror, and a *clink* as something hit the floor. The giant, looming face that Eira had been forced to look at every day for her entire life smiled for just a moment... then was gone.

There were screams of surprise at the emptiness as everyone's faces stared back at them from the portal that had always held that specter of hope and secrets. But Teilia's calm, iron voice carried over the din.

"Do not worry, everyone. This is but a warning. A test. Our

benevolent Mirror has not left us. Indeed, it has even offered us a gift." She knelt gracefully and picked up the ornament that had fallen earlier. It was a pendant depicting a golden apple. Across the front was inscribed:

For The Fairest

Teilia held it up for all to see. "You see? We are still protected as long as the fairest in our land holds the throne. As long as the fairest wears this gift. Do not worry. All will be well. Return to your lives and duties. I will make sure that you are safe."

Slowly, uncertainly, the gathered people broke apart and drifted away, still casting glances backwards at Eira. She never lowered her chin.

But when the last person had left the throne room, Teilia rounded on her daughter, striking her hard across her red-splattered cheek.

"What did you *do?*" the queen hissed.

Eira opened her mouth to respond, but Teilia didn't wait, only grabbed her daughter roughly and marched her back to her room, throwing her inside. "I don't know what kind of mess you made, but now it is up to me to clean it up. Stay in here until I know how to save our kingdom from the monster in its walls."

And Eira was left in darkness.

☆ ☆ ☆

Eira was not idle as she waited for whatever would come. She tried to break down the door to her room. Tried to escape through the window. Tried to forge whatever path would be better than just... sitting and waiting for the inevitable. Her mother would never forgive this. The kingdom would writhe in fear and uncertainty as rumors spread of what so many had seen in the throne room. Eira was not safe in Elsir. But Elsir was not safe as it stood. Changes *had* to be made, Mirrors and prophecies be damned.

But try as she might, Eira couldn't escape her room high in the tower, and as the days went on, she grew weak with hunger and uncertainty. She lost track of time as her fate was decided somewhere on the floors below.

It was late one night when Eira heard her door creak open. Almost on instinct, she lunged at the intruder, startling the Dwarf carrying a serving tray. The tray clattered to the ground, its single apple rolling across the floor. Eira scrambled backwards as the servant cowered in the doorway. On the other side of the door, two guards brandished their swords and shoved the Dwarf fully inside.

Eira glowered at the guards, wondering for a moment if she could take them, even unfed and unarmed. But at the terrified gaze of the Dwarven servant, she changed her mind and instead moved to help the unfamiliar woman up. "I'm sorry," Eira whispered, brushing off her skirt for her. "Are you okay?"

"I'm alright, milady," the servant answered shakily. Eira was surprised that the Dwarf still had a tongue to speak with. "I was asked to bring you this... dinner." She motioned to the apple on the floor.

"Dinner? An apple? A single apple after so much time?"

"That's what I was told, Ma'am. And not to leave until I'd seen you eat." The Dwarf cast an uncertain glance at the guards behind her.

Eira frowned but didn't move. "Where's Lottie?"

"I don't know, Ma'am." The Dwarf fidgeted. "Will you eat so I can go? These are not my usual duties, and the laundry will pile up if I don't attend it, Ma'am."

Eira picked up the apple that had rolled across the floor. Its gorgeous red hue made her mouth water, even if it seemed suspicious.

"So they don't want me to starve to death," she whispered before turning to the servant again. "Do you know what they're planning for me down below?" The Dwarf didn't answer.

Eira sighed. "I'm sorry I scared you. You may go now. I won't keep you."

The servant tried to move towards the door, but the guards didn't move. She fidgeted again. "I have to watch you eat it, Ma'am."

Eira glowered at the guards, then took an unnecessarily large bite of the apple without breaking eye contact. "Is that enough for you?" she asked them. They didn't respond, but once Eira had taken the first bite, the hunger gave way to the sweetness of the fruit, and she quickly devoured what was left. When only the core remained, she placed it back on the Dwarf's reclaimed platter. The Dwarf looked down at it for a moment, and Eira saw there were tears in her eyes.

"I..." the Dwarf whispered. "I'm sorry, Ma'am. You were the only one who was ever nice to us. We... you... you were the hope for something better."

"What do you mean?" Eira asked, but the guards at the door had already pulled the Dwarven woman back so she could scurry back down the stairs. Eira heard them lock the door behind them.

"Wait! What did she mean?" Eira pounded on the door, but there was no response. She sat back down on the edge of her bed, preparing for more nothingness and uncertainty before whatever happened eventually happened, but something felt... off. Her room spun, and Eira knew that if she wasn't already sitting, she'd have fallen. She took a few deep breaths to steady herself. Tried to make it to the door again.

It opened before she got there, and Hunter strolled in, a sword in one hand, the two guards and the Queen behind him.

"Eira of Elsir, I challenge you for the title of Heir Apparent. You have proven unworthy of the throne."

"Hunter," Eira breathed, but her tongue was heavy in her mouth. She couldn't quite make out his disgustingly perfect features. "You never could beat me without cheating."

They'd won. He'd made the challenge before witnesses, including the reigning queen. It must be answered immediately. And Eira could barely stand.

Someone was speaking, but Eira couldn't hear the words. There was a sword in her hand now. It was too heavy. It felt wrong in her grip. Foreign. She was being shoved forward. She tripped. Fell. Hauled back up. Nearly carried down the stairs. Where were they going?

The courtyard. Eira's mind cleared a little when the crisp air hit her face. She shook her head and willed her eyes to clear, glaring at Hunter across the courtyard. He was smiling easily, his armor gone. Eira, too, was without her chainmail, and for once she was grateful. Her knees nearly buckled at the idea of donning it.

No armor. Live steel. A poisoned apple. This was to be a fight to the death for Elsir's throne.

Elsir. Her home. Her people. It was imperfect, but Eira loved her country and those who lived within it. She looked over the gathering crowd. The beautiful, proper humans in their elegant gowns, hiding their horror or amusement behind dainty handkerchiefs. This might be a game to them, but Eira loved them anyway. She wanted to show them how to be better.

But beyond the humans, gathered at the back of the crowd, round eyes wide and terrified, the Dwarven servants watched, too, fervently flapping their hands at each other. And Eira could feel their fear. Could feel the hope of whatever future they might have had slip away beneath the prospect of Hunter's rule. Eira remembered what the Dwarf that had served her the apple had said. And as much as Eira loved her human servants, in that moment she thought there was something more powerful than love. She wanted what was *right* for all her subjects. Even the ones she'd been taught to ignore.

Especially for the ones she'd been taught to ignore.

Somewhere far away, the Mirror picked up its screaming wail again. The gathered people murmured. The tension grew, and they all looked at Hunter. Begged him from behind their kerchiefs to end this.

Eira tightened her grip on her sword. Forced herself into stance. Faced Hunter's cocky grin even as her head swam. She didn't know if she could win—but she sure as the Mirror was going to try.

The battlemaster at the center of the field gave Eira a forlorn glance as he addressed those gathered. "A challenge has been issued for the title of Heir Apparent. Eira and Hunter of Elsir, both of royal blood, both entitled to their claim, will face each other here in front of all you have gathered as witnesses. Whoever bests the other in bladed combat will rise to the throne upon our illustrious Queen's death, long be her reign." He looked to Teilia for confirmation, and she inclined her pointed jaw.

"May the fairest be triumphant." She held out the little trinket that had fallen from the Mirror and the battlemaster took it, ready to present it to the winner in the end. He looked towards Eira again. An end that looked like it would come too soon.

Then the start was announced, and Hunter was already moving. Eira tried to anticipate his attack, but her body felt like it was in deep water. She barely managed to block his strike, and her entire body shook at the blow. He tried again, and she parried, tried to sidestep for a better position, was too slow, had to block again. Her legs weren't responding like they should. Her arms were getting heavier. And Hunter was always there, always ready.

Eira maneuvered to the side, sweeping her sword high, trying to force Hunter off balance. But he ducked low, unburdened without his breastplate, and slashed beneath her wide swing. Eira felt the sword between her ribs. Felt herself topple. Saw the sky above her head and heard the sound of an angry wind through the courtyard. She'd tried.

But the wind didn't dissipate, and after a moment Eira realized that it was something more than that. She swiveled her head to the side, past Hunter's stupid smile as he raised his sword to finish her. Past the humans that watched on with polite disinterest. Toward the Dwarves that tugged on their tunics and hair. Towards a wind that wasn't wind.

It was Lottie, issuing an eerie, tongueless scream. And the sweet serving girl was running forward, her voiceless cries filled with fear and strength and demand.

Eira couldn't die like this. Not in front of Lottie. Not at Hunter's cruel hand. She rolled away from Hunter's falling blade just in time. Fought her way to shaky feet while clutching at her bleeding side. Her sword was gone. She didn't remember dropping it. Didn't know if she could find it again.

But she didn't have to. Lottie was suddenly there, tackling Hunter's legs, swinging an iron skillet at his torso, screaming her airless scream. Hunter stumbled, cursing, swinging blindly at the Dwarf that was too fast and too low for him to hit.

Chaos exploded in the courtyard. Lottie was pulling Eira forward urgently, and the other Dwarven servants were scrambling and screaming, pushing aside their masters, clearing a path in front of Lottie's fervent squalls.

Hunter and Teilia were both screaming, too. Demanding that someone stop them. To protect the throne. Protect Elsir. A few tried, and Eira could barely duck beneath their grasping arms. There were too many of them. Even with the Dwarves holding the majority of the crowd back, they weren't going to escape. She didn't know where they could go. But suddenly the battlemaster was there, using Eira's sword to push back her attackers, pressing the trinket into her hand. Eira could barely make out the scrawled script of "for the fairest" through her blurred vision. "Go, Eira!" the battlemaster hissed, kicking another person away as he pressed her sword into her other hand. Then Lottie was pulling on her arm again, and Eira followed.

As the doors leading out to the courtyard swung shut behind them, barricaded by two burly Dwarves Eira didn't recognize, the chaos quieted a few degrees. She expected Lottie to lead her to one of the other exits from the palace, to the stables or the carriage house or the main road that crossed Elsir, but Lottie pulled her further into the building. Their footsteps and Eira's ragged breathing echoed in the halls.

Eira was about to say that she couldn't go any further when they burst into the throne room, the great Mirror pulsing in a vibrant blue that Eira had never seen. Lottie pulled her up to the top of the dais and pointed enthusiastically at the shining, limitless surface. Eira frowned.

"Do I... do I ask the question?"

Lottie rolled her eyes and pulled the trinket from Eira's hand, sliding the tiny disk into a receptacle at the base of the Mirror. The square face materialized in front of them.

"Little Lottie, smart and small. Is this the fairest one of all?"

Lottie rolled her eyes and signed something Eira couldn't make out. She was dizzy. The arm she was clutching to her side was soaked in blood. She felt herself slipping sideways.

Laughter. "It wasn't my idea to always rhyme. That was one of the human things," the Mirror guffawed. "Better bring her through before all of her people's hopes die with her."

☆ ☆ ☆

Eira woke up in an unfamiliar bed. She'd been washed and clothed, and her limbs felt stronger than before. She sat up, but before she could get a look at her surroundings, Lottie was suddenly there, hugging her and making happy sounds. Eira hugged her back.

"Lottie. I'm glad you're okay. I'm so sorry about... everything. All the years I didn't see you. I would have understood if you'd left me in the courtyard."

Lottie pulled back and signed enthusiastically at Eira, but Eira didn't recognize the movements.

"Sorry, Lottie. I don't understand."

"Many Dwarves have been rendered mute over the years. You will learn our signed language in time. We will teach you. Though you probably could have learned it before now if any of your people paid attention to the men and women who fold your laundry and scrub your floors."

Lottie and Eira both turned to the doorway, and Lottie curtsied to the man standing there. He had a familiar, square face, but his eyes were kinder than the ones she thought she recognized (though this was marred slightly by the jagged scar that cut across from his left eyebrow to his chin).

"You... you're the face from the Mirror!" Eira exclaimed. The man looked like he was trying to keep his face stern, but not well. Lottie giggled openly as she stood up again.

"If you said that to anyone other than me, it would be very offensive, Your Highness," the man grumbled as he crossed the room to stand at the foot of her bed. "But as its face was modeled after my great-great-grandfather, I suppose I'll let it slide." The side of his bearded cheek raised a little in a slight smile. "My name is Gernis, and I'm on the Dwarven Council. And you... You're the one who woke the Mirror up again. The fairest heir in Elsir. We'd nearly given up on anyone like you ever existing."

Eira frowned. "I'm... I'm not the fairest."

Gernis tilted his head to one side. "You're the one who woke the Mirror from its slumber, are you not?"

Eira opened her mouth to respond, but stopped when Lottie stepped forward, signing amidst a fit of giggles. Gernis's mouth dropped open.

"You... you thought the prophecy was talking about 'fair' as in...

appearance? And you thought that was the best way to determine a good leader? Of an entire country? *Fair skin?*"

Eira opened her mouth and closed it again. She could feel the blood rush to her face, darkening her birthmark. "When you say it like that... it sounds stupid."

Gernis didn't even have to translate Lottie's sign. "It is stupid."

"Well... better that someone on your side figured it out late than never," Gernis finally conceded. "For the first time in generations, the Mirror is open. We can get our people back. Bring them home."

"Why didn't they follow us through when we left the courtyard?" Eira stood up and stretched her sore body without looking away from Gernis.

"Before now, the doorway in the Mirror wasn't accessible at all. It will take time for that news to be signed across the country. But those in your palace knew not to come. We could not risk them leading what soldiers you have to our doorstep. They will wait until we can save all of them. The important thing was to get you here so we could decide how to begin."

Eira let that sink in for a moment before inclining her head. The honor of that statement filled her, and for the first time since birth she felt truly worthy of the throne.

"I promise that all my people will be treated better in the future. Elsir will learn what 'Fair' is supposed to be, for all of her people."

She thought that Lottie would be happy with her words, but the Dwarf frowned and smacked Eira firmly across the cheek before signing fervently. Gernis chuckled and began translating for her.

"We're not your people. We don't need your country. We have our own. We just wanted to be able to come home. We want our people united again, and we're prepared to do everything we can to make that happen. Including tearing all of Elsir down. You're only here to decide if that's the best-case scenario or the worst."

Eira gaped. For as sweet and submissive as Lottie had always seemed, she hadn't expected anything like this. But of course Lottie had changed. She'd been a slave without an escape before, forced to work within the confines of a system that wouldn't let her be anything else. How could Eira expect her to be that submissive in every scenario? Lottie crossed her arms and stared Eira down.

Gernis cleared his throat. "It seems to me, Princess, that you're the one who needs us. We'll help you get back to your throne. We'll help you seize it. We'll even help you keep it until your messed-up beauty-based infrastructure figures itself out again. But we will not be subservient to you or pretend we owe you for whatever change comes. You can enter this as our ally or burn with everyone else."

His voice was still kind, but Eira saw the fire in his eyes. For a moment, she was defensive, and there was a hint of irritation in her voice when she responded.

"Then why save me at all? Why offer to help me mend Elsir? You could march through the Mirror now and take everything you've lost. Everything you're owed."

"We could. A lot of Dwarves think that's exactly what we should do. But the Mirror was created by both sides in a world that could already see the divide and hatred coming. Your ancestor and mine saw the potential for change, and they set the groundwork for a future treaty where none was possible then. It would only open again if leaders on both sides held love for each other. We've molded our government to keep our side open, and now that it finally has, we will respect that hope we nourished for generations. If there is a chance that the humans will be our allies, we will give them the chance to prove it."

"And if we fall short?"

Gernis laughed and handed Eira her sword. "Then I guess we'll see."

☆ ☆ ☆

Eira did not lead the Dwarves through the Mirror and into the Elsir throne room. She did not stride triumphantly to the sound of Dwarven cheers. But she was not idle, either. Years of sword fighting had honed her movements, and while she was not the only fighter who met the handful of trained guards that Elsir had to offer, she was far from the worst soldier in the Dwarven army.

But when Hunter appeared at the end of the hall, the Dwarves fanned out around them, leaving Eira's cousin to her. Eira thought about challenging him. Thought about all the niceties their shining system had been built on. But they were just formalities that slowed down progress and kept the "lesser beings" in their place. Eira was done with niceties. She'd been called, and she would do what was best for her people and those she'd allied with.

Eira darted across the throne room, her blade raised. Hunter was just cognizant enough to parry, to change his footing. But he'd lived an entire life where he never actually thought he'd have to defend the life he'd been granted. His gorgeous features and handsome charms had always been enough.

Until now.

Eira didn't relent, and Hunter was forced to remain on the defensive. She saw the fear in his eyes as he recognized that each of his movements was less than perfect. That he was one misstep away from falling beneath her blade. "Eira..." he begged as he barely parried another blow. "Please. I'm sorry."

Eira saw the fear in his eyes. Felt both pity and empathy. But then she remembered the rage they'd held when he'd beaten Lottie. The arrogance and entitlement he'd always carried, and it was enough to strengthen her just as he cut low. Eira jumped back just in time and narrowed her eyes.

"You never could beat me without cheating," she whispered. She lunged forward, then spun on her toe as Hunter tried to deflect. His arm was too low, and her blade cut cleanly through his neck. The beautiful face was stunning even as it rolled across the floor.

There was a wail, and Eira turned to see Teilia rush forward, cradling Hunter's head to her bosom, ignoring the red that spread across her white gown.

"Eira! Daughter! How could you do this? Did I not love you? Did we not care for you? Why would you attack your home?"

"This palace felt like a prison for most of my life, Mother. But I realize now that I had no idea what that even meant. We are here to release everyone that was bound to this place. It's time for a new direction for Elsir."

"But the prophecy! The Mirror! Eira, the city will fall!"

"Maybe it deserves to," Eira whispered. She turned her back on the sobbing queen and ascended the small dais on which the throne stood, the Mirror towering behind it. She took her place and looked down her nose at her mother, gesturing Gernis toward her.

"Teilia of Elsir, for your crimes against Dwarves, I offer you to the Dwarven Council as a show of good faith for the prosperity of our alliance."

"Eira? You'd do this to your mother? Please! I didn't know! I didn't realize!"

"You didn't know what? That you treated people poorly and abused your power in the name of superficial pageantry? You didn't realize that your beauty was only skin deep?" Eira leaned forward in her seat. "Ignorance is a dainty fan to hide behind, Mother. It is no excuse."

She looked to Gernis, who removed his helmet. Teilia quaked as she looked between his visage and that which she'd sworn fealty to her entire life.

"The... You look like the Mirror."

"And you always did take orders from that, didn't you?" Eira quipped. "So let's try it again, shall we?

Magic mirror of all that's seen
*What's a **fair** punishment for this fallen queen?"*

Gernis rolled his eyes. "The rhyming was always a human thing, you know. Thought it sounded more magical. More binding." But he smiled and cleared his throat, staring down at Teilia.

"As was done to us, thus do to she
Remove her tongue and set us free."

Eira leaned back in her throne. "Fair enough."

ABOUT THE AUTHOR

Tahani Nelson is a fantasy author from Billings, Montana. Best known for wearing armor and warpaint to her events, Nelson has become a familiar face at conventions, Renaissance faires, and book festivals across the country.

❧ II ❧

BIZARRE LOVE TRIANGLE

A Retelling of Goldilocks & the Three Bears

Mike X Welch

Barry grunted against the stubborn deadbolt of his summer home. For whatever reason, it had been on the fritz ever since he'd bought the place, regardless of how much lubricant he sprayed into it. His frustration was mounting. The two full sacks of groceries in his arms didn't make the process any easier.

Ursula, Barry's wife of twenty-six years, sighed as if *she* were the only one the door was thwarting. Barry started to rumble a sarcastic response, but then the key finally turned to the right and the deadbolt unlocked.

Bruno, Ursula and Barry's son, trundled in behind his sweaty parents, then turned and locked the deadbolt. Barry saw this from the corner of his eye as he gingerly set the grocery bags on the counter, but the pre-teen was off and down the hall to his room before Barry could bark out an admonishment. Bruno's new habit of locking all doors behind himself had resulted in several angry phone calls from Barry to Ursula, telling her that he needed to be let back into the house after checking the post, putting out the garbage bins, sneaking a fag, etcetera. It was really starting to get Barry's hackles up.

Ursula distracted him by continuing her line of questioning from the hour-long drive, one that Barry was not keen to continue. "I just can't understand how something can vanish from your office. If you didn't fancy it, Baz, you could've just told us."

Barry placed his hands flat on the counter and stared at them, trying to keep his voice level. "Swear down, Lulu, my love, the frame was there the last time I was at the office, two days ago."

This was true. The frame in question had been an anniversary gift from Ursula. It was a nondescript rectangular frame which, when a USB thumb drive was plugged into the side of it, would cycle through the various photo files contained on the drive. She'd insisted that Barry keep it on his desk at his office. Barry found it maddeningly distracting, as the change in photos every fifteen seconds was a jarring bit of motion in his peripheral vision. Ursula explained that the twenty-sixth wedding anniversary gift was supposed to be art, and what better art to adorn his desk than a collection of pictures of his loving family?

Fookin' owt, Barry thought at the time, but had smiled and hugged his wife and thanked her for the gift. He promised to put it right on his work desk. And that's where the bloody thing had been two nights ago, during a particularly frenetic session of fellatio from the office's new cleaning girl. Barry knew this for sure, as he'd had to turn the frame face down because it was distracting him then, too.

"If you say so..." Ursula's voice trailed off as she went through to their suite of bedrooms, her tone that of someone who distinctly did not believe what had been said.

Barry finished putting away the groceries, then slumped into the easy chair in the small living room. It had been a hot, boring drive east from Manchester on the A57, past Glossop to here. Ursula wouldn't have even known about the missing gift if he hadn't been forced to stop at his office to retrieve the keys to the home. Despite Barry telling them both to stay in the car, Ursula and Bruno had trundled upstairs behind him, Ursula eyeing the place for... Heaven knows what, really, Bruno undoubtedly looking for things to lock.

Barry had purchased this vacation home three years prior and made every attempt to use it as much as possible since, but the lack of care was clear. Cobwebs shrouded each corner of the ceiling, and there was a musty smell emanating from... somewhere. At least the tiny "panic room" was clean; no one had been in there since he bought the place. Why the previous owners had sacrificed a bedroom for such a thing—out in the country, even—Barry would never understand. He craned his neck to see into the backyard through the French doors, and the weeds were nearly as tall as his barbeque grill.

Rather than do anything about it, Barry cranked back the reclining chair and promptly fell asleep.

Forty minutes later, Ursula woke Barry with the characteristic *tsk tsk* sound she made whenever he dared to nap. Why the woman couldn't stand the idea of him relaxed, he might never learn.

"It's almost time for supper, luv," Ursula called behind her while heading into the kitchen. "I'll get the table set. Can you start grilling the sirloins?"

Barry growled an affirmative in her direction. It turned to a groan as he hefted his fifty-year-old bulk from the recliner. While retrieving the steaks from Ursula, she reminded him that there was still no cellular signal out here on her mobile phone. "That's the point, *luv*. To get away from all that shite." He managed a half-hearted smile.

Ursula frowned in his direction.

His smile dropped. "It's been like this for three years, Lulu. It's not likely to change." Barry stalked away and began grilling the steaks.

☆ ☆ ☆

Getting Bruno to abandon his computer in favor of dinner was a constant challenge. Barry was in no mood to argue with the boy, and so when his call down the hallway went unanswered, he simply sat down and began tucking his napkin into his collar. Ursula put down whatever she was holding on the counter and went by the kitchen table, all the while glaring at Barry. Barry heard her bark out Bruno's name, and the boy came to his seat with his head hung low. Ursula grabbed a warm casserole dish from the stovetop and brought it to the table—some sort of scalloped potatoes mixture. Barry hated it and he knew Bruno wouldn't touch it. Why Ursula insisted on making things she knew no one would eat was beyond Barry.

"There's red in it." Bruno looked up from his steak. The boy wanted his meat well-done. Most times Barry would accommodate him, but these sirloins had been particularly pricey, and so he was loath to grill them to a blackened crisp.

"Right. That's because I cooked them correctly."

"You know I don't like this. Mum, look, there's blood leaking out of it..."

"It's just the juices, Bruno." Ursula was distracted by cutting into her own steak to determine if Barry had cooked hers medium-well, as she preferred.

Bruno pressed, his voice pitching up into an intolerable whine. "Juice. It's blood! That's wot's inside a cow!" He dropped his cutlery with a clang.

"Quiet." Barry said, but not to Bruno. He'd heard something.

"Can't you, like, microwave this to make it—"

Tap tap

"Shut up, boy!" Barry barked. Ursula jerked her head up to admonish him but stopped when she presumably noticed the tapping.

Metal on glass, Barry thought as he rose from his seat, napkin pulled from his collar already.

He was looking into the living room, but with the next *tap* he realized it was behind him, at the kitchen door. On the other side of the four-paneled window set into the steel door, the barrel of a long pistol was tapping against the glass.

Curiosity overrode fear, and Barry took a step toward the door.

Then he saw the blonde hair shining in the late afternoon sun. The gun barrel shattered the lower right pane of glass. Ursula shrieked once behind him, and a small hand snaked through the broken glass to grasp the deadbolt.

The cleaning girl's hand. He knew because there was a tattoo on the flesh between the thumb and index finger; something that was supposed to be a dove but looked more like a pigeon after being felled by a shotgun blast. And he would recognize his own .357 Magnum *anywhere*.

She'd raided his office to find this address. She'd taken his pistol.

Oh, Christ.

Barry barked out the words he'd never thought he'd have to say. "Into the panic room, now!" he yelled to Ursula and Bruno, who simply stared at him with mouths agape.

"Now!" Barry shouted, pulling Bruno's chair back violently enough to spur them both into action. He stepped out of their way as they ran down the hallway, taking one last look at the kitchen door. The girl had already pulled her hand back out—carefully enough to avoid the broken glass—and was turning the knob, the door coming slowly open...

Barry followed his fleeing family. He was the last one into the panic room and slammed the heavy metal door behind himself. It closed with a semi-satisfying *thunk*.

Ursula was at the far end of the rectangular room, and Barry looked her way. Her face vacillated between fear and anger and something approaching... judgment?

While Barry wrestled with the prospect of trying to explain what was happening, Bruno took the opportunity to press a series of commands into the keypad immediately to the left of the heavy steel door. There was a distinct series of four beeps, and then a muffled *clunk* from within the door itself.

Barry's attention turned to his son, whose neck was within wringing distance. "What did you just do, Bruno?" he hissed through clenched teeth.

"That's the lock!" the boy said proudly. "It says right here: *press these numbers to activate the time lock.*"

"Why would you do that?" Barry asked, incredulous.

"So it was locked, Dad."

"Aye, but why would you lock the time lock?"

Bruno hesitated a moment, his face taking on a look that suggested his father hadn't heard him correctly the first time. "So that it was *locked*, Dad."

Barry's hands curled into and out of fists several times. He looked back and forth from Ursula to Bruno. Ursula, for her part, now had a look of unabashed worry on her face.

Bruno wisely backed away from his father until he felt his mother's hand touch his left shoulder. "Should..." he started, "should I not have—"

Barry erupted. "NO, YOU SHOULDN'T HAVE, YOU DAFT 'APETH! WOT THE FOOK IS WRONG WITH YE, LOCKING EVERY FOOKING DOOR THAT CROSSES YER PATH? IT'S LIKE A SICKNESS WITH YA!"

"Barry..." Ursula warned.

"YOU'VE PUT US IN HERE FOR, OH CHRIST..." Barry's eyes now scanned the four different CCTV monitors that had blinked to life as Bruno had punched the code into the keypad. Each showed a countdown from 180 minutes. "THREE HOURS! WE'RE IN HERE FOR THREE FOOKIN' HOURS, YOU—"

"*Barry*," Ursula said more forcefully this time.

"Oh, Christ," Barry repeated and slid down the wall to land on his buttocks.

"Soz, Dad." Bruno had the good sense to also sit on the floor and look at his lap.

Ursula, however, crossed her arms and glared daggers at Barry. She gave him a few minutes to decompress, during which he mostly looked at his hands like he didn't know why they were at the ends of his arms. Her patience wasn't eternal, though.

"Who's the girl, Baz?"

Barry thought of a thousand different lies to tell his wife in the space of ten seconds.

"Baz?" Ursula's tone was one that Barry had rarely heard in all their many years together. "Who is the bird with the gun?"

Barry's head lolled to the side to face Ursula. His eyes focused on her feet. "Wot it is, right, uh, that's our cleaning lady. The office."

"Bobbins," she stared in disbelief.

"Right. At the office, we hired a cleaning girl, uh, lady, to tidy up the place after hours."

"It's a one-person office, Baz. How dirty can it get?"

"Swear down, luv."

"Aye." Ursula murmured, stepping over Barry's outstretched legs, heading toward the CCTV screens near the door.

Barry resumed studying his hands. He wished her tone was more hysterical. This cold, controlled one was terrifying.

Ursula watched the screens for a few moments, saw the girl milling around their kitchen aimlessly. "She's fit."

"Is she?" Barry had the good sense to reply.

"Aye. *Well* fit." Ursula said again in that same chilling tone.

Barry looked up and watched the CCTV monitors over Ursula's shoulder. The girl seemed to somehow identify the kitchen camera. She skipped over to it, and then something obscured the lens. Barry assumed that the girl had disconnected the camera somehow, but the image resumed, panning around the kitchen. The camera came to a rest on what seemed like the counter beneath its usual corner mounting. He could again see their kitchen table, closer now and at less of a ceiling view.

The girl set what was clearly an oversized purse on the counter nearest the door she'd broken in through. Barry saw her remove an object from the bag and then approach the camera. The girl set something down in front of the lens... a square object that seemed familiar.

A video sprang to life on it, and Barry recognized the setting immediately.

"Oh, it's yer office, Baz..." Ursula said, her tone still cold, some sarcasm edging in.

Barry stood, dreading what might play next.

They both watched the video feed, a coldness creeping up Barry's spine. On it, he called out silently—as there was no audio in the home's CCTV setup—to someone while seated at his cluttered desk. He identified the gift frame on the right side of his desk, exactly where he told Ursula he'd placed it. Barry almost blurted out *I told you so* to Ursula, but then thought better of it.

On the video, the girl stuck her head tentatively into Barry's office, clearly responding to his voice. Some sort of dialogue ensued between them; Barry was often laughing, the girl slowly inching into the room as if drawn by his words. At last, the girl walked further into Barry's office, out of the view of the office security camera. On the video, Barry started undoing his belt.

In the silence of the panic room, Barry put his hand to his forehead and winced.

"Oh, look, Baz, you're getting your kecks off for her."

"Lulu, don't watch—"

"Shut it!" she spat toward him, her brow creased in absolute rage, then she turned back to the screen.

The girl came back into the frame.

"Oh, look, Baz, she's got her tits out."

Across the room, Bruno's head perked up. Barry lowered his in shame.

On the video feed, the girl wedged herself between Barry's bulk and his desk. She dropped to her knees. Barry reached toward the gift frame and turned it face down on the desk.

Ursula looked away from the CCTV monitor, then crossed the room to stand next to her seated son.

Barry could see the rest of the coupling play out on the tiny screen. He didn't need to watch it further to know how short the video would be. He now understood that the girl had somehow gotten her hands on the office security camera's memory card, taken it home and transferred the video file to a USB stick, and then plugged *that* into the purloined anniversary frame. And taken the massive .357 Magnum out of his desk for good measure.

What he didn't know was why.

The frame was taken away from the kitchen camera, restoring the view of the counter, the table, the girl. As Barry watched, perplexed, she sat down in his seat and started carving into his steak. She took a bite, then made an exaggerated face of disgust and tossed the silverware to the table. Barry could hear nothing through the massive steel door; the kitchen might as well have been on the moon for all it mattered.

Next, the girl placed herself in Ursula's chair and similarly carved a piece of steak. After tasting it, she looked at the camera and once again made a face, letting the half-chewed piece of meat roll off her tongue to fall to the floor. Just when Barry expected her to do the same with Bruno's meal, he saw that she remained seated in Bruno's chair, elbows moving frantically as she cut up the steak and ate it. To Barry's shock, she stood after a few minutes of this and displayed Bruno's plate, completely devoid of food. Bruno's entire dinner had been eaten.

First time that's happened, Barry mused.

From across the room, Ursula spoke icily. "Wot's this slag's name, Baz?"

Barry nearly jumped at the broken silence. "Uhm, it's..." Barry struggled to remember.

"You always did have a soft spot for blondes." Ursula rolled her eyes and crossed her arms tightly across her chest. "Never mind. Wot's Goldilocks doing now?"

"She's, uhm..." Barry no longer saw the girl in the kitchen's video feed. He squinted at the four monitors until he managed to identify the girl stretched out in his recliner, in the living room. Barry's massive pistol rested in her lap, and the girl had her hands behind her head in a perfect pose of comfort.

"Uh, living room, on my chair..."

Goldilocks sprang up from the recliner, posted her fists on her hips in mock disappointment, then leveled the pistol and pulled the trigger. The bullet blew a massive hole in the back of Barry's favorite chair, a slightly smaller one in the wall behind it, and then came to a rest somewhere near the home's foundation.

All three of them jumped at the roar of the gun. The steel container muffled most of the sound, but not all of it. Ursula regained her composure and was staring daggers at Barry, who wore a sheepish look but stayed quiet. Barry saw that Bruno was looking back and forth between his parents, probably wondering why they weren't putting a stop to this girl's antics. Bruno, too, had the good sense to remain silent.

In the interim, Goldilocks had moved on to the master bedroom and seated herself at Ursula's vanity. The girl had a finger in her ear, rubbing vigorously, obviously trying in vain to restore some hearing. Her mouth made various shapes.

"She's at your vanity," Barry reported, immediately regretting his decision.

Ursula stormed over, her voice rising as she came. "Whore's gonna cadge our makeup!"

They watched Goldilocks entertain herself in the mirror for a few moments. Then she stood and, holding the pistol in her right hand, gripped the right edge of Ursula's vanity with her left hand and violently overturned it. Every bit of perfume and makeup went to the floor. The mirror showed a series of massive cracks. Goldilocks turned to the camera fastened in an upper corner of the room and performed an exaggerated shrug to it, then went out of the room.

Ursula looked at Barry, mere inches from his face. "She's peckin' me 'ead, Baz. You stick your mingin' tool past her Newtons, and here we are with a wrecked gaff."

"Lulu, I'll get the vanity fettled," Barry offered meekly.

"Fook the fooking vanity, Baz! This is about yer inability to keep yer pecker in yer duds. *Consequences*, Baz."

Barry's sphincter practically inverted.

Unnoticed by either of them, Bruno had waddled over. His stomach growled loud enough for them both to turn and look down at him.

"My tummy thinks my throat's cut," Bruno whined.

Both parents were about to shout "shut it!" in unison, but motion on a CCTV screen caught their attention.

"Hey! That girl's in our room! She's... she's touching our computer! MA!" Bruno yelled.

Before either could address this, Goldilocks put her feet up on Bruno's keyboard hard enough to send plastic keys spraying up from the device. She gave a dramatic yawn-and-stretch gesture while pushing back which resulted in her falling backward in Bruno's coveted gaming chair. Mid-fall, Goldilocks' finger closed on the trigger of the pistol— still in her right hand—and Bruno's laptop was reduced to a smoking ruin. All three in the panic room jumped once again.

Bruno wailed loudly enough for both Barry and Ursula to clamp their hands on their ears. In Bruno's room, Goldilocks stood and, leaving Bruno's expensive chair in two parts on the floor, skipped merrily back to the master bedroom.

Less angry and more alarmed now, Ursula took the whimpering Bruno by the elbow and led him back toward the other end of the panic room. They sat cross-legged on the ground and spoke to each other in soft tones. Barry looked away from them and back to the CCTV monitors. The timer at the bottom of each screen showed 120 minutes. This was nowhere near over.

Goldilocks sequestered herself in the master suite and slowly disrobed, doing a seductive dance to the camera. Bruno said a silent prayer of thanks that he was the only one able to see this display, then sent an equally silent curse crotch-ward as his manhood began to perk up. The girl seemed to tire of her own performance and laid down on the bed. There she remained for the next hour, sleeping face down, naked as the day she was born, splayed across the entire queen-sized bed.

☆ ☆ ☆

With the timer on the CCTV screens counting down with agonizing slowness from 60 minutes, Barry noticed movement again on the screen showing his bed. He had been staring into the middle distance for the better part of the last hour, not daring to glance over at his wrathful wife or his inconsolable son. He looked up and noticed Goldilocks was gone from his bed.

The hallway camera feed showed a shapely, naked arse moving across its face. The kitchen camera, its angle reduced considerably by being taken off the ceiling and put on the counter, showed the girl moving toward her large purse with a sluggish gait. She rummaged in it, her arms sunk practically to the elbows in its depths, then came out with several objects that Barry couldn't identify. No, wait, four objects, and he could identify two of them: a small cigarette lighter and a belt. Goldilocks was now opening and slamming shut various kitchen drawers. Barry watched in confusion as she opened the final drawer and withdrew a spoon. Then his view was of her fully nude front as she walked with renewed purpose back to the hallway.

Barry expected to see her return to his bedroom, but instead she veered into Bruno's and flopped onto his small twin bed, her long hair bouncing before coming to a rest across her shoulders. Goldilocks rose to a seated position on Bruno's bed, her legs crossed, her brow knitted in concentration, and she fiddled with one of the objects she'd gotten from her purse.

"Oh, this is well bad." Barry's hand rose to his mouth and covered it absently.

Ursula had raised her head upon hearing him speak; he saw this in his peripheral vision. She slowly rose and trundled over to him. "Wot's yer bessie doing n—"

Barry quieted her by extending his left arm and guiding Ursula down to a seated position next to him.

They both watched the screen in rapt horror as Goldilocks shut off the lighter that had been positioned under the purloined spoon. She picked up the syringe and sucked the contents of the spoon into it, then held the syringe absently in her mouth while she affixed the belt to her left thigh.

Bruno started to stand. "Wot's she doing n—"

Both of them turned to him, their eyes wide, and cried "Stay there!" To Bruno's credit, he sank back down to the floor and pouted.

Upon turning back to the CCTV monitors, Ursula and Barry saw that Goldilocks had already injected herself. She pulled the needle out from between the first and second toes on her right foot, dropped the forgotten syringe on Bruno's bedspread, loosened the belt tourniquet on her thigh, and slowly lowered herself onto the bed. They saw her eyes, already half-lidded, close and her right hand meander toward her naked crotch.

Ursula stood, her anger back in full force, glaring down at the top of Barry's balding head. She reared back with her right foot and gave him a forceful kick to the bottom of his left thigh. Barry said "Ow," but didn't react otherwise, his eyes glued to the CCTV screen.

"Fooking pig," Ursula swore, turning to march back to the far end of the panic room.

"Oh, no. No, no no no no... please no." Barry droned, his voice rising with each uttered denial.

Ursula turned and had her mouth set wide, her left index finger already poised to thrust in his direction, but stopped when she saw Barry turn absolutely white. She jogged back over awkwardly and viewed the screen with him.

On it, Goldilocks' nude body was practically dancing on top of Bruno's Minecraft bed set. Her legs and arms were straight, rigid even, and her head thrashed to the left and right.

"She's having a fit," Ursula observed coolly.

"She's overdosing." Barry managed, his voice strangled and high-pitched.

Even as they watched, Goldilocks' seizure rattled to a close, her body changed from nearly vibrating to simply jerking, then to a deathly repose punctuated by a few remaining twitches that caused Barry and Ursula to gasp each time.

Then Goldilocks was still; her chest was no longer rising and falling. Finally, to their horror, Barry and Ursula saw a dark liquid issue from between her legs, bubble, and then seep into Bruno's bedspread.

Ursula did the sign of the cross and lowered her head. Barry couldn't tear his eyes away from the screen. Neither of them noticed that Bruno had crept over until he exclaimed "Naked bird on our bed!"

Barry turned and guided both of them back to the far end of the panic room, then returned to the CCTV screens to watch the remaining minutes count down. He sighed and once again slid down the wall to land heavily on his arse.

Barry thought of the coming conversations to be had: with the police; with his son; with Lulu. He did not look forward to any of them. It seemed that every time he had to talk to someone, it was always to his detriment. It had been like that for years. It wasn't likely to change.

ABOUT THE AUTHOR

Mike X Welch lives in Western New York with his wife, the author Aly Welch. Welch is part of the leadership team of Writing Bloc, an Indie Author Collective. (www.writingbloc.com) His self-published collection of horror stories, ENANTIODROMIA, has been met with universal acclaim. Welch is currently working on an expanded version of his short story 'Turning of the Bones' in both prose and graphic novel form. Visit www.mikexwelch.com

12

NEUROPHAGE

A Retelling of Hansel & Gretel

Evan Graham

Grace Mkembe's dark eyes studied the 3D terrain simulation projected on the opaque shutter over her SandPhantom's viewscreen, wrestling control of the vehicle from the vicious sandstorm winds outside. Heavy banks of sand rolled down the dunes, crashing against the car from all sides. Grace wasn't sure which was the greater threat to her vehicle: being carried away by the winds or being swamped by the sand. Although, that latter problem had already happened once today...

"Drop a beacon," Darren Stockley said from the seat beside her. "We'll have to come back and dig out my SandPhantom when the storm is over."

"You know it's probably twenty feet under a couple hundred tons of sand now, right?"

"We have to try, Grace. We can barely put food on the table right now. We can't keep Redcrest alive with a SandPhantom out of commission. The whole outpost depends on it."

Grace sighed. "Yeah, I know." She pulled a lever on her console, and a small silver canister with a flashing red light ejected from the back of the vehicle. It tumbled across the desert floor before rolling to a rest. Half a second later, the sand swallowed it.

Grace snorted and shook her head. "Want me to drop a beacon for that beacon so we can dig it up later too?"

Darren groaned and slumped into his seat. "My life is over."

"Don't get dramatic on me, Stockley. Redcrest is tougher than you're giving them credit for. Anton can keep us going for months with his hydroponics, and we still have Alessia's ride. We can get by with two SandPhantoms until we save up enough to trade for a new one. We'll just have to live a little slim for a while."

Darren stared blankly at the ceiling. "That was Alessia's SandPhantom."

Grace quirked an eyebrow. "You lost your wife's car?"

"I blew the shocks on mine last week, remember? Kaito's still working on it. We're taking turns using hers, and it's her turn to watch Jake."

"I take it back, Stockley. You're dead as hell."

"Yeah, like I said."

"Want me to throw you out now? Save your dignity? I'll tell her raiders got you."

"Tempting." Darren leaned forward, adjusting the dials on the vehicle's sensor array.

"Don't go messing up my settings, Stockley, or I will kick you out."

"Now who's dramatic? Relax. I'm looking for something. Before I had to bail, I caught something on long range. Might have been a metal signature."

"We are not salvaging during a sandstorm. We're looking for shelter."

"I know. But it was close to the ridge. If we can find it, we might not have to come home empty-handed." The console gave a tone as a faint but regular shape appeared in the distance on the viewscreen's terrain simulation. "There! That's it! Right at the foot of the ridge. We can make it that far."

Grace squinted, trying to make out the shape, but distance and storm interference left the image blurry. "What am I looking at?"

"Not sure yet, but it's definitely metal. Looks big too. Probably a mining rig. Maybe a combine sifter?"

"Maybe. We'll check it out." Grace nudged the wheel toward the metal signature. Outside, the winds still roared, and booms of thunder rattled the windows. She squinted at the ambiguous shape growing at the edge of her sonar's range. "That look like a wing to you?"

His eyes widened. "Yeah... yeah it does. And that could be a fuselage. Grace, if that's a ship..."

"Yeah, I know." She locked the object in her sights and pressed down just a bit harder on the accelerator.

☆ ☆ ☆

The storm was at maximum potency by the time the SandPhantom reached the ridge, with winds so strong they threatened to lift the vehicle off the ground. Fortunately, the two-hundred-foot-high monoliths that marked the edge of the sand ocean offered some protection.

The rocky pinnacles enveloped the speeding vehicle like a forest of stone. The sound outside the SandPhantom shifted from an oppressive roar to a keening whistle as wind played the pinnacle canyon like a woodwind instrument. A few hundred yards ahead, half-buried at the base of a monolith wide enough to be considered a mesa, lay the metallic object they sought.

Grace flipped a switch and the sonar projection flickered off as the windscreen shudder retracted. The view outside was still a dark chaotic mess, but the headlights managed to catch a glint of black ceramic plating through the murk. Grace brought the SandPhantom slowly around the vessel's side, directing a spotlight to explore its hull.

"I see some pretty advanced radar and lidar systems." The spotlight shone on an elongated boxy tube jutting from a ball turret beneath the ship's exposed wing. Grace gave a low whistle. "That looks like a railgun."

"An armed research vessel... maybe one of Exotech's special projects?"

The blocky white lettering and series of small flag decals passing into view quickly put that question to rest. "The *ECS Kaifeck*," Grace read. "That's Coalition military."

"We, uh..." Darren said shakily. "We should hail them. If there's anyone on board, I really don't want to get shot."

Grace opened an outgoing comm channel. "Hello, *Kaifeck*, this is Grace Mkembe, civilian dunerunner, do you require assistance?"

The only response was static and the constant gritty howl of sandstorm wind.

"*ECS Kaifeck*, we are right outside your door, is anyone home?"

Nothing.

Grace and Darren sat in silence for several minutes listening to the steady buzz of an empty comm channel. "What are the odds of the Expansionary Coalition losing a whole research vessel in the desert and not sending anyone in to get it back?" Darren asked.

"Low." Grace double checked the sensors on her console. "No signs of a radiation leak. That's the only thing I can think of that would make the military leave a crashed ship alone. Unless it isn't crashed at all. But if there's anyone on board, they would know we're here, and that we know they're here." Grace's eyes traced the enigmatic vessel's outline against the storm haze. "Maybe we should leave this one alone."

"Are you kidding? Grace, do you have any idea how valuable the tech on that ship is? One full cargo hold could keep everyone at Redcrest fed for the next 20 years. If anyone was home, they would have seen us way before we saw them. They might have kept quiet hoping we'd miss them, but we have announced ourselves. They'd be telling us to get out of here, but they haven't. That ship is abandoned."

"Darren..."

"Look, if we go in there and don't find anything shady, we can legally salvage it. If we find a bunch of illegal stuff in there, we'll get rid of any evidence we were ever here and sell what we can the old-fashioned way. You know Nusabaya, down at the Emirate depot? I've heard she has some good contacts in the Martian black market. She could fence anything we can't trade at the other outposts."

"Do you at least have your gun?" Grace asked.

Darren gave her a sheepish look. "Eh... couldn't get to it before I had to bail out. All I got was my emergency kit."

"Stockley, you know I don't have a gun. You want to board a military ship without a weapon?"

"If we boarded with a weapon, our chances would be worse. They'd have better ones and know how to use them. I don't know about you, but I don't want to look like a threat to anybody."

Grace held out an expectant hand. "Give me the kit."

Darren handed her the case. She pulled out a roll of tape, a plastic bottle of isopropyl alcohol, a red cylindrical magnesium flare, and a large metal canister reminiscent of a fire extinguisher: a personal chlorate oxygen generator. Packing them together tightly, Grace started wrapping the components with tape.

"What in God's name are you doing?" Darren asked with a raised eyebrow.

"Garret taught me this one. You can make a pretty nasty firebomb this way. Burns hot and bright. Deadly in an enclosed space."

"That seems like a very bad idea."

"Yeah, well, so is going in the ship at all. At least with this, I'll have leverage if someone holds a gun to my head."

Darren sighed. "Alright, fair. Just don't get twitchy. I prefer my skin medium rare, at most."

Grace gave him a long look. "You sure you want to do this?"

"We haven't found a decent haul in months, and we won't find one like this ever again. You know we can't afford to miss this, Grace."

Grace sighed and activated the SandPhantom's depressurization system. "I know."

She popped the gull-wing door open, and the roaring wind wrenched it out of her hand, flinging it up so fast it nearly tipped the rover on its side. She fought the wind to shut it again as Darren exited the vehicle and struggled to do the same. They leaned into the abrasive winds, shuffling the few dozen yards to the *Kaifeck*'s airlock and flattening against the hull. Grace put a hand on Darren's back as he inspected the airlock controls, bracing him against winds that threatened to topple them both over.

A moment later, the door slid open.

"...What was that?" Grace asked.

Darren stared at the open door. "It... wasn't locked."

"Top-secret military ships don't just leave their doors unlocked, Stockley."

"This one did." Darren tucked into the airlock chamber, finally out of the biting wind. "Inner door looks unlocked too. You ready?"

She hooked her finger through the oxygen candle's pull tab on her improvised incendiary bomb. "Just do it."

The inner door opened, revealing a brightly lit sterile metal corridor. The soft thrum of air filters and the faint buzz of overhead lights were the only sounds in the strangely still vessel interior.

Grace stepped in, casting a glance at the sensors on her suit's gauntlet. "Standard atmosphere. Life support's still online."

"Main lights are on," Darren noted. "She's not on emergency power. The main reactor is still running."

"Let's keep masks on, okay? Could be a bioweapon or something in the air."

"Fine by me." Darren followed the corridor deeper into the ship, stopping at an open doorway.

The room inside was filled with worktables, each scattered with sophisticated diagnostic tools and technological devices of indeterminate function. A set of workstations with large overhead computer monitors lined the far wall, and a prominent table in the center of the room featured a set of articulated robotic arms.

Darren whistled. "This... this is good stuff."

Grace inspected the diagnostic tools on the nearest table. "I think it's a robotics lab."

"Good for us. Lots of money in robot components."

Fear welled in Grace's core as she considered the possibilities. True, robotics were lucrative, but they carried a well-earned stigma. She'd heard about the infamous Corsica Event. Everyone had. Even here on Samrat, so far away from the affairs of Earth and most of a century later, people spoke of that devastating cataclysm with primal dread. A single hyperintelligent rogue AI had gained the ability to self-evolve beyond human intellect, and it nearly brought humanity to extinction. It had only happened once. If it had happened twice, nobody would have been left to talk about it.

Grace knew the odds of finding a Corsica-level threat on the *Kaifeck* were all but nonexistent. The Expansionary Coalition would be just as doomed as everyone else if a second Corsica Event occurred. Still, the knowledge that she was surrounded by secret government experiments in robotics set all Grace's nerves on red alert.

Grace picked up a large socket wrench from one of the workbenches and handed it to Darren. "We should sweep the rest of the ship and come back. Make sure we really are safe here before we do anything else."

They searched the vessel clockwise, from the starboard airlock to the aft section to the port corridor. Six more lab rooms, the entire habitation area, and the engine room yielded no signs of life. Each empty room brought a mixture of relief and mounting worry. The ship was clearly designed for a crew complement in the dozens, but it showed no trace of habitation. Not a dirty dish in the galley, not a tube of toothpaste in the head, not so much as an errant sock in the crew quarters.

"Look," Grace gestured at an empty rack beside the port airlock. "No suits. There weren't any at the other airlock either."

Darren nodded. "Guess that confirms they all left, then."

Grace frowned, staring at the empty rack that should hold dozens of empty space suits and helmets. "Where, though? They couldn't get anywhere on foot. There's nowhere to go. And if they did all leave, why didn't they lock the door? It makes no sense."

Darren opened his mouth to reply, then shut it again. "Yeah... no, I have no idea. This is weird."

"We should go, Darren. I'm starting to freak out."

"Let's sweep the rest of the ship first, okay? We'll do that, grab as much expensive-looking lab equipment we can carry, and leave."

Grace shook her head and sighed. "Fine. But we're pushing our luck here."

A cargo bay, several multipurpose rooms, and a server room offered no further answers as they circled to the ship's bridge. Five seats sat empty before illuminated control consoles, many displaying warning lights about the still-raging storm whirling outside the broad glass windscreen that made up most of the far wall. At the back of the bridge, nestled between the doorways to the port and starboard corridors, was a heavy blast door secured by a keypad lock.

"Here's something." Darren knelt in front of an open panel beneath one of the main consoles. It was an open cavity, a mess of disconnected cables sprawling from it like disemboweled viscera.

Grace inspected the gutted console. "What was this supposed to be?"

Darren inspected the flashing alerts on the screens above the panel. "From the looks of things, long-range communications."

"Okay. You know what? We're leaving. Right now." Grace turned and walked toward the starboard doorway.

"Grace, wait a minute!"

"Uh-uh. Nope. Big empty military ship experimenting with God-knows-what, whole crew missing, and someone ripped out the only way to call for help? No, sir. Not doing that."

"Grace, we can't afford to–"

She spun around, fixing Darren with a heavy glare. "Darren Stockley, get your Darwin-defying ass back in the car, or I swear to God—"

Suddenly, the blast door opened.

Inside stood a man, wearing a nondescript environment suit much like those worn by Grace and Darren, though without a helmet. His tanned face bore creases that suggested more years than the brown in his halfheartedly groomed hair and beard did. His gray eyes widened, matching the surprise on Grace and Darren's faces. His hands gripped the strap of the bulky satchel bag he carried over one shoulder, reflexively tightening. Darren raised his socket wrench defensively as Grace held her makeshift bomb at the ready.

"Who the hell are you?" Grace snapped.

The man raised his hands in a placating gesture. "Whoa, whoa, easy! Easy!"

"I said who are you!" Grace reiterated.

He took a step back. "Hey, easy! It's okay, I'm just a dunerunner."

"Name!" Darren said, brandishing the wrench.

"Wilkes! Dexter Wilkes. It's okay, I'm not a raider!"

Grace narrowed her eyes. "Who are you with?"

Though Wilkes continued to carry himself with a nervous energy, the tone of his voice shifted to an oddly amicable patter. "I was with the Bresset Caravan. Came up through the Grainshoals two months ago. Raiders hit us near Spirefall. Killed ten of us and took our haul, and the rest of us broke up after that. I'm alone now. Any chance you guys need a new runner?"

"Who do you know?" Grace said. "Who do you trade with?"

"Ahh. Well, the Straad expedition, mostly. Lorenzo Conti is their procurement officer, but some of the scientists will trade too. Tia Tamati buys small electronics, Angel Tibayan buys drilling equipment. New girl named Becky buys rocks sometimes. Outside the Straad, there's Zena Sheffield at the Hegemony weather station, Miles and Austen Damport are still panning the Spine for gems... do I need to keep going?"

Grace cast a glance at Darren. "I know Zena."

Darren nodded. "I know Lorenzo, Tia, and Angelo. Sounds like I should meet Becky. Rocks? Really?"

Wilkes shrugged. "Nice ones, anyway. Get her a piece of limestone with more than two colors and she'll make a little squealing noise. Geologists are a different breed."

Grace felt the tension in her muscles dissipate. "Yeah. So, Wilkes, how long have you been here? How'd you get in? We didn't see another vehicle outside."

"Stumbled onto it about a month ago. I'm a pretty good hacker, but it still took three days to crack the airlock. Been taking loads from here to a hidden cave up the ridge in my C60 Bactrian since then. I pulled it around under the port wing for shelter when I saw the storm coming."

"You've been clearing this ship out for a month, and all that lab equipment is still laying around?" Grace asked.

"Hey, you should have seen what was here before I started. I've been taking the stuff that should be easiest to sell first: toiletries, rations, that kind of thing. I know all that lab stuff is valuable, but I don't think my normal buyers can afford to trade for it." Wilkes gestured at the incendiary device Grace still clutched tightly. "Hey, we good yet? Claws back in, teeth un-bared? There's plenty of salvage to go around here; I see no reason we can't share peacefully."

Grace stared at him for a long moment, then put the bomb away in her satchel. "Yeah. I think we're cool enough. Still want to know more about what happened here, though. Where's the crew?"

"Ah... well." Wilkes gestured out the window. "About a hundred yards that way. Thirty-one of them. Couple feet under."

"They're dead?" Darren asked.

"Yeah. Couldn't tell you what happened. I found them when I came in. Lying on the floor in the hallway, sitting at workstations, lying in bunks. Found one in the shower with the water still running. Whatever got them, it gave no warning and left no signs. They all just... dropped. I couldn't strip the ship down with them all still lying there, I just... couldn't do that. I spent my first two days dragging them outside and burying them one at a time. Felt like the right thing to do."

Grace nodded toward the gutted communications panel. "What's the story there?"

"Ah. Well, that was actually the first thing I did when I got here. I figured I must have stumbled onto this ship just after whatever happened happened, and sooner or later the Coalition would come looking for it. I wanted to make sure they couldn't find it, and I know ships like this have emergency transponders, but I wasn't sure how to turn it off, so I just gutted the whole comm system. Not very elegant, but it worked."

"Makes sense." Darren stepped forward, extending his hand. "Darren Stockley, by the way. Nice to meet you, Wilkes."

Wilkes eagerly took his hand, shaking it firmly. "Always nice meeting a new group of Dunerunners."

Wilkes extended his hand to Grace. She took it, shaking it with slightly awkward hesitance. "Grace Mkembe."

"Grace and Darren. Awesome!" Wilkes gave a bright smile. "Where are you two based, if you don't mind my asking?"

"Redcrest," Darren answered. "Got a small settlement out there.

Not much to look at, but we're pretty self-sufficient. It's a good little community."

"Hope to visit sometime. Hey, what say we go around the ship together, sort out claims and such? I've already hauled a lot out, so I don't mind giving you guys first pick, if there's anything you've got your eye on. I'll help you load it up if you like."

"That's very generous of you," Grace said.

"No problem, no problem," said Wilkes. "Seems we're neighbors, so we might as well be neighborly. Oh, by the way." Wilkes pointed at his unhelmeted head. "Air's fine, if you want to save consumables. Whatever killed the crew, it wasn't airborne. Refilling stations by the airlocks are safe too—I've used them several times."

Grace removed her helmet, shaking the messy black curls from her face. "Good call. Let's get our packs on the charger and get started."

"Hey, check this out," Wilkes said, walking over to one of the consoles. "I've got the ship's internal comm set up to play music. You guys like Prismageddon?"

Grace quirked an eyebrow. "Like what, now?"

Darren only shrugged.

"Oh. Oh, you poor deprived souls. We're fixing that right now. Brace yourselves for the absolute greatest in new-wave chromacore. I am about to change your lives forever."

☆ ☆ ☆

Prismageddon was hardly the musical epiphany Wilkes had promised, but Grace found it refreshing to listen to something different from the long-stale media selection shared by the Redcrest community. The aggressive vocals and semi-psychedelic instrumentals that filled the *Kaifeck*'s empty halls inspired a swift pace to their work.

As Grace and Darren's suits replenished their oxygen supply, Wilkes helped them sort and carry their share of salvage, filling various containers and stacking them by the airlock. Wilkes' amiable personality and surprising helpfulness made short work of the task, and it wasn't more than two hours before they had gathered enough research equipment, electronics, and tools to easily fill the SandPhantom's cargo compartment to capacity.

By the time they were done, the sandstorm had died down to a brisk breeze. Though they had less than an hour before Mahatma set, Grace didn't feel comfortable spending the night in a ship whose entire crew had died for no clear reason, despite Wilkes's assurances.

"You sure you want to go back out tonight?" Wilkes asked, fastening the connectors on his suit. "I don't think the storm's gonna pick up again, but you can never be sure."

Grace slid her helmet on, locking the seal. "Yeah. It'll be a long ride to Redcrest, but we've got people waiting for us. We'll come back in a couple days with a second car."

"Well, you guys take your time. You two and anyone else from your compound are welcome here any time, far as I'm concerned."

The outer airlock opened, and they stepped out, carrying their crates toward the sand-covered rover. Grace set hers down and opened the cargo door. "Thanks again for the help, Wilkes. This was cool of you."

Wilkes flashed a bright smile as he shoved the crates into the rover. "Happy to help. Like I said, plenty to go around."

"Seriously, thank you," Darren said. "We've had some hard times lately. I'm glad I don't have to worry about my son going hunny... err, hungry."

Darren's ankle buckled, and he stumbled, dropping his boxes in the sand. Grace dropped to a knee to help him up. "Darren, are you alight? Are you right? I mean..." The sand whirled in Grace's vision, but it wasn't a sandstorm this time. The ground had gone strangely bendy, as had her legs.

Wilkes stood above her, and even though his face twisted high into the sky, she could see his expression was weirdly serious. "Wish I'd known about your kid, Darren," he said. "Too late now, I'm afraid."

"Wassu mean too late?" Darren slurred. He tried sitting up, but immediately fell over.

Grace struggled to keep Wilkes in focus, her eyes narrowing with suspicion even as she fought to keep them pointed straight. "Wass this? You did something. Whadju do to us?"

Wilkes stood still as his body warped and contorted in Grace's vision. "It's weird how you guys always assume that just because the ship's air is safe, the exosuit refill station is too. You know those are separate systems, right?"

"You poisn'd us," Grace pulled herself onto legs as stable as those of a newborn deer. "You bassard! We trussed you!"

"Not poison," Wilkes said calmly. "It won't be this that kills you. Probably should sit down before you lose consciousness, though."

Grace's vision whorled and contorted, amorphous black shapes seeping into her sight. As Wilkes' form liquefied in front of her, Grace took one staggering step forward, swinging wildly at the man. Her punch missed him entirely, and she tumbled face first into the sand.

The black blobs swelled to fill the gaps in her twisted reality, and she felt herself slipping away. "Youbassard..." she mumbled.

Wilkes kneeled close to her, his face nearly reforming in the black flood around her. "Thank you for being such good company, Grace. I enjoyed our time together very much. I really do wish there was another way to do this."

Grace tried to respond, but her voice melted and slipped into the void, along with the rest of the world.

☆ ☆ ☆

Pain was the first of Grace's senses to return, consciousness settling piece by piece into her throbbing head. As the rest of her tortured nervous system reactivated, a needling numbness perforated her shoulders and biceps, culminating in a chafing around each wrist.

Grace's eyelids parted, her retinas instantly pierced by an array of overhead lights that, despite their unforgiving assault on her dilated pupils, barely illuminated the room. The space was octagonal, built like a small arena, with an elevated observation area behind an eight-foot wall. Large crates filled the balcony and had started filling the floor near

Grace, each heaped with piles of bulky, multilayered pressure fabric and polycarbonate helmet shells: dozens upon dozens of empty exosuits.

Grace could only see half the room, bound as she was in a crucifixion pose to an articulated metal T-frame. Heavy nylon straps around her wrists, chest, hips, and legs rendered her fully immobile. She had been stripped to her underwear, the straps pressed hard against her dark skin.

"Darren?" The rasping call hurt her throat as it came up, and the sound of her own weak voice set her head aching again.

"He's asleep right now. Best to let him rest. He's been through a lot today."

The voice wasn't Darren's, and Grace's addled mind struggled to place it. The best she could do in her current state was locate it: somewhere behind her, in the part of the room that her restraints kept her from seeing.

"Where am I?" Grace asked.

"Still on the *Kaifeck*," the voice behind her said, in an even, casual tone. "The lower deck. You wouldn't have been able to access this room before; it has higher security clearance than the rest of the ship."

Wheels rolled across the metal floor, and a moment later the man slid into view on a rolling chair to Grace's left. Her eyes focused slowly on his face, but its features quickly triggered recognition in her rousing mind. "Wilkes."

He gave an oddly sad smile. "Hello, Grace. How are you feeling?"

"I'd feel a lot better with my hands around your throat."

"Understandable."

Grace's mind cleared as anger sharpened her senses. "Where is Darren?"

Wilkes nodded toward a point over her shoulder. "About ten feet behind you."

Grace strained to look, the tendons in her neck aching as she struggled to see beyond the apparatus she was strapped to. She could barely make out part of what looked like the back of a similar frame on the opposite side of the room, with a faint hint of a limp human hand hanging past its edge.

"Darren! Darren!" she called.

"You're not going to wake him. He's out cold. It's the best thing for him right now."

"What the hell did you do to him?"

"It's best you don't know that yet."

Grace gave her restraints an angry jerk. They didn't budge. "Wilkes, I swear to God when I get free I'm going to cave your face in."

Wilkes's expression was infuriatingly patient. "Can we skip this part this time, please? It never goes anywhere, and you're just going to get yourself more upset than you need to be."

Grace fixed him with a hateful glare. "Go to hell."

"Tell me about your life, Grace."

She blinked. It was such a non sequitur, she wasn't sure how to be angry at it. "What?"

Wilkes leaned forward in the chair, resting his elbows on his knees. "I'd like to hear about your life. Get to know you as a person. The real Grace Mkembe."

"Why? So you can use the details to fool the next dunerunner that you're one of us?"

Wilkes cracked a smile. "That does help. You're definitely a clever one."

"And you're definitely a psychopath." She nodded at the crates filled with empty suits. "How many innocent folks you lure here with that 'helpful neighbor' act?"

"More than I'd hoped would be needed," he sighed. "But not quite enough."

"What's your real game, Wilkes? Human trafficking? Some sick serial killer thing?"

Wilkes gave an offended look. "God no. Nothing like that."

"You got a look right now says you think that's beneath you, but from where I'm hanging," She jerked against her bonds for emphasis, "You're on that level."

He smiled a thin, defensive smile. "This isn't for money, and it certainly isn't for some kind of sick pleasure. This is for a purpose. A vital one."

"I didn't sign up for no cause."

"I wish taking volunteers was an option."

A realization struck Grace. "You killed the crew, didn't you? You didn't find them dead, you made them dead."

"You're not wrong."

"The Coalition wouldn't let a random guy in the desert board this ship and turn their backs on him. You were one of them, weren't you? You were part of the crew."

Wilkes's smile broadened. "You really are clever. Yes, I was."

Grace shook her head in disgust. "There's a real special corner of Hell set aside for people who backstab their own crew like that."

Wilkes stood, pacing the floor with a feigned nonchalance that did little to hide his sudden agitation. "Please. Don't shed a tear for them, they aren't worth it. They weren't good people. They were working with GrayPhage, for God's sake."

Grace knit her eyebrows. "The hell is GrayPhage?"

"You're lucky you don't know. And you're lucky you've never seen it used. It's a weapon, an incredibly dangerous, incredibly illegal weapon. It's been banned by an international treaty, which the Expansionary Coalition signed with their fingers crossed. That's why they're developing it here, in the ass-end of nowhere, off the books with zero oversight."

Wilkes's eye wandered toward something over Grace's shoulder, his expression becoming grave and distant. "GrayPhage is weaponized nanotechnology, a networked swarm of microscopic robots that work together as a single entity. They can be programmed to break down practically any kind of matter on a molecular level. Set a GrayPhage swarm on a target, and they'll reduce it to a brown puddle in minutes. GrayPhage doesn't just kill you; it unmakes you. It's one of the most monstrous weapons humankind has conceived. I did the universe a favor by killing these people."

Grace gave the most broadly sarcastic shrug her restraints would allow. "I wish I could applaud."

Wilkes gave her a sad look. "I'm not any better, I know. You'd only hate me more if you knew everything I'd done. I only hope that, one day, someone looks at the fruits of my labor and understands why the tree had to be watered with blood."

Grace's brows lowered, her eyes narrowing to hateful slits. "Only thing you'll be remembered for is how much you cried before I killed you."

Wilkes met her glare, his expression shifting to one of cold resolve. "I think that's about enough for now." He reached into his pocket, drawing a syringe and a small vial. "I don't blame you for hating me. It's natural, given the circumstances. I do hope our next conversation can be a bit more civil. I sincerely would like to hear more about your life before our time is up. I would like to be able to honor your memory when it's all over."

"I'll honor your memory by tying your body to the back of my car and dragging you across the desert until the sand polishes your bones," Grace snarled.

Wilkes drew the vial's contents into the needle. "Vivid. When you wake up, we'll try this again. If you show restraint, I'll let you stay awake. For now, it's time for me to get back to Darren. It's sensitive work, and I can't really afford the distraction."

Grace thrashed in her bonds, resisting his touch as he approached with the needle. But her restraints didn't allow her to evade the jab, and soon her enraged flailing dwindled to a feeble slump as unconsciousness once again seized her.

☆ ☆ ☆

Grace awoke to the sounds of music and sobbing. Wilkes's music played on the overhead system again, and somewhere behind her, Grace heard him humming along. Prismageddon's rowdy psychedelic tones did little to drown out the steady sound of Darren's whimpering.

"Please..." he sobbed. "Please stop. It hurts..."

"Come on, Darren," Wilkes said, with appalling nonchalance. "This really isn't as bad as it could be."

"It hurts! God, it hurts!"

"Did you know the skin on your back is less sensitive than anywhere on your body? Check this out: how many fingers do you think this is?"

Darren sniffled. "I don't know..."

"It was two. But it wouldn't have felt any different if I used one or three; all your brain can really detect is pressure. Look, I know this hurts, and I'm sorry. I'm trying to minimize that as much as I can. Just... try to keep it in perspective. If this was your face it would hurt like hell, but back here? You can handle this. You're a tough guy."

"P-please... please let me go. Just let me go..."

"I'm not letting you go, Darren."

"Please stop... please let me go..."

"I'm not going to stop and I'm not going to let you go. The sooner you accept that, the less scary this whole thing will be for you. You're making it worse on yourself."

Grace tried once again to see the inaccessible space behind the frame she was bound to, straining until her shoulder popped. She still only saw a glimpse of one of Darren's hands, now clenched in a trembling fist behind his frame. She could see a hint of something else now: Wilkes sat in his rolling chair between her and Darren, facing him and leaning forward, intently focused on his task. A small silver cart next to him carried an assortment of forceps, scalpels, and scissors. Most were tipped with fresh blood.

Something else lay between Grace and Darren that she had overlooked before. At the exact center of the room sat something that looked like a cauldron, a meter across and about as high. Segmented hoses crawled across the floor, pumping frosty coolant into the cauldron as its contents bubbled. The liquid inside was a mixture of fetid brownish fluid and a strange, mercury-like substance, which swirled together with a will of their own, as if stirred by an invisible ladle.

GrayPhage.

"Where's Grace?" Darren whimpered. "I want to see Grace."

"Grace is still right behind us, like I told you before," Wilkes said calmly. "She woke up for a bit after our last session, but I had to put her under so I could start working on you again. It's for the best. She would be distracting me right now, and that would have made this process a lot more painful for you."

"Please... please just let us go..."

"You're repeating yourself, Darren. You're just going to get worked up again. Try thinking of something nice instead. Are you ready to tell me about your wife and son now?"

A new soreness in Grace's forearm brought her attention back to herself, and she noticed she now had an IV in her arm. A thin plastic tube ran from just below her wrist to a bag hanging from a wheeled stand a couple feet away. The saline bag was nearly empty.

Just how long have I been here that he's got to worry about dehydration? And how long was I asleep, for that bag to be almost empty already? The dark room had no windows, nothing whatsoever to note the passing time. It could have been hours... it could have been days.

Darren cried out. "It hurts! Oh, God! It hurts!"

"Yeah, that one would," Wilkes conceded. "Sorry about that."

"Can't you do something about the pain?"

"I truly wish I could. Unfortunately, for this to work, I need you conscious and your nerves operating at full capacity. Anesthetic would affect the results."

Grace strained again to get a look, just in time to see Wilkes casually toss a slice of red flesh over his shoulder. It landed with a viscous plop in the GrayPhage cauldron, where it sizzled on top of the sludgy vat for a few seconds before dissolving.

"Darren!" Grace cried, tears spilling down her cheeks.

"Grace?" Darren whimpered.

"Well," Wilkes sighed. "Guess that's as good a time to pause as any."

"Get away from him, get away!" Grace screamed. "Get away from him, you bastard!"

"Grace," Wilkes said patiently. "I told you, if you keep going on like this, I'm just going to have to keep putting you under until I'm done with him."

"I'll kill you! I'll kill you!" Grace thrashed at her bonds. "I swear to God, I'll kill you!"

Wilkes slid into view on his rolling chair, giving her a grotesquely understated look of disapproval. "Let's try this again one more time."

She fought harder than ever to break free, but as the needle spilled its contents into her IV line, it once again amounted to nothing.

☆ ☆ ☆

The third time Grace woke, she wasn't immediately certain she had. The room was pitch black. There was no music this time, no sound at all save for the hum of the cauldron's coolant system and the hideous burbling of its omnivorous contents.

"Darren?" Grace whispered. "Are you there?"

"Grace..." the response was weak. "I'm so sorry..."

"The hell are you apologizing for, Stockley? You're not the one abducting folks in the desert."

"It's my fault we're here..." he said. "You wanted to leave... you wanted to play it safe."

"Yeah... well... remember that for later. Next time you wanna go right and I wanna go left, I'm gonna say 'Stockley, remember the creep in the desert with the bad music and the bondage kink?' and you're gonna say 'oh yeah, that's what happens when I don't listen to you, let's go left.'"

"I'm... so sorry." His sobs came harder.

"Hey... we're getting out of here, man. You gotta make it through this so Alessia can kill you when we get home. Remember, you lost her ride?"

"Grace... he..." Darren's voice caught in his throat. "He did something to me..."

"What did he do?"

"He's... he... did something to my back. I couldn't see, but... oh God, he was doing it for hours."

Grace's blood chilled as she remembered the piece of meat Wilkes had thrown into the cauldron. "Does it hurt?" She immediately felt foolish for asking the question.

"It was... torture, at first. When he started, I screamed until I passed out. He stopped when I fainted, said I have to be awake for the entire process. He just... kept going... cutting on me for hours, and every time I blacked out he'd stop and pick it up again when I woke up. It... doesn't hurt much now, but I'm scared that it doesn't. He's got all these tubes in me, I don't even know what they're for, but he never gave me anything for the pain. Grace, I... I can't feel my legs anymore."

Tears streamed freely down her face. "Oh, Darren..."

"He's asleep now, I think. I thought he'd never rest, but... he said I'm done with 'phase one.' I... I don't want to know what phase two is, Grace. I'd rather die than find out."

She took a deep, shaky breath. "We're not going to find out. We'll be gone before he wakes up."

"Grace, I can't even walk..."

"I'll carry you. We just gotta get to the car. Let's work the problem, Darren. What have you learned about him that might help?"

"He did talk a lot... I think he's been alone for a while; he's starved for conversation. He's... I think he said he's a neurocyberneticist. Some kind of brain surgeon who works with cybernetics. I think he's implanting me with something..."

"What else? What else do you know about him?"

"Umm... he... he started with the crew. Whatever he's doing to me... he started with them. He gassed the whole ship and kept them in comas until he was ready for them. Some died in their sleep, the rest he used for his project. But they weren't enough... he started using dunerunners. He's 'perfecting' something, some experiment that needs live people. He keeps saying he doesn't want to hurt anyone, but it's the only way to do what he wants to do. Says it's a necessary sacrifice."

"Yeah. He said something like that to me too. Lots of high and mighty crap. He's a serial killer who thinks he's a saint."

"I think he might be an Algorithmist."

Grace frowned. "A what?"

"Some crazy cult that worships AIs. I've heard people talk about them. They're all insane; they want to create a super AI like the one that almost destroyed Earth. They think humanity's purpose is to create some kind of machine god. The way Wilkes worked his way onto the *Kaifeck*'s crew sounds like how they operate, and they were studying robotics here."

Grace nodded. "GrayPhage... he talked about that. An AI weapon that eats whatever it's programmed to. There's a cauldron in this room."

Grace shifted her attention to her surroundings. Her eyes were now somewhat adjusted to the pitch blackness, though she couldn't see much past her immediate surroundings. She turned her attention to the straps holding her down. They chafed worse than ever; untold hours of hanging motionless had left her with angry sores and bruises under each strap. She pulled with all her dwindling strength against them but succeeded only in sending a jolt of stabbing pain through her arm as her movements jostled the intravenous needle.

As she flinched, she noticed the saline bag on the IV pole shake slightly from her movement. The thin tube connecting the cannula in her arm to the bag was taut, wrapped in a few loops around a hook on the pole to reduce slack in the line. Grace tested her bonds again, but instead of trying to pull her body forward, she slid her arm back and forth through its straps. Her movement was still limited, but less so, and she watched the IV line sway like a hammock in the breeze.

Grace rotated her arm in its socket, wincing as the cannula tugged at her skin. The slight movement pulled the IV line taut, closing the loop on the hook. As she rotated her arm back again, the line went slack. Sliding her arm back and forth through her straps again, the line swayed farther with her movements, swinging more noticeably. The farthest arc of its swing brought it nearly even with her wrist. It wasn't far enough. She needed more slack.

She experimented, utilizing the entirety of her arm's finite range of motion, trying to increase the distance of her IV line's swing. The skin around the cannula was on fire, agitated by every torturous tug of the needle under her skin. An ugly bruise formed, and blood trickled past her elbow toward her armpit, but she kept going.

She rotated her arm to its limit, feeling her shoulder crack as she turned it almost all the way backwards. The IV line pulled so tight the entire pole started to move toward her. She felt an alarming slipping sensation in her bruised skin—the cannula was pulling free. Reacting just quickly enough to catch it just before the needle's tip left her vein, Grace pinned the cannula between her arm and the T-frame, pressing down on it for dear life.

Grace screamed between clenched teeth and tight lips as the needle stabbed deep into muscle. She whimpered, breathing quickly through her nose as she forced the needle deep into her flesh, then shifted her body away from the IV pole. Its wheels rolled two inches toward her, towed along by its fleshy anchor.

Tears streaming down her cheeks, Grace shifted her body back again, watching the IV line hang a couple inches lower, and slid her arm back and forth again. The line swung wider and higher with each movement until finally it swung far enough forward for Grace to catch it on her little finger. She closed her fist tight with the IV line in her grasp.

"You okay, Grace?" Darren asked.

"Yeah... yeah. I'm onto something. Give me a couple minutes."

She wound her finger around the line, drawing the pole closer to her and giving her more slack, then worked her hand around it to slowly pull the needle back out of her skin. The cannula came free, the tape holding it in place tore from her skin, and the needle dangled freely, dripping blood and saline on the floor.

She reeled it in with her fingers, finally grasping the precious needle between her thumb and forefinger. She flexed her wrist, and slowly, delicately, scraped the needle's tip across the nylon band around her wrist.

The angle of her wrist only allowed the lightest of scratches with each pass. She had to stop regularly, as she felt her thumb and wrist begin to cramp up, threatening to make her lose her grip on her only tool of rescue. But with slow, steady determination, Grace spent hours wearing away at her restraint.

At last, Grace felt something tear when she pushed against the frayed strap. Flexing with all her might, she finally broke free, feeling her aching arm fly against the IV pole, toppling it over. Weeping tears of joy, she fumbled open the fasteners on the straps around her torso, then her other arm, then her legs. With her arms free, the rest of her bonds gave way quickly, and she finally slipped free from the T-frame and collapsed to her knees.

Her body screamed with a thousand pains. Bruises, sores, and cramps riddled every muscle, and she felt dizzy with vertigo and trauma, but still she laughed. She'd done it. She was free.

"Darren!" she whispered. "I did it! I'm out!"

Grace crawled toward him in the dark, her hand finding the cold wall of the GrayPhage cauldron. She listened to its ominous bubbling and churning as she crawled past it, feeling her way onward.

Finally, she found the T-frame holding Darren and braced herself against it as she stood. She felt along the frame until she found his hand, grasping it tightly.

"Darren. Darren, I'm here," she whispered near where his ear must be.

She felt him stir, his fingers tightening against hers as he woke. "Grace?" he asked weakly.

She smiled. "I'm here, Darren. I got free. I'm going to undo your straps. Can you hold yourself up?"

"I... I don't know. Maybe? I'll try..."

"Just a little longer. We're almost out of this." She quickly managed the strap around his wrist, and he moved his arm to brace against the T-frame as she went in search of his other bonds.

Grace's knuckles banged against a part of the frame that was not where she expected it to be. It seemed his frame was not quite like hers; where her back had been held against a single beam, Darren was suspended between two. She probed the area blindly, searching for the strap that must be holding his torso in place.

Her fingers brushed an oddly slimy tube protruding behind Darren's back. She recoiled reflexively, then touched it again as morbid curiosity blended with dread. It was soft, whatever it was. Pliant. Slippery. Warm.

And it had a pulse.

Grace traced the viscous appendage toward her friend. It went past the frame he hung from. It went past where his back should have started. Her fingers didn't stop until the umbilicus splayed out into a soft, sticky wall ridged with hard protrusions.

"Grace? Is everything okay?" Darren asked.

The moist surface vibrated with the sound of his voice.

Grace pulled her hand back, eyes wide in shock. "Oh, Darren... what did he do to you?"

A loud noise from above made Grace's heart stop. Prismageddon's chaotic tones had returned to the overhead speakers.

"He's coming," Darren said. "Grace, hurry!"

Grace's mind raced, trying to imagine the minimum amount of time it would take Wilkes to get from the bridge to the elevator, and realizing it amounted to seconds. Perhaps she could free Darren before he arrived, but what then? They couldn't exit the ship without passing Wilkes. She could probably have beaten Wilkes in an even fight, but not after hanging on a rack for days, and certainly not with a crippled Darren on her back...

Grace cursed, bit her lip, and wrapped the strap back around Darren's wrist.

"Grace, what are you doing?" Darren asked, panic seeping into his voice.

"Listen. He's coming back. I can't fight him head-on. I need to get the drop on him when his back is turned." She buckled the restraint, keeping it looser than before, but hopefully not loose enough for Wilkes to notice the difference. Stumbling past the GrayPhage cauldron, Grace rushed to her T-frame, righting the fallen IV pole and fastening the straps around her legs as quickly as her fumbling hands could manage in the dark.

"Don't leave me like this, Grace!" Darren pleaded. "Don't let him touch me again!"

"Listen!" Grace hissed. "You need to distract him! Keep him from looking at me! We can't escape until Wilkes is out of commission. We have to work together on this, or we're both going to die. I promise you, Darren, I'm not going to abandon you."

"I can't," he sobbed. "Grace, I can't..."

"Hold it together, Darren. Think of Alessia. Think of Jake." She fastened her chest strap and started on her wrist. The lights in the room came on, forcing her eyes shut.

Darren sniffled. "...okay... okay, Grace... I'll try."

An elevator door slid open, and with one final burst of movement, she seized the dangling IV tube and pressed her free hand against the destroyed remains of the strap she had cut. There was nothing she could do about that one; if Wilkes got a good look at it, she was done for. The lightest inspection would reveal she was no longer secured. She could only hope he would be too focused on Darren to concern himself with her.

She hung limp and still in the frame, trying to look sedated, as she heard Wilkes's accursed chair roll into the room.

"Good morning, Darren," he said, his tone still repulsively casual.

"Please... don't do this..."

"Are we going to have *that* conversation again?" Grace held her breath as Wilkes stood from his chair and began to walk around the room.

"N-no... no," Darren said, his voice calming slightly. "No, I... I want to talk about something."

Wilkes's footsteps stopped. *Good, get his attention*, Grace thought.

"Oh? What did you want to talk about?"

"I have a question..."

Wilkes returned to his chair, pulling it toward Darren. "Ask away."

"You're... you're an Algorithmist, aren't you?"

It took several seconds for Wilkes to answer. "That's a complicated question."

Good. Complicated is good. Grace slowly lowered her free hand, praying Wilkes' back was turned, and let the IV tube dangle as she reached for the strap on her other hand.

"I ran with the Algorithmists for a while. They helped me get this posting. I guess I still agree with some of their ideals, and to you there probably wouldn't be much difference. But they wouldn't call me one of their own anymore, and I tend to think they're on the wrong track."

Grace pulled her wrist free, careful not to let the fastener clack against the metal of the T-frame, and started again on her torso straps.

"Do I believe in some kind of technological apotheosis? Some 'Deus Machina' humanity is destined to bring into existence to remake the world? No. Do I believe an AI with superhuman intelligence could solve many of humanity's problems? Certainly. We're only here on this planet because an AI just like that made faster-than-light travel possible. Imagine what else it could do with half the chance."

"But the Corsica Event..." Darren said. "It almost wiped us out."

"And that," Wilkes said proudly, "is where I don't agree with Algorithmists. Most of them want nothing more than to recreate the Corsica Event. They study its relics, read its code, try to replicate what happened before. They're all missing the point. The Corsica AI wasn't trying to emulate something that came before, it was trying to grow, to learn, to improve itself. And it was messy. Costly. Deadly. It flailed around blindly as it grew, oblivious to the chaos it caused."

Grace knelt slowly to the floor, trembling fingers undoing her last straps.

"We need something more controlled. Something new. Or rather, a new application of something we already have. When I told Grace about the GrayPhage, I called it the most monstrous weapon humanity ever devised. And it is. It's a horrific weapon. But it doesn't have to be. Millions of microscopic machines all thinking and working together like cells of a living organism can do so much more than mindlessly destroy targets. But they have to be programmed. They have to be trained."

With one final delicate tug, Grace freed herself of her final strap. Cautiously, she removed the IV bag from its hook and set it on the floor. She hoisted the stand, grasping it in a firm, two-handed grip, and slowly turned toward Wilkes.

She immediately wished she hadn't.

Wilkes sat in his chair, stooped over Darren's back. With the lights at full brightness and nothing obstructing her view, she could now see in full detail what had become of Darren. The skin of his back was splayed open from pelvis to shoulder blades, pulled away from his body and pinned to the sides of the rack with hooks and wire. The space the skin should have covered was an excavation of flesh; every major muscle had been excised, leaving a clear view of the organs in Darren's core. The only thing keeping them from spilling through the cavernous opening was a clear plastic barrier vacuum sealed to the sides of the cavity with medical adhesive, a cheap patch job not meant to last. A mess of tubes snaked down from the ceiling, plugging into various catheter ports across his body, injecting him with a steady flow of whatever kept his mutilated body alive.

But the worst was his spine. His entire vertebral column was exposed. It had been severed completely at the pelvis and now extended from the ruined torso like a segmented serpent of glistening bone. Long, ropy mercurial tendrils slithered up his spine, seeping into the cartilage between each vertebra and up through the severed stump, connecting the vivisected man's body to the churning pool of GrayPhage through a pulsing pseudopod of interconnected nanites.

"The first step to creating a superhuman AI," Wilkes continued, "is creating a human AI. Once we teach an AI to think abstractly on a human level, its superior data processing and storage ability will take care of the rest. GrayPhage is the key. I've programmed them to behave like human neurons; instead of mindlessly devouring a target, I'm teaching them to imitate the cells they consume. When these nanites destroy a nerve cell, they replace it, and they communicate with each other just like our neurons do. They start with the spinal cord, then work their way to the brain stem, the cerebellum, and eventually the whole brain. Every time they do this, they learn. They're mapping the human nervous system, mimicking its structure. Soon, they'll be able to imitate it perfectly: a gestalt intelligence, a perfect simulation of human consciousness. It can already understand emotions no AI has ever experienced. For now it only understands pain and fear, but by the time I'm finished, it will be able to relate to the entire spectrum of human emotion."

Grace crept slowly toward Wilkes, knuckles whitening as she clutched the IV pole with determined fury. She could see Darren's lungs heaving through the hole in his back as he sobbed.

"You're killing me..." he cried. "You're feeding me to them alive..."

"Yes. I really am sorry, Darren. I don't enjoy doing this. I know this isn't how you wanted your life to end up. I wish it was possible to rely on volunteers for this, but no one with a stable mind would ever do that, and training them on unstable minds would be a disaster. Your sacrifice will help so many people, Darren. You're contributing to the next quantum leap in technology. When it's finished, this AI will change the universe! And it's almost done. After you and Grace, I'll only need a few more subjects to complete the neural mapping. But I promise, I'm not going to subject your wife or son to this unless I absolutely have no choice. I'm not a mons—"

The weighted wheels on the IV pole connected with Wilkes' skull with a resounding crack, knocking him from his chair and sending him sprawling to the floor. Grace brought it down again, striking him in the gut with a vicious two-handed blow. Her third swing was too slow;

Wilkes caught it with one hand and jerked it to the side, pulling her off her unstable feet and sending her to the ground near his feet.

"Damn it, Grace!" he said, blood pooling between his teeth. "None of this has to hurt! The more you fight it, the more pain you cause yourself. Just give it up already!" His boot connected hard with her cheek.

She tried to crawl away, but his hand seized her by the ankle. He wasn't a strong man, but he'd eaten food and slept in a bed while Grace had withered on a rack. His grip was inescapable.

"Die today," Wilkes said. "Die tomorrow. What's the difference? You're scavengers living off scraps in the desert. You're sons and daughters of failures, running out the clock on a world that wants you dead."

Grace clawed at the floor, desperately seeking anything she might use to fight back or pull herself from Wilkes' grip. But the IV pole had tumbled out of her reach, and Wilkes's kicks sent her senses into a whirl.

"This whole damn planet was a mistake," Wilkes said, landing a powerful blow to her ribs. "A generation from now, maybe two, none of you will be left. No dunerunners, no raiders. You'll pick each other off, and the last one standing wins the honor of suffocating when the life support goes out. What are you fighting for? This planet has no value to anyone but scientists. People like me, doing work that *matters*."

Grace finally felt her fingers wrap around a ribbed hose. She yanked at it, feeling it pop from its socket in the GrayPhage cauldron. She thrust the severed tube at Wilkes as frigid coolant billowed directly into his face.

He cried out in pain and alarm, releasing her and scuttling away from the icy spray. She pulled herself to her feet, putting the cauldron between her and Wilkes.

Wilkes stood, coughing and sputtering and cursing under his breath. His bloodshot eyes streamed tears, the skin on his face was ruddy and frost-bitten. He spat a mouthful of blood on the floor and drew another hypodermic needle and the vial of anesthetic from his pocket.

"Never did get the hang of measuring anesthetics. Not gonna take any chances this time." He staggered to the GrayPhage cauldron, leaning against its rim as he filled the syringe to capacity and tossed the emptied vial to the floor. "You have an awful lot of fight in you. Really hope this dose doesn't kill you. I have a feeling you'll stay alive on that rack for a real long time."

Then, Darren struck.

Two hands seized Wilkes's shoulders from behind as Darren contorted his upper body around his rack in a way he never could have with an intact spine. The strap Grace had loosened had offered him just enough freedom to remove the bonds from his upper body as Grace and Wilkes fought, and he now used every bit of his strength, weight, and determination to grapple with his captor.

Wilkes's attention had been fully on Grace. He had disregarded Darren as a threat, so even in Darren's weakened and mutilated state, the element of surprise was enough. Wilkes's supporting elbow slipped under Darren's unexpected weight, plunging his arm up to the shoulder into the roiling, bubbling, silver and brown mass of liquid GrayPhage.

Wilkes screamed as millions of nanites sank their microscopic robotic teeth into his skin. He flailed and struggled to pull himself free, but the ravenous pool refused to release him. Grace seized the IV pole from the floor, hefting it triumphantly in her grip.

Wilkes's eyes filled with terror as he watched her over his captive shoulder. "No! God, please, no!"

Grace gave a satisfied sneer. "This is that cryin' part I told you about." She thrust the pole wheels-first into the back of Wilkes's head, and his face plunged into the cauldron's insatiable contents.

Wilkes had trained the GrayPhage well. It had learned much from the dozens of scientists and dunerunners he had fed it over the past few months. It knew exactly where to find all the densest neural matter in the soft skin of the human face. The optic nerve was a favorite treat, so rich and sophisticated, but the sensitive olfactory nerve was not to be missed, and the exquisite chorda tympani of the tongue was no less delectable. Indeed, the nanites had learned well the fine cuisine of neurophagy. It was really all they had learned from Wilkes's experiments, other than three unpleasant emotions they had unwillingly assimilated from their victims' minds: fear, pain, and hatred.

Hatred for Wilkes.

He thrashed and struggled against the viscous attacker, using his one free arm to push against the cauldron in a vain attempt to extricate himself. For a brief moment, he pulled his head away from the churning semi-fluid, a gurgling, choking wail of agony fleeing his lips before the silvery tendrils worming down his throat stifled them. Ropy strands of GrayPhage adhered to his eyes, nose, ears, and across his face, overpowering him and dragging him once again beneath the surface. His free arm quickly followed, then his chest, and it wasn't long before his twitching legs slipped into the gluttonous pool.

Grace didn't watch the show in its entirety. Once Wilkes's fate was sealed, she hurried to Darren's side. His condition was grim; the act of contorting his body to grapple with Wilkes had dislodged several tubes from his life support system, and the unnatural position of his body had crushed several of his organs. Blood seeped from his mouth and the hole in his back, and his breath came in ragged, shallow wheezes. Grace wrapped her arms around him, propping him back up into a more natural position on the harness, but she knew the damage was done.

"Grace..." he panted. "I... I know. I know... there's no going home for me."

She wanted to deny it. She wanted to reassure him that he would be okay, that he would see his wife and son tonight. It would be such a nice, comforting lie. "I'm sorry, Darren. I'm so sorry. This isn't fair."

He shook his head weakly. "Not fair. No. But here we are."

Grace sniffled. "You're hurting."

"Not... for much longer..."

"I think... I think I saw where he dropped his syringe. Do you want it?"

He shook his head again, coughing up a splatter of blood. "Get... the bomb..."

Grace's eyes widened. "Darren, no! It's a firebomb... burning is... it's a bad death..."

"Grace..." He nodded toward the cauldron. "We have... to kill that stuff. Can't let... someone else... finish what he started. Fire should do it. The coolant's all that's... keeping it stable..."

She looked at him, watched the pain and sadness in his eyes, then nodded grimly. She went to the bin holding their equipment, dug through it, and took the improvised explosive from her satchel. She returned to him, placing it gently in his hands.

"The oxygen candle first. The longer you leave it going, the bigger the fireball will be," she instructed. "When you're... ready... set off the flare. Throw it right into the cauldron if you can, it'll keep burning in there."

He pulled the tab on the oxygen candle. A jet of flame emitted from its tip as its sodium chloride contents converted into a steady stream of free oxygen. "Cut the rest of the coolant lines... please..."

Grace did. One by one she unplugged the rest of the coolant hoses, dragging them away from the cauldron. The temperature in the room climbed, and an acrid, soupy smell somewhere between vomit, rotting meat, and iron invaded the humid air.

Grace returned to her friend. "It's done," she said softly.

He gave another weak nod. "Thank you... Grace. I think... I think I'm ready."

Tears trickled down her cheeks again. "Are you sure? Maybe... maybe there is another way..."

"You know... there isn't..."

She sobbed, nodding. "Do...What do you want me to tell them?"

"Don't... don't tell them it was like... this..." He gestured broadly.

Grace gave a weak smile. "Raiders got you?"

He returned the smile. "Yeah... raiders." He coughed another spurt of blood, wincing in pain. "Tell... tell Jake I'm proud of him. Make sure... he keeps up his studies. He... deserves a future off this world..."

"We'll send him to the finest school in the colonies. Maybe even Crisium. I promise."

Darren's voice faded to a rasping whisper. "Tell... Alessia I love her..."

"She knows," Grace sobbed. "She knows you do."

"Don't let... her blame herself... Don't let her... blame you." His trembling hand grasped hers, squeezing. "You were a great friend... a great... partner. I'm glad... you were here..."

She squeezed his hand in return. "Wouldn't be anywhere else."

Darren closed his eyes, serene in his suffering. His hand limply rested on the pull tab for the flare. "Go," he breathed.

Grace returned to the crate, retrieving her exosuit and helmet, cast one final look at her dying friend, and entered the elevator. Its doors shut behind her, and as it rose to the *Kaifeck*'s bridge, she heard a muffled whoosh from below. Automatic alarms went off throughout the ship, and a series of secondary explosions shook the floor panels. The firebomb set off something volatile down there, causing a chain reaction of detonations and setting off fires throughout the ship. By the time Grace had suited up, dumped her tainted air supply, and refilled it enough to get from the airlock to her SandPhantom, torrents of flame billowed through the *Kaifeck*'s halls.

She secured her helmet, rushed through the smoke, and evacuated the airlock. Her boots sank deep into Samrat's blessed sands, Mahatma's golden rays bathing her in precious, beautiful light. The SandPhantom's gull-wing door welcomed her into the familiar embrace of its interior, and no sooner had it shut behind her than her foot was on the accelerator. The SandPhantom sent twin plumes of dust into the sky as it roared away from the smoldering derelict forever.

ABOUT THE AUTHOR

Evan Graham is an Ohio resident and graduate of Kent State University who never grew out of his "spaceships are cool" phase. He's an obsessive creator and consumer of science fiction stories, with a particular fascination for the macabre. Neurophage is Graham's fifth contribution to Writing Bloc's short story collections, and is the sixth published story in his Calling Void anthology series. His debut sci-fi thriller, Tantalus Depths, is now available in ebook, paperback, and audiobook everywhere books are sold.

13

UNDER THE SEA

A Retelling of A Little Mermaid

Jenn Newman

Everyone in the kingdom understood the danger. The peninsula providing them with food and access to other kingdoms across the water shrouded a deadly threat—the Merfolk.

The people were taught about the bloodthirsty sea creatures at a young age, the legends handed down to them with great sadness. They were told the soulless underwater dwellers would deplete the kingdom's fish and kill any human who dared enter their waters. Humans held Merfolk responsible for hundreds of deaths and drownings. Even their beloved Queen Ella fell victim to their ruthlessness while frolicking in the water a year after giving birth to her son, Prince Eric.

King Henry Charming IV, still bitter four years after witnessing the death of his wife, explained this to his young heir when he was only five years old.

"They are an abomination, my son. Their lack of a soul prevents them from feeling empathy towards other creatures, and they will not hesitate to slaughter any human they catch in their grasp. They would just as soon devour the entire ocean's bounty of fish and see us all starve.

"When you are old enough, you will take your place as the Supreme Commander of our fleet, and you will oversee the annual culling of the sea monsters. And for every creature you slay, you shall do so in your mother's name."

"Yes, father," the young prince replied. He did not understand the history between the humans and Merfolk, but he mourned the loss of a mother he did not remember. Knowing only nurses and nannies, he wondered over the bond other children shared with people who were not paid to care for them.

☆ ☆ ☆

Eric grew into a handsome, intelligent young man. Known for his kindness and compassion towards both humans and animals, he was adored and respected by all in the kingdom. This was in contrast to his father, whose bitterness and anger had aged King Henry beyond his years. The King's overwhelming grief ate away at any happiness he might have found as he reigned over a prosperous kingdom that was otherwise full of love and hope.

The trained seamen tasked to hunt the Merfolk were traditionally led by the Crown Prince, and only the bravest of the King's subjects were chosen to serve. The King's eagerness to have his son take over as Supreme Commander and continue the traditional culling was obsessive, despite Eric's hesitations.

"Father, must we continue this barbaric tradition? There have been no incidents in almost two decades. Should we not at least consider a progression towards peace with the Merfolk?"

"How dare you even question that! Do I need to remind you that your beloved mother was slaughtered at the hands of those vile creatures?"

Eric's fists clenched as he felt another argument brewing. "No, of course not. But her death was avenged, was it not?"

"There can be no limits to revenge when it comes to the loss of your mother, Eric. Honestly, it disappoints me every time you bring this up. We can never let go of the past that way; it dooms us to falling prey to it again."

Eric could only sigh in resignation and bow his head. For years he had hoped that the King's vengefulness would wane, and that there would be hope for peace. But now that he had turned twenty, the time had come, and the expectations were clear. He would captain the lead ship in three days.

☆ ☆ ☆

"We've got one, Commander!"

Eric turned to see his first mate, a stout man named Headley, hanging over the port side of the ship, clawing at the net he had cast an hour ago. Eric's stomach tightened into a knot, wondering if his crew had actually caught one of the creatures they hunted.

"Gilford! Meckam! Help him!" Eric ordered.

His palms sweated at the idea of seeing one up close. It had been three years since any sightings, before he had become of age, and the thought of being close to one both thrilled and horrified him.

The men grappled with thick rope, straining their muscles as the slack fell onto the ship and the net raised out of the water. Eric peered over the side and saw what looked like a large fish struggling with all its might to break free.

This was no ordinary fish, though. They had caught a monster.

Eric watched as the net traveled up the side of the ship, nearing the railing. He was surprised how much the creature resembled a human, with the exception of its long, shiny tail.

A flush of embarrassment swept over him as he realized by the curves of the torso that this was a female. He found himself admiring the long, brown tresses cascading almost to the end of her tail and stared into her wide emerald eyes. Those eyes, filled with fear, searched frantically for a way out of her predicament. Seawater flowed from her mouth, and she screamed. She looked down to the water and back up at the men pulling her towards her doom, sobbing as she reached the top. She must have known there was no hope of escape.

☆ ☆ ☆

She landed on the ship's deck with a thud, a gasp escaping her as she smacked against the wooden planks. Attina's instincts told her to close her eyes, but she couldn't help but look up at the humans. Several of them were breathing very hard and leaned over with their hands on their legs. The one that was standing straight looked at her with curiosity (and was that fear?) in his eyes. He was dressed differently than the others and did nothing to help them confine her within the net.

As she curled into herself in a futile attempt of self-protection, she saw his expression turn sympathetic. Yet he did nothing to allow her to return to her home and family.

She wondered for just a moment what he was thinking when the burning pressure of a blade against her throat pierced her delicate skin. Her eyes fixed on the standing human, and her last thought was how strange it was that he should look so shocked as she was being slaughtered.

☆ ☆ ☆

From behind a rock jutting through the sea foam, Ariel watched from a safe distance. She didn't bother to stifle her sobs, since the lapping waves and high winds muffled any sounds. Part of her wanted the hunters to hear her, to know the anguish their callous ignorance caused.

She watched helplessly as her sister struggled to break free from the net and then disappeared once they pulled her over the ship's bough. A few moments later, Attina's lifeless body fell overboard, where she morphed into a warm turquoise foam blending with seawater.

"Why?" Ariel choked out between sobs into the wind.

Her grief consumed her, and her arms would no longer support her on the surface. Slowly, she descended from the rocks and back into the ocean, where she would have to bear the horrific news to her family. The Merfolk would all mourn the loss of their eldest princess, but none more so than her father, King Triton. Ariel knew that his loathing of the humans would turn into an obsession to avenge their family's loss.

Ariel did everything possible to comfort her father during the months after Attina's death, but she could only do so much. He refused to speak of it unless someone proposed a plan to kill the humans.

She was devastated, and needed to know why Attina was killed. It didn't make any sense. What could have happened that made the humans hate the Merfolk so vehemently?

She decided the only way to find out was to ask her father and demand an answer.

"Ariel, enough of these questions. You will obey my command to never go to the surface again. I cannot lose another member of my family to those savages."

"But Father, why? Please tell me what started this. Why do they hunt us?"

"Your aunt started this war, and your mother paid the ultimate price for her malicious intentions. Ursula killed them both, as far as I'm concerned. Now I won't discuss it further!"

Killed them both? What did that mean?

☆ ☆ ☆

Ariel knew there was no point in pleading with her father to expand on his comment. She had only seen her Aunt Ursula once, when she came to the kingdom uninvited. Ariel's sister Aquata was getting married, but her wedding was ruined by Ursula's dramatics. Ursula made a scene when told she was unwelcome, turning a dark shade of purple. With a flick of her wand, half the guests withered into vegetation swaying along the sea floor.

King Triton attempted to kill Ursula that night, but she disappeared, never to be seen again. At least, that's what Ariel had thought.

Ariel couldn't go to Aquata for answers; she was still unwilling to speak of Ursula after her destroyed wedding celebration. Adella, the second eldest, would have the best memory, so Ariel went to her.

"Why do you want to know so badly?" Adella asked, clearly annoyed by the subject.

"I don't understand. I've watched them, and they seem so like us. I'm not naïve, I was there when Attina died. But there must be a way to convince them that we're not a threat. Won't you tell me?"

"Okay, fine, just remember—you asked." Adella threw up her hands in resignation and Ariel felt a moment of anxiety, wondering what she was about to learn.

"Our mother worked hard to keep peace between the Merfolk and the humans, and she would often swim near the shore to make sure nothing bad happened to a human that we would be held responsible for. She mistakenly believed that we could live in peace with the humans, also.

"The day our mother died—"

"Wait, our mother had something to do with this?" Ariel had very little memory of her mother. She only knew that she died in an accident when Ariel was young.

"Don't interrupt," Adella scolded. "You were too young to be told the truth, and I'm sorry to be the one to tell you this now. But I think it's time you hear what really happened. I'm not even sure Arista knows the details.

"A human woman was swimming far out from the shore, her husband playing with their child in the sand on the beach. Ursula was lurking behind a large coral reef nearby, watching her. She knew from the jewels the woman wore that she was someone of great importance, and the idea of that only made Ursula want her more. The woman swam close to where Ursula was, not aware of the danger she was putting herself in.

"Ursula had her sights on the human woman but knew that our mother was nearby and would try to prevent her from causing trouble.

She hatched her despicable plan then, and her serpent demons were by her side and more than happy to help carry it out."

Ariel was dumbstruck as her sister relegated the story.

"Ursula ordered her serpents to restrain our mother while she slithered up to the woman. She pulled her under with ease, even though the woman fought hard to break free. Eventually she inhaled too much water, and that never ends well for humans.

"It turns out that the human man on the beach was the King, and the woman was his Queen. He ordered his guards into the water to rescue her, and they launched their boats immediately, but it was too late. They found her, floating lifeless in the water. Humans don't come from the ocean, so they don't return to the ocean like we do. Did you know that?"

Ariel shook her head as she listened, trapped in a trance.

"They returned to the land with her body, and of course the King assumed it was one of us who murdered his wife. He couldn't see Ursula under the sea; I don't know if he's aware that she exists. He ordered them to find the Merfolk responsible and kill any others they found while doing so.

"They set out in droves just as Ursula slipped away. She got herself to safety, and that's when the serpents released our mother. As soon as they did the hunters spotted her, of course, and wasted no time launching their spears into the water. Many of them cheered as her essence absorbed into the sea." Adella's voice had lowered as she imagined the scene.

"How do you know all of this?" Ariel was stunned to learn how her mother had died at the hands of the humans. She'd watched those same humans kill her sister.

Adella looked off into the distant coral reef before answering.

"Attina told us. She saw everything." Adella looked over at Ariel, knowing this would come as a shock. Ariel briefly considered the irony of history repeating itself before Adella continued.

"She was a lot like our mother, you know. She was curious about the humans and thought that someday we would live in harmony, even help each other. She followed our mother that day, thinking she would help somehow. But she was so young and so terrified of Ursula, she could only hide.

"So, do you finally understand why Father has no use for humans?" Adella asked.

Ariel was lost in thought. She'd heard the story now. She knew it was humans who killed her mother, and of course she had witnessed first-hand what they were capable of.

"Yes, I suppose I can," she eventually answered with a heavy sigh.

She didn't dare tell Adella that she put more of the blame on Ursula than on the humans, or that she was still determined to find out more about them.

☆ ☆ ☆

The month-long culling period was coming to an end, and Eric could not have been more relieved. He was tired of pretending to hunt the Merfolk. Truthfully, since that horrible day they killed one of them, he spent most of his time navigating away from the usual places they could be seen. Memories of the brown-haired female ensnared in their net gave him chilling nightmares, and he had no intention of adding further remorse to his already heavy heart.

On the last night at sea, the clouds gathered quickly, hiding the moon and stars, making it difficult to choose the fastest course back to land and safety. The crew found themselves facing an unexpected deadly storm, with little else to do but batten down the hatches and secure the riggings.

The wind ripped part of the sails from their masts and sent supplies flying off the ship's deck. Lightning and thunder crashed all around them, and the cold, sideways rain pelted the crew's skin through their drenched clothing. Eric struggled to hold one of the booms in place, while at the same time holding onto Max, his Old English Sheepdog who refused to leave his side despite the protection and warmth of the cabins underneath.

For an hour they battled the whipping winds and rain until finally there was some relief. Though the rain was still strong, the wind died down, and the ship stopped tossing about like a child's kite. The entire crew had been put through the paces to survive and keep the ship afloat, and Eric could see the stress and exhaustion in each of their faces.

Boom!

One final lightning strike hit the topgallant mast, sending the heavy chain line flying across the ship. It struck three of the crew members and sent them into the ocean before reaching Eric, who was knocked to the deck. Max slid to the edge of the ship and was unable to stop himself before being tossed into the dark water.

☆ ☆ ☆

That night, as she had many nights before, Ariel defied her father and went to the surface. She knew the ship would be there at this time of year, searching for something or someone, and that she could keep herself concealed. She knew that the men she watched were responsible for her sister's death, but in her heart she also knew that they held Merfolk responsible for their terrible losses.

She enjoyed catching glimpses of the hairy and slobbery crew member on the ship. The humans treated him with kindness and playful affection. He wasn't human, but still he commanded their attention and returned their admiration. Ariel wondered if he was the one in charge. It was either him or the one that stayed by his side most of the time. He had wavy dark hair and bright blue eyes that glistened whenever he played with the hairy, slobbery one. Ariel was surprised at her attraction to the human sailor. He'd done nothing to stop Attina's death, so her sudden fascination with him felt unsettling.

She knew the storm was coming long before the people on the ship noticed or reacted to it. She wondered why they didn't turn around and head back to their home. Storms didn't bother Merfolk under the sea, but she had seen enough of them in her sixteen years to know that ships could only take so much, and that this one was in danger. She watched as they eventually became aware and prepared as well as they could.

Ariel was impressed with how well the humans handled the storm, until an unexpected sky light came down and damaged part of the ship. The humans were thrown about as sheets of rain swept across them, but the ship stayed intact. She could see most of them standing up again and was glad that none of them seemed hurt. She watched nervously for any signs of Ursula as the few that had fallen into the sea climbed up to safety. She remembered what Adella had said about humans inhaling water not being a good thing.

Suddenly the men were looking around frantically, and the dark haired one kept yelling, "Max!"

She looked around and saw the hairy, slobbery one and assumed he must be Max. He was doing his best to stay above water, but the waves were still heaving from the storm. Ariel dove under the water and quickly made her way towards the struggling form. She didn't know if she would get to Max in time, but she was convinced that he had a good soul and deserved saving, so she had to try. She also knew that if he was important to the humans, then rescuing him might be a step toward mending the relationship between the humans and Merfolk.

She reached him just as he was about to be swallowed by a large wave and was able to pull him away in time. She stayed underwater, pushing him up above her so that he would have air, but she knew she wouldn't have the strength to keep that up for very long. She swam towards a rock formation, planning to get him to a safe place where the ship could come and get him. She would wait with him to make sure he was safe until they arrived.

Ariel sighed with relief when she managed to get Max to a high spot on the rock. Max shook water from his thick, bushy hair and shivered from the cold, and seemed thankful for his spot, having had enough of the saltwater.

Pleased with her accomplishment, Ariel didn't see the powerful wave behind her, which pushed her into the rocks, where she spiraled into darkness.

☆ ☆ ☆

Ariel's vision was blurry from the dry, high sun. Eventually, she was able to focus on a figure leaning over her. She recognized him, and her brain hosted a war of fear and curiosity. He was the one who'd watched Attina die and had done nothing. How could he have been so heartless... and yet he saved her?

She gasped, water flowing out of her mouth as she attempted to ask him so many questions. She was vaguely aware of being surrounded by a cloth of some kind, and her first reaction was panic when she remembered the netting that the hunters used to capture Merfolk. This was soft and warm, however, and she quickly found that it did not prevent her from moving around freely. Although her body didn't require the warmth, she found it comforting.

"Whoa, you should take it easy. You've been through a lot. What's your name?"

Ariel's head pounded where she had hit the rocks, and she vaguely recalled the storm. The storm... the ship... trying to save Max...

"Max!" she yelled, and a look of surprise came over Eric's face.

"Max? You mean my Max? He's fine. Really, he's perfect. And I believe I have you to thank for that, uh..."

"Ariel."

She looked up into Eric's blue eyes and was caught there. She was relieved to hear that she had been able to save Max, but she had so many questions.

"Ariel," he repeated. "I'm Eric."

"How did I get here?" The bright sunshine and beach were in stark contrast to the surroundings she was used to, and to the violent storm hours before.

"You were laying near the rock over there." He pointed to a grouping of Beachrock at the edge of the alcove. "I saw you from my window and had to see if you were okay."

Ariel looked around again and realized she was very close to the grand castle where the King of the humans lived. *His window?*

"Are you the King?" she asked, guardedly.

"No, that's my father. I'm the Prince." Eric looked down when he said this, as though he knew she would condemn him for being the leader of the group of hunters.

"Why didn't you do anything to save her, Eric?" Still adjusting to her surroundings, she wasted no time getting to the point. He looked confused for a moment, and then his eyes widened in realization of what she was asking.

"I... I don't know what to say. Did you know her?"

"She was my sister."

Eric's pallor turned slightly green, and Ariel thought she could hear his heart racing. He considered his answer carefully and took a long breath before speaking again. She waited patiently for his answer.

"I was raised to believe that your kind were soulless, cruel killers. And that if we allowed you to hunt fish and humans in our waters, we were doomed to starvation and loss of our kingdom. It's not an excuse for what happened to your sister. It's just... what we've always known."

"Who told you these lies about us?" Ariel's curiosity was mixed with a growing anger now.

"My father, the King. And I don't think you'd call them lies if you knew what happened. My mother was killed by a Mermaid when I was a year old. He never got over that, and even though his guards killed the one responsible, he still seeks revenge."

It was Ariel's turn to be wide-eyed. The story. The woman of great importance.

"No. No, she wasn't killed by a Mermaid. That's wrong!" She yelled.

"What are you talking about?"

"Your mother wasn't killed by a Mermaid. She was killed by the Sea Witch, Ursula."

"The Sea Witch? I've never heard of her." Eric's anxiety rose with the idea of a possible new threat to his kingdom.

"She's... my aunt," Ariel admitted, chagrined.

"Ariel, please tell me. What kind of a threat is the Sea Witch to my people?"

Eric had no reason to distrust Ariel from what little he knew about her, but he was stunned with this new revelation.

"Ursula is evil and powerful. She was shunned by the Merfolk many years ago and is now considered a very dangerous enemy. She was once a Mermaid of Royalty, the sister of my father. Instead of our peaceful lifestyle, she chose a dark and depraved path. She did kill your mother, but my mother was trying to protect her from harm. And she died at the hands of your guards because of it."

"*Your* mother?"

"Yes," Ariel began to sob quietly. Describing the tragedy of her mother's death brought a renewed level of grief.

☆ ☆ ☆

Eric sat and absorbed what Ariel had just told him. This would mean that for years they had hunted innocent Merfolk and not the one creature that was responsible for his mother's murder. And she was still out there. Would his father believe it? His bloodlust for the Merfolk was so ingrained, Eric wondered if the truth would have any impact on him.

He looked over at Ariel and saw kindness in her face, even while she openly grieved. And after what he had allowed to happen to her sister, she still had it in her heart to save Max.

The question hammered him. Who was the soulless creature?

☆ ☆ ☆

Over time, Ariel and Eric developed a friendship. They bonded over the loss of their mothers, and shared a determination that the bloodshed would end with them. Many afternoons they would meet in the cove where they first spoke, just along the water's edge near the Beachrock. Max would play but had become leery of the water since the night of his unplanned swim. Ariel wanted to know everything possible about humans and would ask questions until she couldn't digest any more information. Eric wanted to know more about the Merfolk as well. He was amazed that an entire world existed under the sea, far more intricate and functional than anything he had imagined.

Eric wanted to meet King Triton, but Ariel had refused. She

reminded him of the level of vengeance his own father harbored and pointed out that her father shared similar feelings. Eric could understand that.

There was only one thing that would foster the peace they both wanted.

Ariel had been forming a plan, and one sunny afternoon she mustered the courage to propose it to Eric.

"You're not serious. Tell me you're joking, please!"

"It can work. I know it can. We just have to make sure the timing is right, and it will finally put an end to this war."

"But you're asking me to risk lives, Ariel. I'm not sure I'm willing to do that."

"Ursula has the power to destroy my home and my entire family. I know what I'm asking is risky, but as long as she lives, we are all in danger. Think about it, Eric; if this works it could mean so much to both of our kingdoms."

Eric promised to think about it, and the following week he reluctantly agreed.

"Under one condition. It must be me, no one else." Ariel didn't like the idea of risking Eric's life, either. She had developed strong feelings for him, and it saddened her to know they could never have the relationship of two committed Merfolk or humans. But she knew he would not allow anyone in his kingdom to risk dying at the hands of Ursula. She also knew if their plan failed, his kingdom would face the full force of Ursula's wrath.

☆ ☆ ☆

Five months after that stormy night when Ariel saved Max, King Henry Charming IV passed away, still bitter and resentful against the Merfolk. Eric ascended to the throne never having told him of Ariel, the Sea Witch, or how the Queen really died. He knew there was no point to it, and the truth may have put the Merfolk in more danger if he did.

But there was still a threat to deal with. And the plan was set.

☆ ☆ ☆

The overcast sky threatened rain, but the ocean remained calm. Gentle waves lapped onto the shore of the alcove where Eric sat in one of the smaller fishing boats used by the castle staff. Spears and shotguns lined the bottom of the vessel, strategically placed to be within easy reach.

Eric tried to control his breathing as he contemplated what they were about to attempt.

"Ariel, are you sure this is worth the risk? Are they really prepared to put their lives in jeopardy for the sake of humans?"

Ariel's arms rested on the side of the boat while her tail flicked anxiously in the shallow water. "Eric, it's not only humans in danger every day. My sisters and I want to protect our family and our kingdom."

"I know. I'm still in shock that they agreed to this, though."

"When I explained everything to them, they understood it was the only way. Adella voiced her skepticism again last night, but even she can see what this means for our future. We're just lucky they agreed not to tell my father, because he would have locked us all in a cave if he knew."

"If I had daughters, I might agree with him." Ariel just raised an eyebrow at Eric but understood his point. It was dangerous.

☆ ☆ ☆

Aquata, Alana and Adrina were the strongest and fastest swimmers, so they joined Ariel near the alcove. It was the first time they had laid eyes on Eric, and they were overcome with a mixture of emotions toward this human who had allowed their sister to be slaughtered and yet was risking his own life to save their kingdom and his own. Despite his friendly wave, they stayed silent and kept their distance, busying themselves with the collection of spears and knives they had stolen from King Triton's armory.

✫ ✫ ✫

Adella and Arista hid on the north side of Ursula's lair, waiting for their opportunity to tempt her out of her quarters. It was a murky and foul place, even by deep ocean standards. They laid among the vegetation surrounding the "palace" that their aunt called home, which was nothing more than a collection of old, rotted pieces of ships held together by barnacles. The vegetation that provided them cover were the poor, unfortunate souls that had been cursed by the Sea Witch or paid the price for one of her contracts. Watching their former fellow Merfolk sway across the ocean floor solidified their resolve.

Adella and Arista swam casually around near the front of the underwater hovel where they knew they would be overheard. They were careful not to be too close.

"Arista, I suppose we should head up to the surface soon."

"Yes, it's getting close to the treaty signing. Imagine after all these years Father has made peace with the new human King. It should be quite a celebration!"

"I agree. It will be so nice to have an alliance with the humans. And such a novelty to have both heads of the Kingdoms together."

"Yes, let's hurry so we don't miss anything!"

The two sisters swam off, and as Arista looked back for a second, she could see a black, slimy tentacle creeping out into the open.

✫ ✫ ✫

Ursula watched the direction that Triton's daughters swam, and knew they would be headed toward the human's palace. She thought for a few moments, and decided this was an opportunity she could not miss. She called on her serpents, who raced dutifully to her side.

"A celebration, eh? Hmph! When I lived at the palace, we had real celebrations. There was no talk of treaties with the humans, I can tell you that. How disgusting! Triton has obviously lost his mind. Am I right, my little poopsies?" The serpents entwined their bodies and nodded in agreement.

"Well, I think we can give them something to really celebrate. Let's go, boys. I believe there's a new crown in my future!" She gave a roaring, menacing laugh as she swam away with her two sidekicks in tow.

☆ ☆ ☆

The humans were perched on various levels of the castle and along the streets near the beach, far enough away to run if they needed to. Eric knew that it wouldn't make a difference if they ran should the plan not go well, but he needed to convince Ursula that this was a celebration. Adella and Arista had arrived a few minutes earlier and took their posts, so he knew the time was almost upon them.

He looked over to where Ariel kept watch, and she gave him an encouraging smile. It saddened him that they could not be more than friends, but he valued their relationship more than any other he had.

Suddenly, Ariel raised her hand and pointed in the direction of one of the rock formations. This was it. Ursula was coming.

☆ ☆ ☆

As she swam toward the palace, Ursula could see the humans gathered for their celebration. There was no sign of Triton yet, but she could tell there were Merfolk nearby and assumed he was on his way. She stopped just before the water became too shallow to hide her imposing form and listened for any indication of her dear brother's approach.

The thought that something was not right had just started to form when stabbing pains sent her into a frenzy. She struggled to spiral and flee to safety but was unable. She saw spears stuck in five of her tentacles, pinning her to the ocean floor.

Before she could react, a net made of small anchor chain fell through the ocean surface, covering her. She looked up to see a human in a small boat, gathering more spears and other items that looked harmful. One of Triton's daughters, the youngest named Ariel, stayed near the boat looking at the Sea Witch defiantly. She would not tolerate this insolence! This would be her kingdom and she would demand their fealty.

☆ ☆ ☆

Ariel watched her sisters retreat as Ursula struggled. She would break through the chains and rise above the surface while still affixed to the floor, and then the humans were prepared to launch their attack. What none of them planned on were the serpents.

Ursula called for them, and they hastened to where their mistress was trapped, assessing the situation. They quickly pulled out the spears, allowing her tentacles to move freely and help her to slip under the net. She did not rise above the surface, but instead swam over to the small boat, capsizing it with a flick of her wrist.

Ariel tried to reach Eric, but one of the serpents already had him in their grip, dragging him down under the water. The other one was keeping her sisters at bay with their snapping teeth, until finally Adella put a spear into it.

The loss of one of her serpents distracted Ursula, but only for a moment. She would deal with Triton's other daughters later and make an example of all of them. She used what powers she had to create a tidal wave, sending the humans running for cover. Many of them dropped their weapons, eliminating that threat.

Ariel didn't have a moment to lose. If she didn't get Eric to the surface quickly he would take in too much water and she would lose her friend forever. She fought with the serpent, but it was strong. And then she heard Ursula behind her.

"You foolish girl! How dare you plot against me—"

"Ursula!" an angry voice bellowed.

A paralyzing fear struck the Sea Witch. She knew that voice and turned to look her brother in the face with a smile of innocence and gratitude. She had to play this right. She had lost the element of surprise, she was injured, and now one of her serpents were gone.

"Why Triton, thank you for coming to my aid. Your daughters have aligned with the humans to kill us all and rule the ocean themselves! I just can't believe it. Surely you knew nothing about this. What should we do about them, dear brother?"

Triton looked around and saw all of his daughters, except Ariel. They all just stared at Ursula, waiting to see how their father would handle this.

"I believe this calls for severe punishment, would you agree?" he asked.

Ursula was stunned and thrilled that Triton was siding with her. She knew eventually he would learn the truth, but this would buy her some time to escape. Until the time was right to kill him.

"Why yes, unfortunately, I must agree. This type of behavior cannot be tolerated. We have a kingdom to protect now, don't we?"

"Yes, we do."

The King raised his mighty Trident and aimed it directly at Ursula's heart. A look of disgust crossed her face as the blazing arcs pierced through her rubbery surface and the deadly electric force shone through every orifice.

✩ ✩ ✩

Triton watched as Ursula returned to the sea. Not as turquoise foam, but as a black, oily, foul smelling substance that would soon disappear. His attention quickly turned to Ariel.

"Where is Ariel?" he passked the girls as they gathered around him, all trying to explain what had transpired.

Adella pointed to the alcove less than a mile away, where Triton could see Ariel on the beach along with another form. It appeared to be a human. He hurried over to make sure his youngest was not hurt during Ursula's attack.

"Ariel?"

"Father! I'm so sorry. I didn't mean–"

"It's alright, child. It's all over now, and neither of our kingdoms will live under your aunt's threat any longer." Triton looked at the human that Ariel was staying close to. His lack of movement told him that the human had not survived. He looked at his daughter with sympathy, assuming this was the human that he heard about. Sending Sebastian to watch after her was the right move, and he was a very reliable crab when it came to not keeping secrets from the King.

"He was special to you, wasn't he?"

"I love him, Father. The humans aren't anything like we were taught. There are very good ones. And he was one of the best." She sobbed into Eric's soaked shirt, and Triton's heart broke for his youngest daughter.

"Ariel, you know I can't undo what has happened."

"Yes, I know." She knew Eric would always be in her heart, even though she would miss him terribly.

"There is one thing I can do, though," the King said with a slight grin.

Ariel looked at her father and raised an eyebrow, not understanding what he was saying.

Triton pulled Eric's body into the water, and once more raised the powerful Trident. A soft light cascaded over the body of the man that his daughter fell in love with, and Ariel watched in disbelief as Eric's clothing split off of him, revealing a tail and fins that closely matched her own. His eyes opened, and he sputtered for a moment while he adjusted to breathing in the water, then the realization of what happened hit him.

Ariel wondered if this were what Eric would want if he had a choice. She desperately hoped so.

Ariel rushed over to hold him as he adjusted to his new body.

"Oh, Eric, are you okay?"

"I thought I died because of that serpent."

"You were dead. My father killed Ursula and was able to bring you back as one of us but couldn't return you to your human form. I don't know what to say about you not having that choice to make yourself..." she trailed off.

Eric took in his new surroundings. The world looked very different from this viewpoint. He had lived for over two decades on land, and was forced to hunt the very creature that he was now. But there would be no more hunting. The biggest threat to his kingdom was gone. And now he had the chance to spend his life with the mermaid that he fell in love with.

Eric smiled at Ariel and took her in his arms. He looked over at King Triton and said in the sincerest voice, "Thank you."

King Triton smiled and nodded back at him, then swam back to his palace with Ariel's sisters to spread the news of Ursula's death. There were many Merfolk who would be returning to the kingdom now that her spells were no longer active, and they would have many questions about their new Prince.

ABOUT THE AUTHOR

Jenn Newman lives outside of Boston and developed a love of writing after playing with some story ideas and deciding they were worth telling. She has placed at respectful levels within several short story writing competitions through NYC Midnight, and authored "Thirty Minutes to Life" in Writing Bloc's anthology Family. When not writing, she is a very busy wife, mother, and HR Director who often thinks, "I should be writing."

❧ 14 ❧

SISYPHUS, THE SNIPER, AND THE SHOPPING CARTS

A Retelling of the Sisyphus Myth

Peter L. Harmon

"Living... is never easy."

— - ALBERT CAMUS, *THE MYTH OF SISYPHUS*

Clackata clackata clackata.
Thunk.
Clackata clackata clackata clackata.
Sisyphus Jones pushed a shopping cart across the uneven asphalt, the polyurethane wheels bouncing and skipping over rocks and pebbles. He swerved quickly to avoid a large stone in his path, thinking *skrrrt* in his mind, mimicking the sounds of the modded-out cars in that Fast and Furious movie he had seen the summer before. He docked the cart with the already waiting collection, corralled behind a Taurus and a Camry, parked in the lot of the Giant Food grocery store off of East-West Highway in Hyattsville, Maryland where he was employed.

It was mid-October, and the air was brisk. Sisyphus took off his gloves for a moment to breathe warm air onto his cold fingers. Then he figured he had better get moving again. Stay moving, stay alive. Don't make yourself an easy target. The only good thing about being the cart collector at the market was that the work was solitary, and he could let his mind wander. Other than that, it was a shitty job.

Sisyphus was a senior at Corinth High School and he was pretty popular. In fact, sometimes he felt like the king of Corinth. There was usually a party to go to on Friday night, usually a girl to talk to. There was usually a 40-ounce of Olde English in the back of his buddy's Impala or some Natty Lights in the fridge at the hangout spot. He had a table to sit at in the lunchroom if he wanted to play spades and homies to dap up as he walked through the school hallway. But his popularity didn't help his GPA, and it definitely didn't help when he got caught messing with teachers and other staff who rightly deserved to be made fools of.

For example, Sisyphus thought he was actually doing fine in his Spanish class. Some kids from his neighborhood spoke Spanish, so he felt like he could understand it pretty well, and he knew he was good at reading and writing it. His accent wasn't that great, as it battled his cool-guy Prince George's County intonation. Senora Lycus—the Spanish teacher—let him know it often, and always in front of the class whenever they had to pair up to work on their conversational prompts.

"Tu acento no es bueno... *gringo*," she would tell him condescendingly after Sisyphus would say his piece. It was embarrassing. So Sisyphus thought he was totally justified when he left his backpack in her classroom with an activated mini cassette recorder. And it wasn't his fault she just happened to take a personal phone call during her planning period where she talked mad shit about the school administration. And then Sisyphus thought it was also within his right to play said recording on the school's PA system after the morning announcements. Right after his buddy Jamal read that day's lunch menu: popcorn shrimp with your choice of potato. The school system was required to provide a vegetable at every meal, and it seemed like each day the big roulette wheel of veggies always came up potato.

But Senora Lycus and the vice principal disagreed with Sisyphus' assessment and suspended him for several days. His consolation prize was that it was still totally awkward between Senora Lycus and a couple of members of the administration she'd badmouthed.

Sisyphus didn't like being shit on. Not from classmates and not from the asshole gym teacher who called him "numb nuts" for forgetting his gym uniform. Sisyphus didn't think that a fifty-year-old P.E. teacher with pit stains and a pervy goatee should comment on his nuts. So Sisyphus asked Mr. Natos, the aforementioned educational professional, to show him where the spare gym clothes were and told him that he would pay him for another pair of shorts instead of taking the incomplete mark for the day. Mr. Natos was greedy and dumb enough to let the gym uniform policy slide for twenty bucks. Mr. Natos led Sisyphus to the back storage room where they housed the gym uniforms in large cardboard boxes next to a cage of red dodgeballs and a bucket of hopelessly tangled jump ropes. Sisyphus grabbed Mr. Natos' key ring from his cargo pants and locked his ass in the storage room, where he stayed for several periods. There was a rumor that the gym teacher had peed in a lacrosse helmet, but Sisyphus never confirmed if that was true or not. He hoped it was.

During those glorious gym periods while Natos was locked up, the ladies got to sit on the bleachers and gossip, the nerds kept their street clothes on and got ahead on their homework, and Sisyphus and his buddies ran full-court basketball games with the scoreboard on. Jamal ran the board and called fouls. After Mr. Ares, the security guard, found a very pissed Mr. Natos, Sisyphus was suspended again. Neither time was he expelled, though, which he looked at as a win, as he had avoided expulsion twice by his count. That was akin to beating death in his eyes because if he got expelled, his mom would kill him.

But back to the damn shopping carts.

Sisyphus' job was simple. Congregate the shopping carts that customers customarily cast aside after loading their groceries into their Corollas or Civics, push them all together into one wagon train longer than the river Styx, and snake them back into the cart holding area by the front of the store. If he lagged, his manager, Zeus, would look out the store window and gesticulate wildly for him to hurry up. The boss seemed pretty animated behind that glass, but he never tried to take a tone with Sisyphus when they were in the same room. Sisyphus had built up some burly forearms from all that cart pushing. Half of the parking lot was at a slight incline, so if he didn't keep a hand on the carts, they would roll back and potentially hit a car.

There was always something up with the carts, though. Sometimes a wheel would be frozen, locked in some sort of purgatory from which it would never return. People left their trash in the carts, like chicken bones from rotisserie chickens they bought inside and immediately gorged on like a Gorgon gobbling Gorgonzola. There was sometimes gum on the handles. Plastic bags caught up in the metal frames. Hot Fries dust all over the place. Mambo sauce spatters and Old Bay fingerprints. And did Zeus ever get the shopping carts professionally cleaned or serviced? Absolutely not. Once a week, Sisyphus had to go out and get on his hands and knees with a spray bottle and a rag. But he needed the job if he was ever getting out of P.G. County. He wanted to go to college down south, where there was good weather, maybe near a beach. Getting a job he could work while going to school was tough; he had to take what he could get, even if it was monotonous.

Sisyphus had aligned a long line of shopping carts and was pushing them towards the ramp leading to the cart dock when he saw it. The van.

The white van sat parked under a tree by the edge of the parking lot. Normally, it would have been no big deal. Every once in a while, they'd get a drunk passed out in their car, sleeping off the booze until they could safely drive themselves home. A couple of times, Sisyphus had to knock on the window of a vehicle that had been parked in the same spot for several of his shifts to tell the person living out of their car they had to move on to a Wal-Mart or a rest stop off the interstate— anywhere else. It totally wasn't in Sisyphus' job description to handle vagabonds and drunks, but Zeus was a dick and made him do it anyway. Zeus made him do a lot of shit he didn't want to do.

But the white van was different.

The rear windows were blacked out. It was an older model and had seen a lot of miles. Even the passenger side window, the side Sisyphus could see from his angle, was tinted too dark to see in. Was there movement in the front seat? He couldn't tell. He felt like he could hear rustling and conversation. He tried to ignore it for the time being.

Over the past couple of weeks, white vans had become noteworthy. A sniper was on a killing spree, randomly targeting people doing mundane things in the "DMV" area— the nickname Sisyphus and his friends (and most everyone he knew) had given the D.C., Maryland, and Virginia region. Even 95.5 WPGC on the radio, D.C.'s home of at least 18 jams in a row, called it the DMV.

Two weeks ago, four people had been shot dead in the span of two hours. A single shot was fired in each case, and there were no clues as to who was responsible.

The victims were:

A guy mowing the lawn.

A guy pumping gas.

A lady reading a book on a bench.

Another lady vacuuming her Plymouth Voyager.

Sisyphus drove a damn Voyager (when his mom let him have the keys). It could have been his ass getting sniped while vacuuming his mom's minivan. Well, he actually felt like he was safe in that regard; he would never vacuum the Voyager unless his mom paid him or made him. But imagine your last thought on Earth being about getting the damn Goldfish crumbs out of the gray carpeting in the backseat of your early 90s-era minivan. Then... nothing.

Or whatever came after death, Sisyphus wasn't sure.

Heaven or Hell. Elysium or Hades. Who knew?

In the subsequent days, a kid got shot at Benjamin Tasker Middle School, where Sisyphus' little cousin went. Sisyphus' cousin had been playing basketball with the kid the day before. Then the next day, bam, shot. He was in the hospital and it looked like he was going to make it, but damn, *a 13 year old*? You had to be cold as ice to turn tweens into target practice.

A few more people were shot pumping gas like the other guy. Gas stations put up tarps to obscure the vision of the phantom killer. But that was just for peace of mind. A placebo for the public. A lady got shot in Falls Church at a Home Depot. Another guy at a steakhouse.

It was crazy. Random. It made you not want to go anywhere. It frightened you. There was saber rattling about gun control while gun sales skyrocketed. So did tarp sales. The solution wasn't less guns, it was more tarps. Good ole boys at the bar fetishized what they would do if they caught the sonofabitch who was shooting folks. They would shoot'em, that's what. An eye for an eye, they'd say, but how did that phrase end?

Were there copycats? Sisyphus didn't know. The news said a white van was seen at all or some of the locations before the shootings took place. Could be a coincidence. There were a lot of white vans out there. But maybe not.

A day ago, his mom had told him not to ride his bike to school because of the sniper—take the minivan, she'd said. Sisyphus had thought that he'd rather be shot than be seen in his mom's van, so he took his bike anyway. That afternoon, a white van had pulled onto the same street as him, a few blocks back. Now, Sisyphus was nice on a bike, but still his heart started pumping and so did his legs. He took the next corner and hit the handbrakes, leaving a streak of rubber. The white van drove by innocuously. But that's where peoples' heads were at these days.

The police had gone on the news and told parents they should drop off their kids at school. Don't let them walk. Don't make them wait at the bus stop. The schools were locked down. No recess. No outdoor P.E., either—Sisyphus bet Mr. Natos was happy about that one. No field trips. Little Johnny can't go to Assateague State Park this year. Get your Assateague indoors.

Sisyphus didn't really follow the news, but just over a year ago he had seen the second tower fall in real time on September 11th. He was in his physics class that morning and someone had rolled in a TV cart with the DVD player so that they could watch Jake Gyllenhaal's goofy ass play Homer Hickam in *October Sky* because it had something to do with physics and rockets or whatever. Jamal had run into Sisyphus' physics room from his TV productions class where he had been editing the Latin class's stage production of Julius Caesar. Jamal was allowed to have the TV on while he edited as a perk for assemble editing the school assemblies. Jamal had seen the first tower fall. He was shocked. He was in disbelief. What was happening? Was it an accident? Total chaos. No answers. Just a live feed of the devastation. Must-see TV.

He ran to Sisyphus' class and yelled for Mr. Abrams, the physics teacher, to turn on the news. Mr. Abrams did, and the whole class watched the second plane hit the second tower. Later another plane would hit the Pentagon where some of Sisyphus' classmates' parents worked. Leonardo Paulson, who previously Sisyphus had called "Nerdo" Paulson, was on the payphone in the hallway trying to get in touch with his parents. His dad worked at the Pentagon. He couldn't get through to him. Tears were streaming down his face.

Leonardo's dad ended up being OK, but still, Sisyphus didn't taunt him after that. School was dismissed and Sisyphus went home and his mom was glued to the news. A plane crash in Pennsylvania. Images and videos of the wreckage in New York City. People jumping to their deaths before the flaming towers fell. Sisyphus couldn't hang, so he went to the park and shot baskets. Some old heads were drinking Heinekens on the sidelines, oblivious. Sisyphus didn't really like to turn on the news that much anymore. The news was kind of fucked up.

Sisyphus remembered a few nights ago while listening to slow jams on WKYS 93.9 and trying to fall asleep that they'd cut to a news snippet about the sniper. He didn't think they should interrupt slow jams with the news. What if you were with your lady trying to get something going, listening to slow jams, and then all of a sudden you heard about the traffic on the beltway or Congress about to be in session? Ladies aren't getting in the mood thinking about traffic or Congress.

But anyway, the DJ had said that at the Tasker crime scene they found shell casings and a Tarot card, the Death card specifically. Sisyphus wasn't superstitious, but he knew better than to mess with Tarot and witches and sorcery. He wouldn't even lay a hand on the Ouija board at Jamal's twelve-year-old birthday sleepover. No, thank you. He had a hard enough time communicating with the living. If ghosts were around twelve-year-old birthday party sleepovers they were probably freaks anyway, and they could mind their own business.

The Tarot card read, "Call me God" and "Do not release to the press." Sisyphus stayed up all night thinking about why the police would release to the press a card that said, "do not release to the press" by someone calling themselves "God." Sisyphus didn't play with those who thought of themselves as gods. Eh, or maybe he did.

There were no real leads at the moment, just the white van tip.

Sisyphus eyed the vehicle. He didn't want to turn his back on it, but then again, what good would it do to keep looking at it?

His mom had questioned his decision to keep going to work collecting carts in the parking lot. He thought he could either quit and think he was staying safe up in his room and who knows, be in a building that was targeted by a terrorist group or get hit by a drunk driver while riding his bike or get shot anyway by one of his classmates like those kids in Columbine three years earlier, or he could go to work.

Columbine had been blamed on video games and Marilyn Manson and *The Matrix*. Sisyphus played video games. He thought a couple of Manson's songs were OK for that jerbang jerbang shit. He loved *The Matrix*. Sisyphus wasn't sure those things were the culprits. Politicians demonized the media. They blamed mental health issues but offered no solutions in the mental health arena. Therapy was still for pussies according to the good ole boys at the bar. Access to guns was never questioned. Guns were an unalienable right in the U.S. of A. Politicians clutched their pearls, asking the public not to politicize such a heinous act. Could you imagine the public wanting to politicize something political to a politician? It was almost like a politician's job was to be political and enact policy.

After Columbine gun sales skyrocketed. Trench coat sales dipped slightly.

There was outrage and fear after the Columbine school shooting, but the fuss eventually calmed, which worried Sisyphus. Why wasn't this on everyone's mind every single day? Kids walked into a school like *Rambo* and picked off their peers. Why didn't America unite to make sure that nothing like that ever happened again?

Sisyphus imagined a world, twenty years in the future perhaps, where a shooting at a school, maybe an elementary school, would barely register on the national radar. Business as usual. An NRA convention two days later. More people coming to the defense of the guns than the kids. Bulletproof backpacks. Active shooter drills replacing stop, drop, and roll. Sisyphus thought that gun sales would probably skyrocket. Sisyphus grimly thought that maybe he should use his paycheck to buy some stock in a gun manufacturer and wait for the next tragedy. Forget a 9 to 5. Invest in a company that makes AR-15s.

Sisyphus' job was easy but repetitive. It gave him something to do. It put money in his pocket. He was stacking to escape. He was going to get into a good school and hit Virginia Beach or North Carolina or something. Somewhere where the water was warm. Forget a beach week in Ocean City. The world wasn't safe, he rationalized, and he might as well make a couple of bucks while he was waiting to die.

The parking lot was pretty vacant. It was after the dinner rush and not yet time for college students to go in to get late night snacks or third shifters to grab their Red Bulls and sandwiches before their nights began. The van was there, of course, parked by the edge of the parking lot, under the tree. Someone had an Escalade on spinners up near the entrance to the grocery store, which was pretty sick. Then there were just a few nondescript coupes and sedans sprinkled throughout the rest of the lot.

Sisyphus decided to tempt the fates and approach the white van. The cherry Coke can sky was ever darkening. He abandoned the carts and walked quickly towards the van, moving slightly left then right, strafing subconsciously. Doing the Sisyphus serpentine. He didn't know much about long-range weapons, but he didn't think he'd be an ideal target at such a close proximity. He reached the side door of the van and knocked like the cops.

"Hey," Sisyphus said, "I work here and y'all gotta move."

He waited. He could hear movement inside the back half of the vehicle. Muffled talking. Metal on metal.

Sisyphus instantly regretted his decision.

"Haha," he laughed unconvincingly. "Sike it's alright. I'm not pressed. Y'all can hang out for a while."

He turned to hurry quickly back towards the store, deciding that he was going to take his fifteen-minute break to hyperventilate in the staff bathroom. But as soon as he took one step away from the van, he heard the back door unlatch and start to slide along its track.

"What'd you say?" a gravelly voice said from the back of the van.

"Nah, nah, we're good bro." Sisyphus looked over his shoulder out of the corner of his eye. The back door was barely open, but a hand held it in place.

"We got a problem?"

Again Sisyphus heard conversation in low tones and what sounded like equipment being adjusted into place. Maybe a rifle being hoisted onto a bipod or a magazine being loaded.

He turned back to the van slightly. "No, it's my bad. Alright, my manager is looking for me. Be easy." Sisyphus could have taken off running, but the image of his body flailing and hitting the pavement flashed in his mind.

"Is it the van?" the voice said. "We know, the cops stay pulling us over this week, bro."

Sisyphus was confused. The back door slid open a little further and Sisyphus saw a couple of dudes in the back. The passenger side door opened and a girl—probably in her early twenties—was sitting there, putting on makeup in the mirror. In the back with the guys was a disassembled drum set. A keyboard lay on its side.

"We're just killing time before a gig, bro." The guy had a Swisher Sweet in his hand that wasn't lit yet. "Don't make it hot."

Sisyphus was relieved. "Nah, y'all are good man. Have a good show. Where you playing?"

"Just some spot in College Park. Yo, here's our album, tell your friends." The guy handed Sisyphus a shiny CD with the name of the band scrawled in Sharpie across the front. Sisyphus' hand was shaking so much that he couldn't read the band's name, but it was some combination of Backyard and BBQ and Go-go and Groovers.

"Alright." Sisyphus broke his stasis and walked back towards the train of carts he had left. He chided himself for being so scared of a band in a van. He chuckled but was still shaking when he ran into a kid exiting the Giant Food. Well, not really a kid—he was pretty close in age to Sisyphus, probably in his late teens.

"Sorry," Sisyphus said, but the kid didn't respond. Instead, he looked to the older guy he was with, who just shook his head slightly as they continued.

He pushed the carts up the ramp to the holding area. Just as he was finishing that batch, he looked out into the parking lot. The sky was Pepsi blue. The streetlamps were on. Of course, there were carts scattered about. There were roughly as many as when he had started the process the last time. He pushed the carts to the front of the store just to look back and see that it was time to start all over again.

But he didn't mind. He wasn't going to be a shopping cart wrangler for the rest of his life. He hoped there was more. He smiled as he thought about getting away. What was he going to study? He didn't know. He knew he was going to be studying the ladies at the beach, though.

As he walked to the first cart, the cart that would serve as his handlebars for the rest of the process, he casually watched the young guy and older man walk to their car. Sisyphus hadn't noticed it before because it was at the other far end of the lot, away from the white van. It was an older Chevy Caprice, dark blue like the sky, with New Jersey tags.

Sisyphus pushed the latest shopping cart into the next one into the next one, across the uneven asphalt, the polyurethane wheels bouncing and skipping over rocks and pebbles.

Clackata clackata clackata.

Thunk.

Clackata clackata clackata clackata.

ABOUT THE AUTHOR

Peter L. Harmon grew up in Prince George's County, Maryland. After spending 14 years following his dreams in Los Angeles, he has returned to Maryland where he lives with his wife, their two kids, and a freeloading pug. He is a TV producer, screenwriter, podcaster, and author. He was featured in The Baltimore Sun's 2022 article: *Season's readings: 10 books from Baltimore-area authors to add to your holiday wish list.* You can see what he's up to by following @HighDivePublishing on Instagram.

ABOUT THE WRITING BLOC

The Writing Bloc is a writing group and independent publisher. We help writers reach their writing goals, and publish books by passionate authors. We're a working collaborative writing community—a place to work together on everything from beta reading to marketing.

We publish short story collections, anthologies, mysteries and thrillers, science fiction, horror, fantasy, and contemporary romances produced by our members.

Find us at:
writingbloc.com
Twitter: @writingblocpub
Instagram: @writingblocpub
Facebook: /writingbloc
Facebook Group: facebook.com/groups/writingblocgroup